TAKE A
DIVE FOR

MURDER

Enjoy !

Millie Mack

MILLIE MACK

ISBN: 1466301899
ISBN 13: 9781466301894

Library of Congress Control Number: 2011916110
CreateSpace Independent Publishing Platform
North Charleston, South Carolina

ACKNOWLEDGMENTS

This book could never have been written without the help and the support of my family and friends.

Any acknowledgement should start at the beginning and that is with my Mom. My mother who in her early years was a librarian, loved to read mysteries. In fact she was known to check the ending first and then read the rest of the book to see if the clues supported the conclusion. We spent many hours together enjoying mystery movies and shows which deepened my love for the genre. She gets all the credit for developing my appreciation for a good mystery.

There are so many other people who supported me but there are a few special people I want to acknowledge. First, I want to thank Deb who is an excellent editor and made terrific suggestions when the book was in its infancy and continued to offer great suggestions as the book was completed. To Nancy who pushed me in a good way to get the book finished and will miss the results of her effort. To Gale who was not only supportive of my writing, but a good friend. And to Stacy who only saw the positive in everything I was doing. She was always the sunshine when I needed a boost and lifted the dark clouds.

I want to thank Mark who did a phenomenal job of developing my website www.darkandstormynightmysteries.com and teaching me everything I needed to know to support the site. And to Pam for her help with designing the various print pieces and for being a good listener.

And to all the members of my family who have always been a source of inspiration and support for all that I do.

To all of these great folks, I offer a big Thank You!

DEDICATION

For Mildred--I probably never thanked you enough while you were here. You were a great mentor of mysteries, a wonderful influence on my life, but most important you were always a friend. This book is for you. I hope it's a mystery you would enjoy.

PROLOGUE

For the first time since he walked to the end pier, Jamie realized his life could be in danger. It was dark on the pier, and he was grateful it had finally stopped raining. He didn't want to do this meeting on a dark and stormy night on the end of a pier. The warm afternoon rain caused a fog to rise off the cool waters of the harbor, and this fog would hide them from the people strolling past on the boardwalk.

Jamie was careful to move his eyes without moving his body. He didn't want the men to know what he was thinking. If he went into the water, he would need to do a sideways dive. He wasn't worried about the maneuver. After all, in his youth he won every swimming event he entered. The real question was what to do after he was in the water. Perhaps go deep under the pier and then come back up on the other side. Hopefully the men would be looking on one side, and he would be swimming on the other. He could swim across to the other pier and quietly edge back to the boardwalk. His plans were interrupted as the men came closer.

"You just wouldn't let it go. You had to keep researching that damn story," stated the man in charge. "A minor mistake in my European operation, and somehow you're back in Tri-City doing an investigation. Why didn't you just drop it?"

"Look, there's a simple solution," offered Jamie. "Just stop what you're doing, and my story will never get published."

"Simple, yes, but not practical," said the smallest of the three men.

"Why would you say that? You know I'm not that way. If a person changes his bad behavior, I'd never expose him."

"Yes, I do believe you would keep your word."

While the man in charge was thinking, the third man approached Jamie.

"Do you think we're fools?" He spoke with an Eastern European accent. "We just walk away and then, what, we all become friends?"

He pushed Jamie in the chest. Jamie tried throwing a punch, but was pushed again. He fell backward, hitting his head on the piling, and rolled into the water.

In the final moment of consciousness, Jamie had two thoughts. First, he hoped his son, Christopher, would remember what he taught him in the years they were together, and this would guide him through the rest of his life. Second, he hoped Carrie would ignore the feelings of the past and respond to his challenge to come to Tri-City. Then the darkness slowly spread over him and wiped out the remaining light.

"There he is—pull him over. Is he dead?" asked the man in charge.

The two men grabbed his legs and pulled him to the pier.

"Yeah, he's dead," answered the smaller man. "What you want to do?"

"You shouldn't have pushed him," the boss said sternly to the third man. "But there's no going back now. Take his shoes and socks and then let go of him."

"What?"

"You heard me. Get his shoes and socks."

The men did as they were told.

"Wring the socks out to get them as dry as possible, and dump any water out of the shoes."

He then took the shoes from the one man and the socks from the other. He draped a sock over each shoe and lined them up neatly on the edge of the pier.

1

It was a typical Tri-City night. The temperature and humidity remained high as a great round orange ball fell slowly toward the horizon. The humidity caused the sounds of the street to be distorted. Ascot spun quickly. No one was there.

Calm down. Calm down. You need to keep your wits about you. You'll never spot those two agents if you jump at every sound, he reminded himself.

Ascot walked with the tourist crowds as they left the Tri-City harbor. But the evening was growing late and the crowds were thinning. Soon this natural cover would disappear. He hugged the sidewalk nearest the stores and walked as quickly as he dared. Most tourists were walking slowly as they dragged themselves to the concrete parking lots. Soon they would return to the comfort of their homes while Ascot was faced with finding a safe route back to his hotel.

He pretended to window shop by looking at an assortment of silk ties. In a typical nine-to-five job, a tie was probably an important purchase. Ascot knew nothing about silk ties.

As the sun's glare created a mirror in the window, Ascot spotted one of his adversaries on the other side of the street. He didn't turn around, but he looked quickly left and right. *Where's the second agent?* He asked himself silently. He was unable to answer his question since the first agent spotted him and was now trying to cross the street through the oncoming traffic. Ascot had one advantage--the time it would take the agent to cross the street. The agent also had an advantage since he knew where his partner was.

Ascot moved quickly, darting between the caravans of families and their strollers. He scooted into an alley. It was closed to traffic, but busy with pedestrians seeking refreshments in the sidewalk cafés and pubs. The alley even had a bank branch with ATM machines so visitors could replenish their funds and spend more.

Ascot was about one hundred feet into the alley when his earlier question was answered. Coming from the opposite direction was the second agent. He was trapped! His mind raced quickly, searching for an escape. There was no escape… when the phone began to ring.

Damn, Carrie thought. *This is awful. I've trapped my hero in an alley where only Superman could do a rescue. I should stick with photography and stop trying to write this book.*

The phone continued to ring. Carrie stood up, ran her hands through her short, curly, light-brown hair and then leaned over and punched the save key on her computer. She perched her glasses on top of her head and crossed to the other side of the room to answer the phone.

"Hello," she answered sharply.

"Oh hello." The voice on the other end was unsure. "I'd like to speak to Carrie Kingsford?"

"This is Carrie Kingsford." She was annoyed but with the status of her story rather than the caller.

"Carrie, is that you? This is Joel Wheeler." The voice was now steady and in control.

"Joel Wheeler," she said slowly. Even with the name in her possession, she didn't immediately recognize it. Then it hit her. "Joel, gosh I can't believe it. How long has it been since you and I spoke—ten, no, fifteen years since..."

"It's been twelve since we spoke, but over twenty since I've seen you. Of course, that could be easily fixed if you would attend one of our alumni events."

"Dare I say it seems like only yesterday when we were attending classes at college?" Carrie's mind recalled a picture of a young Joel Wheeler with dark long hair tied in a ponytail. They worked together on the college newspaper. And then her mind produced another picture of the heated editorial debates, with her and Joel arguing over the newspaper's viewpoint. Joel leaned toward the more radical views of the time, and Carrie was often on the opposite side. His strong booming voice would drown out the other opinions. Jamie Faraday, the assistant editor, would jump in as referee on more than one intense discussion between them.

"Carrie, are you listening?"

"I'm sorry. I was daydreaming." She focused her mind back to the present. "I still can't believe it's you," she said. "What causes one of Tri-City's best lawyers to call me on a Thursday afternoon?"

"Thanks for the compliment. So you do keep in touch with the news of your old town."

"Every once in a while, I grab a Tri-City newspaper. Have you tracked me down for some sort of alumni donation or another event? Although March is a little early, I thought most alumni events were later in the spring."

"I wish it were something that pleasant. Unfortunately, I'm afraid I've some rather bad news." Joel Wheeler paused.

"Bad news...what bad news?" she asked softly.

"Now that I actually have you on the phone, this is harder than I thought it would be. I guess the only way to get through this is just to say it. Carrie, Jamie Faraday is dead."

2

The news of Jamie's death traveled through the time and space of twenty-five years. Carrie could see Jamie with his brown wavy hair and the smile that was a permanent feature on his face. Regardless of the unending deadlines and disputes, he always fully researched his stories and enjoyed the process. Jamie believed that "life is fun because all points of view are not black or white but lovely shades of gray that are fun to explore." He always said this with a twinkle in his brown eyes. *Those beautiful eyes...* and her own eyes filled with tears.

"Carrie, I'm sorry. I felt I needed to call you personally since the three of us were such close friends once."

"Oh Joel, there's no easy way to break this kind of news. I'd much rather hear it from you." Carrie paused for a moment to gather her thoughts and then asked, "Why haven't I seen or heard anything about his death in the media? Jamie is... was a fairly well-known journalist."

"You know the Faradays and their influence in the publishing world. With the exception of limited stories in the local papers, they were able to keep other coverage low-key."

Carrie definitely knew about the Faraday influence in the world of publishing and in Jamie's life. She always wondered if her relationship with Jamie would have been different without their interference. Yet when all was said and done, Jamie worked for Faraday Publishing as a reporter. Faraday Press published four magazines, including the regional *Tri-County Monthly* and *News World*, a global publication. Jamie was an overseas reporter for *News World*.

Suddenly Carrie wanted more answers about Jamie's death. "When did he die?"

"His body was found this past Saturday in the early-morning hours. The funeral arrangements couldn't be finalized until after the autopsy. That's why I waited to call you until today."

"You said his body was found? How did he die?"

"His body was pulled from the harbor. The initial findings are he drowned, but the coroner added 'under suspicious circumstances.'"

"Drowned? You know that's impossible! You know as well as I do Jamie was a champion swimmer." Carrie exclaimed

"The police think Jamie may have hit his head as he dived into the water. They think he might have taken a dare and was trying to prove he was still a champion swimmer."

"Jamie would only take a dare if he was drinking." She paused. "Was he drinking?"

"The newspaper reported that he was drinking earlier in the evening at the Admiral's Saloon, where he discussed swimming with the bartender. That's how the police got the idea he might have jumped into the water to prove something. However, with no witnesses, it's only a theory."

"Hmm, that's interesting. I also remember that Jamie would have been hanging around a bar and talking with a bartender if he was working on a story. Was Jamie researching a story?"

"Now wait a minute!" Joel's deep resounding voice reacted quickly. "I don't have all the answers. In fact, I know very little since the case is still under investigation. I mean, how would I know if Jamie was working on a story?" Then Joel softened his tone. "Carrie, as shocking as Jamie's death is to us, it may be nothing more than an accident."

"Do you believe it was an accident?"

"I honestly don't know. I mean, there are still unanswered questions, but sometimes with accidental deaths, some questions are never answered."

With that, Carrie realized there wasn't much more that could be said except, "Joel, will you keep me informed as details are revealed?"

"Wait a minute. There's another reason I'm calling. Jamie's funeral is Saturday, and you should plan on attending."

"I can't go to the funeral. It's been too many years, and Jamie's family wouldn't want me..."

Joel cut her off. "You've got to come to the funeral, or at least to the reading of Jamie's will. He named you as one of the beneficiaries. However, I think the family would be upset if you came only to the reading of the will without paying proper respects at the funeral."

"Why would Jamie name me in his will after all these years? It doesn't make any sense."

"I thought perhaps, well…did you two keep in touch?" Joel asked tentatively.

"No, we didn't," Carrie said firmly. "We lost touch after college. Occasionally, I read his articles in various magazines, and then I followed him more closely when he became a regular contributor to *News World*. But we never communicated with each other."

"I'm sorry. I didn't mean to open old wounds. The reason I asked is there's a letter for you from Jamie. The fact that he left you a letter led me to believe you two still communicated."

"What kind of a letter?"

"I've no idea. It's in the hands of his lawyer, Simpson."

"Jamie didn't use you for legal matters?" She blurted the question out before thinking. "I'm sorry, that was rude. I just thought since you called me, you were the lawyer handling the estate."

"No, my area of expertise is corporate law, with a special emphasis on import/export laws. I don't do wills and estate planning. Besides, once Jamie returned from Europe, he seemed to be more aligned with his family and their suggestions of how to handle items like estate planning. I think he knew getting along with his family provided a more stable environment for his son after his wife's death."

"I didn't know his... his wife died." Carrie stumbled over the words.

"You knew he was married?"

"I heard he married a younger English woman when he was assigned in London. How did she die?" Carrie had started pacing back and forth across the floor of her study.

"She stepped out in front of a car on one of the busiest streets in London. It seemed suspicious at the time, but the investigation revealed it was just an accident. Soon after her death Jamie started to make arrangements to return to the US. However, it took over a year by the time his son finished school and everything was cleared for his return."

"How old is the boy?" Carrie quickened her pace back and forth across the room as she asked more questions.

"He's twelve, and his name is Christopher. He seems to be a good kid." Joel hesitated and then added, "Maybe I should also mention that Jamie returned home with a woman named Suzanne Redmond. Jamie said she was his research assistant; however, she told everyone they were engaged. She's staying at the Faraday house."

"Did Jamie say he was engaged?"

"That's kind of strange, too. He never denied it, but he also never confirmed it. She started using the 'engaged' word much more frequently after his death." Joel paused and then added, "The only other thing you need to know is the logistics. The church service is eleven o'clock at Grace Episcopal on State Street, with interment at twelve-thirty at Woodhaven. You know the cemetery where we used to ice skate on the pond?"

"Yes, I remember, Joel. Thank you for calling. It meant a great deal to hear the news personally from you."

"You will come, won't you? I really would like to see you again."

"I guess I have no choice. I've been invited by a dead man."

3

arrie never attended funerals. She hated them. She preferred not to have a funeral as the last memory of the person. Plus, she could never be sure of her own emotional state. She found that now that she was older, she could be standing at the gravesite of a person she barely knew, and the tears would stream down her face. When this happened, she wasn't much comfort to the family. She didn't know how she would react at Jamie's funeral, considering their past relationship. But on Friday, she pulled herself together, packed her luggage for several days, and headed to Tri-City in her car.

Tri-City was a point on the map where the counties of Allwin, Dorchester, and St. Thomas all touched. It grew from a crossroad stop where farmers traded and sold goods into a metropolitan city supporting the work force for the entire area.

Carrie's trip was boring, tiring, and unending. She found herself measuring her progress by the number of rest stops she passed. Every forty to fifty miles, the road offered services for the traveler. Some were full-service stops including restaurants and repair garages; others offered fast food and self-service gas. After wasting time at two rest stops and drinking more coffee than she cared to measure, Carrie realized she had to concentrate on her driving in order to make the church service.

She zipped back onto the expressway and pressed her foot down on the gas until she achieved the speed limit and even a little more. She noticed another car followed her onto the expressway from the rest stop and was now keeping pace with her. When she passed a car, this car passed with her and then returned to a position behind her. Carrie didn't like someone pacing her, so she decided to stay in her lane and slow down. Traffic was light, and the car had plenty of room to speed on its way. Finally, when no other cars were in sight, the car made a move to pass.

When the car drew alongside, Carrie couldn't help but look over. She could discern there were two men in the front seat, but saw little else since the windows were heavily tinted. Instead of passing, the car started to encroach into her lane. She slowed down and moved more to the right, but the car moved with her.

Carrie was suddenly frightened. What was this car doing? When she sped up, the car sped up. When she slowed down, it did the same and then tried to move into her lane. Carrie didn't know what to do. The car once again moved alongside her car and was edging closer and closer when, out of nowhere, a deep, resounding blast of a truck horn broke the silence. Carrie jumped in her seat, and the menacing car cut sharply in front of her and sped ahead. As Carrie moved to the right to avoid being hit, her tires caught the edge of the shoulder, and she momentarily lost control. Her car careened off the road and ran along the grass, barely missing a ditch before she was able to get it under control and come to a halt. The trucker who honked his horn pulled his truck off the highway and ran back to assist her.

He waited until she opened the window before yelling, "Lady, you okay?"

"Yes, I thhinnk so," she stuttered.

"What the heck was going on? Did you know that other car?"

"No, never saw it before. I guess it was just someone having a little sport."

"Well, playing games on the highway is a dangerous..." The driver didn't finish his sentence as a state trooper car with flashing lights pulled up behind them.

By the time Carrie convinced the trooper and the truck driver she was fine and ready to continue her journey, she realized she would never make the church service on time. She decided to go straight to the cemetery.

4.

oodhaven was the largest and oldest cemetery in Tri-City and occupied the north, south, and east corners of a major intersection. The Faraday plot was in North Woodhaven, which was the most desirable location because of a large pond located near the center of the property. The pond was fed by a creek, and the sound of the babbling water provided a serenity that the other two locations didn't offer.

Carrie knew the section well because she, Jamie, and their friends spent many a cold winter's night skating on the pond. One night while skating, Jamie showed Carrie the family burial plots. He stretched out on the ground in front of a family tombstone.

"Well, what do you think? How do I look? Peaceful?"

"Jamie, get up from there! You're going to catch cold."

"Regardless of what the family thinks of me now, I think I'll fit in nicely when I join them in this spot."

Carrie shook off a chill as she turned into the main entrance of the cemetery.

The Faraday procession wasn't hard to find. A snake of dark luxury cars were parked around a circle, with the tail of the snake backing down the hill. Carrie's blue sports car made a colorful end to the snake's tail.

She used the mirror in her sun visor to check her makeup. She applied a fresh coat of lipstick and checked her hair. That was the one nice thing about her short, naturally curly hair: a quick run of her fingers through her hair would straighten the stray locks. *Not bad for a woman in her late forties.* She thought.

The burial site was located at the highest point in the cemetery. By the time Carrie walked up the hill, a crowd was formed tightly around the gravesite. But that was okay with her. This was one time when having a front-row view held no attraction for her.

Carrie positioned herself to see between the heads of the crowd. On the opposite side from where she was standing were four people seated on folding chairs. She recognized Jamie's mother, Geraldine Faraday. She sat up straight in her chair. She looked frail, unlike the formidable woman Carrie remembered. Next to her was a young boy. As she was able to position herself to get a better look at the boy, Carrie let out a slight gasp. The boy was a younger image of how she remembered Jamie: the same square cut of the jaw and the soft-brown, wavy hair that fell across his forehead. There was no doubt in her mind this was Christopher. On the other side of Geraldine was a tall, distinguished, good-looking man with silver hair. Despite all the thick, silver hair, the man had a young face. Once more, Carrie angled her position. *Could it be Charles, Jamie's older brother?* She wondered. *That silver hair gives him a distinguished look...* Her thought trailed. She wondered if Jamie had silver hair. What was she thinking? Her hair was probably silver if it weren't for the number ten hair color she periodically applied to her own curls.

Seated next to Charles was a wispy blonde. It was hard to determine her age since the brim of a large black hat covered most of her face. *Maybe this is Charles's wife,* thought Carrie. While the family showed no emotion, this woman was openly crying and dabbing her eyes with a handkerchief. *I don't believe Charles's wife would be this emotional. Wait! Could this be Suzanne, Jamie's assistant?* Carrie couldn't bring herself to think the word "fiancée."

Carrie looked around and surveyed the other attendees. She spotted a man in the second row who she was sure was Joel. Next to Joel were two other men who were extremely well tailored and looked like they might be lawyers, In fact most of the men were older with gray hair and looked like they could be lawyers. She didn't recognize anyone else, but she did notice one other man. Not because she knew him, but because of where he was standing. He stood away from the group on an incline that led to the next section of plots. The man was tall and lanky and probably in his late thirties. He wore a black all-weather coat, unbuttoned, with a dark blue suit beneath it. He had a dark hat, but she noticed no hair showed below it.

"Ashes to ashes, dust to dust..."

There was a slight hum as the motorized mechanism started to lower the casket. Mrs. Faraday, Christopher, Charles, and Suzanne approached the opening in the earth, and each placed a rose on the lowering casket.

Moments later, the entire ceremony was over. The crowd began to disperse as the cemetery crew drew closer, waiting to do their final work. Carrie turned and moved with the rest of the crowd toward the parked cars.

"Carrie, Carrie, wait a moment." She turned to face a man hurrying after her. As he drew closer, she knew it was Joel Wheeler. Aside from his hair, which was cut short with gray at the temples, and about thirty additional pounds, Joel Wheeler looked the same. He was still a big, strapping fellow, with a gait to match.

"You made it!" he bellowed, with a big smile and a kiss on the cheek. "I was worried you weren't going to come, especially when I didn't see you at the church."

"The traffic was much worse than I expected." Carrie didn't want to go into details about the car incident.

"Sometimes I wonder how we can get anywhere. It seems every street is congested with traffic." Joel accepted her excuse without question. "I'm really glad to see you, although I wish it wasn't at a funeral."

"I wish the circumstances were different, too, but thanks again for calling me."

"Funeral or not, we really do have a lot of catching up to do," Joel said. "As soon as the formalities are over, you and I need to spend some time..."

Joel's words were interrupted as Charles Faraday came up behind him. "Joel, excuse me, we need to discuss the Carrie situation. I thought you said she would be here?" Charles' question was direct but delivered in a very calm even tone.

"And so she is." Joel's body was blocking Carrie, so he moved slightly to the right. "Charles, you remember Carrie Kingsford?" It was obvious Joel was enjoying putting one over on Charles.

Carrie forgot how tall Charles was as she looked up into his face. Carrie was always pleased with her five-foot-eight height, but next to Charles's six-foot-two frame, she felt small.

"Oh, hello, Carrie," he stammered. After an awkward moment of silence, Charles continued, "I'm sorry if I sounded cranky a moment ago, but I knew you missed the church service, and, well…I didn't see you at the gravesite."

"Hello, Charles." She extended her hand. "I was delayed in traffic, so I came straight to the cemetery." Charles took her hand and held it gently in his.

"I'm glad you decided to come."

"I told you she was coming," Joel interjected.

They both ignored Joel as Carrie continued, "I'm sorry about Jamie's death. I know it must be very difficult for you and your mother."

"It's been difficult, especially for Mother. The natural order expects children to outlive their parents."

Carrie realized Charles was still holding her hand, and she gently withdrew it. "You were saying you needed to decide about my situation?"

"There is no situation, now that you're here," Charles said with a warm smile. "We can easily follow Jamie's instructions."

"You mean the reading of the will?"

"Yes, the will, but my brother also left you a letter." Charles looked at Joel. "Joel, you did tell Carrie about the letter?"

"I did. I told her Simpson is holding a letter for her," Joel defended.

Carrie looked from Joel to Charles. "Do you know what's in the letter?"

"No idea," Charles answered, "but since we consider the circumstances of Jamie's death suspicious, we're hoping his letter sheds some light on what he was doing."

"Hello, my dear. It has been a long time," Said a soft genteel voice. Carrie turned and faced Geraldine Faraday as she extended her hand.

"Oh, hello, Mrs. Faraday. I'm so sorry about Jamie."

Mrs. Faraday had weathered the years well. Her skin was tight, and she looked much younger than a woman in her seventies.

Carrie barely finished her sentence when Mrs. Faraday turned to the blonde who was walking toward them, holding onto Christopher's arm. "Suzanne, you and Christopher wait for us in the car." Suzanne started to protest, but then turned and followed Christopher to the waiting limousine.

Mrs. Faraday turned back to Carrie. "Carrie, of course you will be staying with us. Jamie asked us to extend every courtesy to you. You remember how to find the house?"

"Jamie asked you? How did he…?"

"We also received a letter from Jamie. He asked us to make sure we reached out to you and have you stay at our home."

"That's very kind of you, but I think a hotel would suit me…"

"It's settled then," Mrs. Faraday said, ignoring Carrie's protest. "We are serving a luncheon at the house, and I have guests waiting. I'll expect to see you and Joel there shortly."

Charles took his mother's arm and led her to the limousine.

Carrie turned back to Joel. "I guess I'm staying with the Faradays."

"Some battles aren't worth the fight," Joel offered. "Hey, can I ride with you? I rode with the family this morning, and my car is parked at their house."

"Sure, you can help me find my way to the stately old mansion," Carrie said as she unlocked the door of her car. Joel slid into the passenger seat.

"You shouldn't look harshly upon Mrs. Faraday. After all, she's old school, and the old school never forgets the rules for proper behavior." He turned to face her. "Of course, you never approved of the old school, did you?"

"I'm afraid you've got it backwards. The old school never approved of me."

"Do you think if they approved, it would have made a difference for you and Jamie?"

"Oh, I don't know. That would be an easy excuse to explain away life's little twists. Over the years, I realized that Jamie and I weren't really meant for each other."

"Really? You two always seemed so close. You don't think you could have worked things out?"

"We were close. We were caring, fiercely loyal, loved each other, but we weren't in love." For the first time, Carrie expressed what she knew in her heart to be true.

"You certainly didn't seem that way at the time. Don't forget to take a left at the next road," Joel prompted.

Carrie turned into a street lined with large old oak trees. Set back several hundred feet from the street were large homes. Each home was different from the next, but all were of a good size and design.

"As I remember, the house is near the end of the street." Carrie was glad the ride and conversation were nearly over.

"Yup, third house from the end on the left. Since you're one of the overnight guests," he said with a slight sarcasm, "you should park behind the house near the garage."

Carrie maneuvered around the other cars along the edge of the driveway and found a parking spot on the concrete pad next to the garage.

"This is where Jamie worked," Joel said, pointing to the garage as they emerged from Carrie's car.

"Jamie worked in the garage?" Carrie asked with surprise.

"Not literally in the garage. He converted the area over the garage into a studio."

Carrie gazed upward at the windows and for a moment imagined Jamie working at his desk.

Joel sensed Carrie was deep in thought and waited before he suggested, "We better go in."

oel and Carrie entered through a set of French doors at the side of the house. They stepped into a large room already crowded with people talking and eating. On the far side of the room was a fireplace nestled between two floor-to-ceiling bookcases. A large crackling fire warmed the room. In the middle was a seating area with two overstuffed sofas and four leather chairs sharing space on a thick Oriental rug. Several groups of people who were engaged in conversations around the room looked up when Joel and Carrie entered.

"Joel, are you sure it is all right for us to enter this way?" asked Carrie.

"We missed the official reception line at the front door, but you were officially welcomed at the cemetery. Besides, this is where the food and beverages are," he said with a twinkle in his eye. "Now, don't worry. You make yourself comfortable, or should I say right at home, and I'll let everyone know we are here. Give me your car keys and I'll have your luggage taken to your room." Joel accepted her keys and made his way through the crowd and out into the hallway.

Carrie moved farther into the room and captured a glass of wine from a passing tray. She found herself standing near two women of Mrs. Faraday's age.

"It seems such a shame. He just arrived home."

"Yes, and he was finally settling down," the second woman added.

"It continues to amaze me how well he did. You know, he barely made it through high school. He had to attend Tri-City State College because his grades were so low. But then he got that second degree from a top journalism school and one award after another for his work."

"Well, as I always say, good family lines are inherited. In some children it just takes a little longer before they appear."

Carrie moved away and heard a second conversation between a man and a woman.

"What will happen to his son? I hear he's just like his father was at that age. A little on the wild side," offered the woman.

"Geraldine and Charles should send him to a good military boarding school. I always say discipline is the way..."

Carrie tuned out the conversation and selected a grilled chicken quesadilla triangle with a tangy salsa from one of the food tables. She picked up the food item as a distraction from the surrounding conversations and then realized she was quite hungry. Carrie looked over the assortment of food. There was grilled fillet of beef on a stick, bite-size crab cakes, cut vegetables, and a display of caviar. *My, my*, thought Carrie, *little Tri-City has become quite cosmopolitan, offering caviar at its functions.* She fixed herself a toast point of black fish eggs topped with a dollop of sour cream. She popped the delicacy in her mouth and was debating what to select next when she overheard pieces of another conversation. She maneuvered closer to the conversation by pretending to stare at the crackling flames in the fireplace.

"I hear the death is still classified as suspicious."

"Was there alcohol in the blood?"

"Not enough to account for the drowning." The two men talking were both in their late fifties and were the same two men standing next to Joel at the funeral. One man was thin, medium height, and balding, in an exquisite dark charcoal gray suit, while the other man was tall with salt-and-pepper hair, a matching moustache, and silver-rimmed glasses. Both men exuded a sense of wealth or "old" money that Carrie associated with the Faradays.

"One of my sources at the medical examiner's office said there was a contusion on his head."

"Jamie could have hit his head on the pier when he went into the water," suggested the man in the charcoal suit.

"It's a possibility," the other man said as he rubbed the end of his chin. "You know, the police have taken all these odd little circumstances and wrapped them in a neat little package. I hate neat little packages. I think they want it to be accidental."

"But, Hugh, if it's not accidental, you're saying you think it could be murder? That part of downtown tends to be very safe. It's well patrolled by the police because of all the tourists. Although I guess it could have been a simple mugging that went bad."

"Look, I did want to ask you something else," said the taller man. "As long as I can remember, James was always writing. Was he working…"

"Oh, there you are." Joel returned.

The two men, sensing people nearby, moved further away. Carrie turned to face Joel. His timing couldn't have been worse, but she smiled. "I felt a little chilled, so I'm just warming up here at the fire. Joel, who are the two men chatting over by the window?"

Joel looked over. "I see only one, but he's someone I want you to meet." Joel motioned for the shorter of the two men Carrie just overheard to join them.

"Carrie, this is Jonathan Stone. He's the general manager and the man who sees that every issue of *News World* hits the streets each month. Jonathan, this is Carrie Kingsford."

"I'm a loyal reader and a longtime subscriber of your magazine," Carrie said as she shook his hand. She noticed that his bushy eyebrows offset his smooth, round face. Although he was balding, the hair on each side of his head was thick and perfectly clipped. His face lit up at her words.

"That's truly a compliment, coming from a professional photographer like you. I'm very much aware of your work and your reputation." He smiled as he acknowledged her.

Before Carrie could answer, Joel said, "I see someone I need to greet. If you'll excuse me, I'll leave you two to chat."

He grabbed a treat of caviar from a passing tray and then darted off to the other side of the room. There was an awkward pause as the two strangers were left to carry on the conversation.

Then Carrie said, "It must be difficult to lose a journalistic talent like Jamie."

"Yes, such a sad occurrence." Jonathan paused for a moment as if he was remembering a special memory and then continued. "He was an editor's dream. Jamie wrote the pieces, could also capture a good photo when needed, and had the mobility to go anywhere in the world at a moment's notice. Of course, I also lost a personal friend, but I understand he was a personal friend of yours, too." Stone accepted a drink from one of the trays being passed by a waiter. Then he set the drink on the fireplace mantle as he straightened the sleeves of his cuff-linked shirt.

"Jamie and I were friends in college, but lost touch over the years."

"Oh, really? Then I wonder why he selected you for this mysterious letter of his." Jonathan realized the implication of what he said and then gently added, "I mean, after all this time."

"Does everyone know about this letter?" Carrie asked trying not to sound annoyed.

"I'm afraid we were all a little curious when your name was mentioned by Simpson. You've no idea why Jamie would write you a letter?"

"Sorry, I don't know. Believe me, his death was a tremendous shock, but his letter is even more of a shock. I'm just beginning to catch up on the details of Jamie's life, and now I'm in the middle of his death. I understand from Joel that his wife also died under unusual circumstances?"

"In light of Jamie's death, I guess people would react that way. The actual truth is Emma, that was his wife's name, was the victim of an accidental hit and run on a London street. That was over two years ago. After Emma's death, Jamie found himself with the sole responsibility of a ten-year-old. He refused to put Christopher in a boarding school and took him on all his assignments. But I think, as the boy got older, Jamie realized he needed the stability of regular schooling and wanted to come back to Tri-City."

"And Jamie had been back in Tri-City for...?"

"I guess about three months. By the time Christopher finished the current school year, Jamie finished his assignments and I arranged for other reporters to replace him, it took me a while to get him home." Jonathan stopped the waiter carrying a tray of caviar. "Have you sampled this caviar, my dear? It seems to be the snack food of choice in Tri-City at the moment, and this brand is quite good." Jonathan took a moment and carefully fixed the treat and quickly consumed it. He then took his napkin and wiped the corners of his mouth. "Quite tasty, are you sure you won't have some?"

"I tried some, it's delicious, but I'm good for right now." Carrie shook her head no, and the waiter moved away.

"The world does seem to be getting smaller, just based on all the different foods we are able to enjoy," added Stone.

"Mr. Stone, you mentioned Jamie's assignments, was Jamie working on a story at the time of his death?"

"Please, call me Jonathan. 'Mr. Stone' is too formal. No, he wasn't writing anything for me. As I mentioned, he was just getting settled, and I hadn't given him any assignments."

"He was to working on a story!" announced a young voice from behind Carrie and Jonathan.

6

arrie and Jonathan Stone turned to face Christopher Faraday.

"Hello, Christopher. Have you meet Carrie Kingsford? She was a friend of your father's from his college days."

"Hello. I saw you at the funeral, but I didn't get to introduce myself because Grandmother made me go right to the car." Christopher held out his hand. "I wanted to talk to you about the letter my dad left you."

Carrie looked into the young eyes of Christopher and saw someone she once knew. She ignored these thoughts and said, "Nice to meet you," as she shook his hand. "You said your father was working on a story at the time of his..." She stopped.

"You can say it...death. I'm not a two-year-old. I understand what happened and, I know a lot about my dad's work."

"Was he working for someone else?" Stone asked sarcastically, "Because he had no assignments from me."

"It wasn't exactly an assignment. He was working on a book." Christopher rushed his second sentence so much it was hard to understand him.

"Did you say a book? What was this book about? A memoir of his years abroad?" asked Stone smiling at the boy.

An annoyed look momentarily showed on Christopher's face, and then he continued directing his comments to Carrie. "It was going to be sort of a mystery. A true mystery, based on stuff he discovered in Europe."

Carrie looked at Stone. "And what stuff did your father discover?"

"I'm not really sure. He just told me that he discovered stuff he thought would make a good book, but he needed to check things out in Tri-City. Plus, Tri-City would be a good place for me to go to school, and Grandma's home would be a good place to live."

"This seems like a very serious business discussion," Charles said as he and Joel approached. "Are we interrupting?"

"Hello, Charles. Christopher was just telling us that his father was working on a crime book," summarized Stone.

"Christopher, your grandmother wants you to meet some folks," Charles said. "They're in the living room."

Christopher's face changed to disappointment, and he looked to Carrie for support. He clearly wanted to stay the center of the current conversation.

"We'll have plenty of time to talk later," Carrie said as she gently placed her hand on his shoulder. "Your grandmother has invited me to stay here in the house."

Christopher brightened at this news and headed to the other room.

"We have to give Christopher a little leeway," Charles said. "Since he's been home, his stories about his adventures with his father are growing by leaps and bounds."

"Isn't there a possibility Jamie did return home to work on a book?" Carrie asked Stone.

"This is the first I've heard of a book," Stone said. "But I'm sure if Jamie was going to write a book, it would center on his experiences during his years in London. As I suggested, more of a memoir about politics, people, and places. Somehow I can't imagine true crime as the subject. It just wasn't Jamie's field."

"Christopher mentioned that Jamie needed to come home 'to check things out.' That sounds like whatever he was writing had a Tri-City connection," suggested Carrie.

"Of course anything is possible, but the subject never came up with me. Jamie had barely unpacked his papers and put his studio in working order before he died. Speaking of papers, here's Hugh Simpson. Hugh, over here." Stone waved to a man who entered the study from the hallway. Carrie recognized him as the man with Stone earlier.

"Hugh, this is Carrie Kingsford," introduced Charles.

"Hello, my dear. Such a sad time, but it is a pleasure to meet you." He took her hand and gently squeezed it. There was something warm and genuine about Hugh Simpson that Carrie liked immediately.

"Has anyone mentioned the letter that Jamie left?" Simpson asked seriously.

They all looked from one to the other, and Carrie giggled.

"I think everyone attending this gathering has mentioned Jamie's letter," she answered.

Simpson smiled, too. "I'm afraid in my efforts to find out who you were and how to contact you, I did mention the letter to several people."

"Do you know what the letter is about?" asked Carrie.

"Haven't a clue! Jamie gave me an envelope about a month ago. It wasn't a legal document, or at least not one that I prepared. It was a gentleman's agreement that if something happened to him, I would open the envelope. After his death, I opened it and discovered another envelope and a note inside. The note said I should deliver the envelope personally to you, Ms. Kingsford. That's the first I knew what was in the envelope and what I was to do with the contents."

Hugh Simpson removed a business-size envelope from his pocket and handed it to Carrie. Carrie felt as if time was in slow motion and all eyes in the room were watching the transfer of the letter from Simpson's hand to hers.

"Perhaps you would prefer to have the letter kept in a safe place until you have the time to review it. I'll be glad to keep it in my office safe until tomorrow," Joel offered quickly.

"I think Carrie will have plenty of time to review the letter here in the privacy of the house," Charles answered. "If she's worried about the letter's safety, I'll be glad to lock it in the safe in my study."

Carrie was sure Stone was about to offer another suggestion, but she interrupted. "Mr. Simpson, you've kept the letter safe since Jamie gave it to you. Would you mind holding it for me until tomorrow? I'm not sure I want to deal with the letter tonight."

"I'll be delighted to do that for you." Simpson slipped the letter back in his pocket.

7

As the last guests were leaving, Carrie slipped away to her room. She still felt uncomfortable about staying in the Faraday home, but the thought of having a bed nearby was comforting.

She found herself sitting on the edge of a queen-sized bed in a beautifully decorated room. The colors were a soft teal shade, with one wall papered in a tiny splash pattern of teal and peach that matched the fluffy bedspread. The room wasn't masculine or feminine, just comfortable, and she found herself fighting the urge to sleep. Her luggage was in the room, and her belongings were neatly folded and stored in the antique walnut furniture.

As alluring as the bed was to Carrie, she needed to do one more task before she slept. She held Jamie's letter in her hand. As much as she liked Simpson, at the last minute, she decided to keep the letter with her. She caught him in the hallway as he was about to leave. She thought Simpson looked relieved as he willingly returned the document. Now, she needed to find a safe hiding place.

She looked around the room. The banker's desk in the corner was too obvious, and her clothing drawers could easily be searched. There were several paintings and framed photos around the room. She looked at one photograph that showed Jamie and a group of people. She recognized Jonathan Stone and Charles holding a copy of the magazine, along with Joel and Simpson. The caption underneath the photo read: "First Issue—*News World.*"

She decided it was too much work to select a picture and then properly tape the letter in place. No, she had only one choice. She slipped off her jacket and dress and put on a robe. She tore open the envelope, removed the letter, and dropped the envelope in the trash can by the desk. She folded the letter several times and placed it securely in her bra. She pulled back the comforter and sandwiched herself between it and the cool sheet.

Carrie slept soundly for two hours. Toward the end of the sleep, she began to dream about her unfinished book.

෨

Ascot was stretched out on a bed in his hotel room, resting. He thought he heard a slight sound outside his door and was on his feet in a split second. In his socks, he bounded to the locked door of his room and held his gun against his chest. The doorknob turned. He placed his finger securely on the trigger. Nothing happened. There was a slight swishing sound, and he looked down and saw a note slide under the door. He wouldn't be fooled by the old trick of bending down to retrieve a note just as a bullet crashes through the wood door. He waited. He heard nothing. He unlocked the door. He opened it slowly and carefully looked out. He saw no one. He moved cautiously into the hallway. No one was there. The mysterious postman had come and gone. He shut and locked the door. He picked up the envelope and felt around the edges. It was flat with no signs it contained anything dangerous. He used his penknife to slit the envelope on the short end and took out a single sheet of paper. Written on the paper was, "I know who did it, and he's closer than you think."

～

Carrie woke up and sensed a presence in her room. Was it the dream, or had someone also come to her room? She looked around but nothing appeared to be out of place. She thought of her character, Ascot, and wondered how he escaped from the two agents in the alley. She would work on that problem later. She thought of the note Ascot received, and she reached into her bra. Her letter was still there. Ascot's note didn't say much. She hoped her letter from Jamie held more answers.

She moved over to the desk and smoothed out the creases of the letter. As she was about to read it, there was a knock at the door. She quickly returned the letter to its hiding place.

"Come in," she called.

"Good evening, miss. I hope I'm not disturbing you."

The young woman who entered was a member of the Faraday household staff. She was in her late twenties, thin with auburn hair piled loosely on top of her head. Her glasses sat precariously perched on the end of her nose. It made her look somewhat bookish as she stared over the top of the frames.

"The family asked me to inform you that a light supper will be served in a half-hour. They are currently in the study, if you would care to join them for cocktails."

"Thank you…and you are…?"

"Oh, I'm Mary, Miss. Shall I announce that you will be joining them?"

"Well, I'm not quite ready yet, Mary, perhaps in a few minutes. Mary, did you put my clothes away?

"Yes, I did. Oh, was anything wrong?" Mary's face showed concern.

"No, no not at all. It was quite nice and a pleasant surprise. I was tired after my trip, and it was nice not to worry about unpacking. I just wanted to thank you."

Mary looked pleased. "I appreciate you saying something. Mr. Jamie was the same way. He always thanked me, too, when I kept this room for him."

"This was Jamie's room?" Carrie asked, somewhat surprised.

"This was…is one of the guest rooms. But Mr. Jamie used it when he came home. He wanted his son to have his old room."

"I see. Well, thank you, Mary. I'll be down in just a little while. Does the family dress for dinner?"

"Oops, glad you asked. I was supposed to tell you to dress casual." She smiled sheepishly as she closed the door behind her.

Carrie knew that dress casual in the Faraday house didn't mean jeans and a T-shirt. Instead she put on navy slacks and a matching turtleneck with small snowflakes along the neckline and around the sleeves. She brushed her hair and removed a new lipstick from its packaging. As she tossed the package into the trash can, she realized the can was empty. Someone had been in her room! But why take the empty envelope? She wondered about the empty trash can as she left her room to join the family for dinner. Maybe Mary had emptied it while she napped.

When she arrived on the first floor, she could hear voices coming from the study. She couldn't make out the words, but the discussion sounded lively among Charles, Suzanne, and Mrs. Faraday.

She quietly approached the study door. The words coming from inside were clearer now.

"I don't see why you invited her to stay here in the first place. After all, what does a photographer know about..." Suzanne stopped.

"Were you about to say 'murder'?" Charles asked.

"I was about to say Jamie's work," Suzanne defended. "His death has not been ruled a murder. His death will probably turn out to be an unfortunate accident, but I think this mysterious letter has stirred up all these thoughts about murder," added Suzanne.

"I wonder..." Mrs. Faraday's voice sounded weak.

"Mother, what are you thinking?" Charles asked gently.

"I was also wondering why Carrie. Jamie hadn't seen her in many years, and from all indications they didn't keep in touch," she added.

"Maybe Jamie's death has something to do with the past," Charles suggested. "Someone they both knew or some story they both worked on for the college newspaper."

"Charles, if you're right, then Jamie's letter must contain clues. I think we should insist that Carrie show us that letter!" Suzanne stated firmly.

"See, Suzanne, you do understand why we invited Carrie to stay with us. The best way to learn what Carrie knows is to have her under this roof," Mrs. Faraday said, and then added, "So, children, no more bickering."

Carrie did not like Mrs. Faraday's last comment. *Let them have supper without me*, she thought. She spun around to return to her room and crashed into Christopher.

"Hey, how come you're spying on everyone?" he asked.

Carrie jumped. "Christopher, you shouldn't be sneaking up on people!" she scolded.

"Look who's talking. You were sneakin' up on them, weren't you?" Christopher tilted his head toward the study.

Carrie hoped her face wasn't showing the guilt she was feeling. "I didn't exactly sneak up. I was waiting for the right moment to enter the room."

"That's a good one. I'll have to remember that excuse the next time I get caught."

"Ah, so you've been caught listening to other people's conversations, too. That means we're both spies. Maybe we can get side-by-side cells when they cart us off to prison."

Christopher started to defend himself, when he realized Carrie was pulling his leg. He placed his thumbs inside his belt loops and boasted, "You might say I've overheard a few conversations in my time."

"Glad to hear it. In that case, I think we should make a deal. You don't tell on me today, and I won't tell on you," Carrie offered.

"But you haven't caught me at anything!" Christopher protested.

"Let's say you're buying security for your future."

"Future options...hmm," he said. "I like that. Grandma and Uncle Charles are always talking stock options. Okay, I agree, with one condition."

"What's the condition?"

"I get to choose when to exercise my option," he stated.

Carrie smiled at his use of the phrase and said, "You do understand finance. It's a deal." She held out her hand, and they shook on it.

"What are you two plotting?"

They both jumped.

"Looks like high-powered negotiations going on out here, especially when the negotiators look guilty as sin." Charles was standing at the door of the study.

"Nothing's going on," Carrie said calmly. "We were just coming into the room."

Charles led the way as Carrie gave a wink to Christopher, who responded with a grin.

After drinks in the study, the group adjourned to the dining room. Mrs. Faraday was the perfect dinner hostess, orchestrating the serving of the entrée and vegetables. Charles seemed at ease as he managed the conversation. He asked Carrie about her photography and if she was doing any writing. He asked Christopher how he was progressing on his science report for school and asked Suzanne what she liked most about Europe.

It wasn't until after dessert, and Christopher left to do his schoolwork, that Suzanne brought up the letter. The adults were enjoying the last of the coffee when Suzanne asked, "Were you planning on reading the letter tomorrow at Simpson's office?"

"I'll read the letter before the reading of the will." Carrie answered Suzanne's question without mentioning she had the letter in her possession. "I just wanted some time before I made any decisions."

"Decisions?" asked Mrs. Faraday.

Carrie placed her coffee cup on the saucer and turned to face her hostess. "I'm very saddened by the loss of Jamie, as I know all of you are. However, I'm just not sure what my role is and why Jamie..." She paused.

Charles supplied the missing word. "Involved you."

"Why do you feel Jamie did involve you?" Suzanne interrupted abruptly.

"I haven't seen Jamie's letter yet. However, my assumption is that he felt that if he died under unusual circumstances, he needed someone outside his immediate circle of family and friends to look into his death," Carrie responded.

"Does that mean you're not satisfied with the accidental death verdict?" Charles asked the question as if this suspicion were being raised for the first time.

"I don't know whether to be satisfied or not. I won't know until I read the letter and see what Jamie was thinking."

"You can't make a decision until you read the letter, but you give the letter back to Simpson," said Suzanne.

"Suzanne is right, my dear," stated Mrs. Faraday. "We could have read the letter together and then worked with you to determine the next steps."

Carrie was thinking how to respond when the phone rang, and Charles went into the hallway to answer. The conversation stopped while they waited for Charles to return.

"Hello. Yes, this is Charles Faraday. Yes, of course I know him...has something happened...When? Is he all right? ... That seems unusual. What hospital is this again? ...I'm on my way. It will take me about twenty minutes to get there."

"What is it, Charles?" Mrs. Faraday asked when he returned to the room.

"It's Simpson. He was mugged."

"Is he hurt?" Suzanne asked.

"He's at the hospital, but he must be okay. The hospital is calling because they want someone to accompany him home. He's ready to be released."

"Was anything taken?" Suzanne was full of questions.

"According to the person from the hospital, the police said he was attacked, but his money and credit cards were left."

"That is most unusual," remarked Mrs. Faraday.

"I don't understand," piped in Suzanne. "What's so unusual about that? I bet a lot of thieves don't take credit cards."

"Perhaps, but Simpson is known for carrying several hundred dollars in cash," said Mrs. Faraday. "And while some thieves may not take credit cards, I've never heard of one that doesn't take cash."

"Mother and I have warned him several times that he would be a target for a mugger carrying that kind of money," added Charles. "Then when he does get mugged, the mugger doesn't take the money?"

"Maybe they didn't know he was carrying money," Suzanne said as she went to the side table and poured herself another cup of coffee.

"I think it means he wasn't looking for money. Anyway, I better get going. I'll have more answers once I talk with Simpson."

"Charles, Hugh's wife is out of town visiting their daughter. If he needs a place to stay while he mends, be sure to bring him here," added Mrs. Faraday.

Carrie was surprised by the continued show of hospitality on the part of Mrs. Faraday. First she extended her home to Suzanne, then provided a room for her, and now a place for Simpson to heal. After what she overheard earlier, Carrie couldn't help being cynical about Mrs. Faraday's reasons. Did she want everyone related to the case gathered under her roof?

"I wonder..." Suzanne looked directly at Carrie. "I wonder if the muggers were after the letter."

Suzanne asked the very question Carrie was thinking. Was her letter the cause of Simpson's mishap?

"Suzanne, unfortunately in this day and age, many people get mugged," stated Mrs. Faraday. "To assume this attack occurred because of James's letter has no foundation. Besides, it was my understanding, Carrie, that Hugh gave you James's letter this afternoon."

Carrie never had a chance to answer because Suzanne jumped in, "He did, but Carrie gave it back. She asked him to hold it until tomorrow."

Mrs. Faraday looked at Carrie, and Carrie nodded her agreement with Suzanne's statement. Carrie still didn't want to reveal that the letter was back in her possession.

"Then we'll have to wait until Charles and Hugh return to get more details." She looked past Suzanne to Carrie. "This has been a very tiring day, and I'm going to my room." With those final words, Mrs. Faraday left the two women sitting in the study.

After Mrs. Faraday left the room, Suzanne started in again. "I agree with Mrs. Faraday."

"I beg your pardon?" Carrie asked.

"I think it raises some questions about your judgment. It's not right you let Simpson get hurt over Jamie's letter. We could have all read the letter together right here in the safety of the house."

Carrie was irritated by Suzanne's accusations, but she kept her annoyance under control. She answered, "I've three thoughts on the matter. First, Suzanne, that isn't what Mrs. Faraday, said. What she said was we don't know if the letter was the reason Simpson was mugged. We'll have to wait and see. Second, I'm sorry Simpson was attacked. However, if the letter was the cause of this mishap, I could have placed everyone in this house in jeopardy. The mugger might have broken in here to find the letter."

Suzanne sat quietly and then said, "What's your third thought?"

"If the letter was the reason for the mugging, only a limited number of people knew Simpson had the letter. So I can't help but wonder if someone closer than we think informed the mugger." Carrie realized she used the same phrase Ascot found in his note.

Suzanne didn't reply to Carrie's comment. Then Carrie added, "I agree with Mrs. Faraday on one thing. This has been a very long day. If you will excuse me, I'm going to my room." Carrie left Suzanne sipping coffee in the study.

When Carrie arrived at her room, she saw the door wasn't completely closed. Yet she was sure she had closed it securely when she left. Perhaps Mary returned to turn down the bed and straighten the room.

She entered the room cautiously. The bed was not turned down, there were no fresh towels, but Carrie was sure someone had been in the room. She gazed around, and her eye was drawn to the wastebasket. The envelope from Jamie's letter was now hanging over the lip of the basket. Someone else knew that Carrie, not Simpson, had the letter. It couldn't have been Suzanne. Suzanne was with Carrie the entire time. That left Charles, Mrs. Faraday, Christopher, or members of the household staff.

Carrie decided now was the time to read the letter, before anything else happened. She took it from her bra, grabbed her reading glasses, and sat on the edge of the bed. Jamie's letter was handwritten, and Carrie immediately recognized his tiny cursive script.

My dearest Carrie,

The years cannot take away all that we meant to one another. On more than one occasion, I've questioned whether we made the right decision not to marry. And I can't help but wonder if you haven't asked yourself this same question.

Carrie stopped reading for a moment and held the letter. Jamie was always so direct. She continued.

I know our decision was made by two people who thought they logically and calmly came to a mutual conclusion. We both had talents that needed to be developed. We both had freshly printed degrees in hand that gave us the opportunity to go off and search the world. I think we both did fine.

Now I find myself in desperate need of that cool, calm, and logical way you had of analyzing situations: black and white, without all the shades of gray. I'm not sure how bad it is, but I'm beginning to think I'm in deeper than...well, deeper than I can perhaps handle.

Remember the story we worked on together in college for the paper, the one about the records being altered in the registrar's office? We stayed up for two nights hiding out in the registrar's office trying to catch the person. We never caught him, but the problem just stopped. I'm working on a story with a similar situation. Waiting in the dark, hoping the person will stop. If not, I'll have to try to catch them in the act. I know this isn't much information, but if something does happen to me, I don't want to cloud your analytical ability with my theories.

If the worst happens—be careful. I'm placing this incredible burden on you because I know you're a good photographer who can analyze a situation without being influenced. Good analysis is like a photo. A photo never lies because it sees things exactly as they are.

If it becomes necessary to deliver this letter, I've asked my family to have you stay with them in our house. I can hear you saying, "Thanks a lot," but I have my reasons.

First, I have a son. His name is Christopher. He's a wonderful kid, and I'd like for him to meet you. In many ways he reminds me of you. Staying at the house will allow you to be near Christopher. I think you will enjoy the experience. Second, the house will provide you with protection. Be open-minded toward Mother and Charles. I've learned to accept them for the good people they are. Third, all of my belongings, notes, photos, and papers are at the house, and staying there will provide convenient access to them.

Asking you to help is harder than any story assignment I've had, but I know I've done the right thing. I

*pray I'll see you someday in person, and this letter will
never be delivered.*

*Carrie, there has always been and will always be a
place in my heart for you.*

With love,

Jamie

*P.S. Remember, good analysis is like a photo. It
always reveals the truth.*

⚬⚬

Carrie turned the letter over, but there was nothing on
the back. Through her tears, she read the letter several more
times. She was looking for some clue in the words as to what
Jamie was investigating, but it just wasn't there. The only
thing the letter did imply was that Jamie might be working
on a story.

The next question was what to do with the letter. It was
too dangerous to keep it there. Then she had an idea. She
went to the desk and wrote a short note explaining where she
was and asked for the enclosed envelope to be held until
she was able to retrieve it. She enclosed Jamie's letter in a
new envelope and placed it in a second envelope addressed
to her parents in Pear Cove, a resort town about seventy-
five miles away from Tri-City.

She slept with the envelope under her pillow. But sleep didn't come easily. Her restless dreams were of Jamie swimming in the harbor and Ascot running through the streets of Tri-City. In each case they were trying to escape from someone wanting to murder them.

9

When Carrie awoke the next morning, it was only four-thirty. Unable to go back to sleep, she took the time to write down a couple of notes for her mystery book based on her recent dreams. She wondered if all writers dreamed of their characters.

When the first light showed through the windows, she put on her jogging outfit and left the house. The morning was beautiful. She liked March mornings, with their promise of spring. The air was crisp, but not so cold that you couldn't enjoy running. She jogged into the small village near the Faraday house. The village consisted of a deli/convenience store, a garage, an antique shop and craft store, an interior design shop, a pub, and a post office. She jogged around the village a couple of times to be sure her movements weren't being observed. When she was sure no one else was around, Carrie went to the post office and dropped her letter in the mailbox. She wasn't a dedicated runner, so she decided to walk briskly on her trip back to the house. Her character Ascot was a good runner. After all, Ascot was an agent and he often needed to run to escape the danger he was facing. Carrie was a photographer and there was no danger in her life so walking was just fine for her. Plus, walking allowed her to clear her mind and reflect on the words in Jamie's letter.

What did he mean by waiting for the person to stop? What was this person doing? Did this person kill him? What did he mean by "my things are at the house"? Did he mean actual clues were in the house? Was Jamie speaking literally or figuratively when he said photos don't lie? She had lots of questions, but few answers. If Jamie was writing a story, she needed to find out what that story was and then follow his same path of research.

Carrie arrived back at the house as Mary was bringing a tray of coffee to her room.

"Good morning, miss. Mr. Charles saw that you went jogging and thought you might enjoy a cup of coffee when you returned."

"That was very kind of him," Carrie said out loud, but wondered where Charles was positioned that he saw her leave the house.

"Miss? Miss Carrie. Are you all right?"

"Oh, yes…yes, I'm fine. I'm sorry, Mary. I was daydreaming for a moment."

"May I pour you a cup of coffee?" Mary was standing by the tray ready to pour from the two-cup pot.

"Well, that depends. Do I have time to shower before the big breakfast with the family?"

Mary giggled, and the freckles on her face seemed to pop from their hiding place. Then she caught herself and replied, "Oh, yes, miss. Actually, the 'big breakfast' is a buffet. Mrs. Faraday thought that would be easier, with today being special. However, it won't be served for another thirty minutes. I believe you and Mr. Charles are the only ones up and about."

"I assume today is 'special' because it's the reading of the will?"

"I'm sure that's part of it, but I think it has more to do with everyone eating at the same time. Normally, for breakfast each person comes to the kitchen and tells either my aunt or myself what you want, and we prepare it. Mr. Charles, Master Christopher, and Mr. Jamie, when he was here, ate early because they needed to go to school or work. Mrs. Faraday likes her breakfast served in her room at eight, and Suzanne...well, she can appear at anytime."

"Suzanne is not an early riser?" Carrie asked.

"It isn't so much she's a late riser as she's inconsistent. Sometimes she would eat with Mr. Jamie causing a delay in his schedule. For several days she bothered Mrs. Faraday. Other days she wouldn't come down at all, which interrupted my aunt's schedule, waiting to see if she wanted something. Now she tries to time her breakfast to coincide with Mr. Charles. Master Christopher is the only one Suzanne completely ignores, but that's probably okay with him."

"Not the best of friends?"

"She treats him like a kid, which he doesn't like. They seem to have a mutual understanding just to leave each other alone. Plus..." she covered her mouth. "I probably shouldn't say this, but I just figure there isn't anything for Miss Suzanne to gain from buttering up Master Christopher. There I've gone and said it!"

"Mary, you can say anything you want to me, and it will stay between us. I appreciate your honesty and trust. By the way, do I detect a bit of an accent?"

She smiled. "Yes, miss, I come from Ireland. Mrs. Cavanaugh is my aunt and she's been with the family for years. She started as a maid, too, but now she's in charge of the whole house." Mary said these words with a great deal of pride. "Mrs. Faraday is sponsoring me. I help with the chores around the house, and in return I have a place to stay, plus Mrs. Faraday pays for my college tuition."

"That's wonderful. Good luck with your studies and thanks for the coffee."

"Thank you, miss." As Mary left, Carrie found herself thinking about Mrs. Faraday. Here again was Mrs. Faraday doing something nice for another person. Mrs. Faraday, whom Carrie always thought of as cold, was sponsoring Mary in this country and providing for her education.

Carrie took a quick shower and then sat down wrapped in her robe to savor Mary's coffee and think. She initially thought she might be jumping to conclusions that Jamie's death was murder, but his letter validated that she was on the right track. She would have to stay alert and be careful as she followed in Jamie's shoes. She finished her first cup of coffee and thought about a second, but then decided, *nothing is going to be accomplished with me sitting here drinking coffee. I wonder what you wear to the reading of a will.*

Two hours later, Carrie knew she made the right decision about what to wear. Her smoke blue dress with her navy blazer blended in nicely with Mrs. Faraday's charcoal suit and the other assortment of dark suits worn by the men. Only Suzanne showed up in a brightly colored flowered dress, with little-girl lace trim on the collar and sleeves.

The first order of business was to see how Simpson was feeling. Carrie thought he looked rather intriguing, with the white bandage cocked over his left eye.

"Really, folks, I'm fine. These things happen all the time when you live in a city." He seemed embarrassed by all the attention. "Perhaps if you could all find seats..."

Carrie took a seat at the back of the room and left the chairs closest to Simpson's desk for the family. Joel started to take the chair next to Carrie, when Charles slipped in next to her.

"I'm sorry, Joel, did you want to sit here?" Charles asked innocently.

"No, no, it's fine. I'll sit next to Stone," Joel responded.

Carrie turned to look at Charles, but he never turned his head to meet her eyes. Nothing was said between them, and they both sat silently as the proceedings started.

Carrie was surprised by the lack of anticipation from the group because she was certainly experiencing a sense of excitement. She could feel her rapid heartbeat and there was an empty feeling in her stomach.

"It looks like everyone is here, so let's get started." Simpson took his place behind his massive mahogany desk, opened his center drawer, and broke the seal on an oversized blue envelope. He carefully unfolded the legal-size paper and began to read. "I, James Wesley Faraday, being of sound mind and body…"

Sometimes the strangest thoughts would come to Carrie at the oddest moments. She realized she never knew Jamie's middle name was Wesley. She also knew his classmates at college would have teased him mercilessly if they had known this piece of information. She focused back on Simpson's reading.

The first bequests were items Carrie classified as mementos rather than items of real value. Jamie left his boxes of personal photos and a Scottish tea set of Emma's to his mother, a chess set and watch to his brother, his beer stein collection to Joel, several first-edition books to Stone and a small bequest to Mrs. Cavanaugh. Then Simpson proceeded to the more substantial bequests. Suzanne was left a sum of fifty thousand dollars, with a thank you from Jamie "for giving up her career to be my companion." Carrie thought this was a generous sum of money, but Suzanne showed no emotion. Simpson continued the bequests by announcing that all of Jamie's remaining assets, including life insurance, investments, any royalties from his writings, plus Jamie's share of his father's estate, were left to Christopher. Charles was named as guardian of Christopher and his newfound wealth.

"I name my brother, Charles, as administrator of Christopher's money, until he reaches the age of twenty-five. I know Charles

would accept this duty without being asked, but I wanted to make my wishes clear. I want someone who will invest his funds wisely and help Christopher make the right decisions. And, Christopher, be sure to seek Uncles Charles's help, especially when you don't think you need it. He will be a dependable and valuable resource for you."

Carrie glanced briefly at Charles and sensed he was pleased. He reached out and placed a hand on the shoulder of Christopher, who was sitting in front of him.

"My last bequest goes to a person I've always considered to be one of my very best friends. We may not have been as close in recent years, but I know there isn't anyone I would trust more with this final bequest. To Carrie Kingsford, I leave my entire collection of past and present work. I ask that she be given complete access to my studio and all of my writings, papers, and photos. Upon review and cataloging of these works, I know Carrie will see the appropriate parties receive them."

Carrie sat stunned as she heard an intake of breath from several of the listeners seated around her. She felt a cold chill pass through her body. She knew exactly what Jamie was doing. He was giving her access to the same story materials that may have led to his death. Her thoughts were interrupted as Suzanne jumped to her feet.

"This certainly doesn't make any sense. Why would an award-winning writer leave his works to a picture-taker? After all, I'm the one who traveled and worked with him. If anyone should catalog his work, it's me."

"Suzanne, do sit down," Charles demanded.

Suzanne, realizing her reaction may have been a bit strong, looked around the room and muttered, "You have to admit it really doesn't make sense."

After she sat down, the room remained quiet for what seemed to Carrie like an eternity. Then, finally, Joel came to Carrie's rescue.

"I, for one, am delighted. This means you will be staying with us for the near future and I plan on taking advantage of your extended stay. In fact, let me start right now. Carrie, will you join me for lunch?"

Charles quickly piped in, "Carrie should really return with the family. There are some things we probably need to discuss."

Carrie ignored Charles's attempt to regiment her schedule and answered, "How thoughtful of you, Joel. Thank you, I'll be happy to have lunch with you. However, I need to spend a few minutes with Mr. Simpson. Tell me where you want to meet for lunch and I'll join you shortly."

Charles stood by helplessly as Joel took a business card from his wallet. "Why not come to my office? There's a garage across the street for parking, and then we can walk to one of the nearby restaurants."

"Great, I'll see you around twelve-thirty?"

"I'll be waiting." Joel quickly excused himself and left the room.

Then she turned to Charles and very calmly said, "I'm sure we do need to discuss some items. However, I think it will wait until after lunch, don't you?"

Charles remained silent. He didn't answer her rebuke. The family left Simpson's office rather quickly, with Suzanne leading the way.

Jonathan Stone came and took Carrie's hand. "Carrie, I know that was an awkward moment for you when Suzanne expressed her thoughtless opinion. But I think Jamie's choice was an excellent one. If I can do anything to help, I hope you will call me. I approved or edited most of Jamie's story ideas over the years, so I may be of some help in your sorting. I was thinking there may be additional stories that would be suitable for publishing that I would love to see." Stone took a business card from his billfold and handed it to Carrie. "I know you probably think of me as part of the family, but after so many years as an editor, most people find me quite objective."

"Thank you. I really appreciate your words, especially today."

Jonathan Stone left the office, leaving Hugh Simpson and Carrie alone to discuss the terms of Jamie's will.

10

arrie spent the next twenty minutes reviewing the requirements of her responsibilities with Simpson. She was concerned about managing Jamie's files and records from inside the Faraday home. However, Simpson suggested it might make sense to do the preliminary work right in Jamie's studio. He was sure a great many materials could be thrown out or packed for distribution to the appropriate parties rather quickly. Then she could ship the remaining materials to a more convenient location of her choice. Simpson assured her she had complete authority to destroy materials, pack up files, give items away, and move the remaining work anywhere she wanted. Carrie liked Simpson's suggestion for handling the work.

She was getting ready to leave when she decided to take advantage of the time she had alone with him. "Mr. Simpson, what's your take on Jamie's death? A simple case of someone losing his balance and falling off a pier, or is there something more sinister out there?"

Simpson leaned back in his chair. He thought for a moment and then looked directly into Carrie's eyes. "One could easily take the evidence we have about James's death and formulate a case to support either theory. But, of course, that doesn't answer your question, does it?" He paused a moment longer, as if he was determining whether he could trust her with his insights. "Although I rarely had the opportunity to talk with him, I found James quite bright and extremely astute. Regardless of the evidence, I don't believe James would have asked you to question his death if he hadn't believed he was in danger. That's what he asked you to do in the letter, correct? To question his death if the circumstances were out of the ordinary?"

Carrie also hesitated for a moment, not really knowing whom in this lot of friends and family she could trust. She liked Simpson, and Jamie must have trusted him, too. After all, he chose Simpson to draft his will and to leave her letter with him. She decided to tell Simpson the truth. "Yes, that's what he asked me to do."

"In that case, I would simply advise you to be extremely careful. There must be danger out there. James obviously thought you could handle yourself or he wouldn't have asked you to help. But then I always thought James could handle himself and look what happened to him."

"Mr. Simpson, what about the mugging last night? Do you think it was related to this case?"

Simpson did not hesitate with his answer. "Oh, yes, it's related." Simpson didn't miss the surprised look on Carrie's face. "I see you're surprised at the quickness of my response. I haven't told anyone this, including the police. The muggers came up behind me and clunked me on the head."

"There was more than one mugger." Something was nagging at Carrie based on what Simpson described, but she couldn't quite place what it was.

"Yes there were definitely two of them," answered Simpson.

Simpson touched the bandage on his forehead. "I pretended to be out cold, but I heard them say they were looking for the letter."

"Mr. Simpson, I'm so sorry I was the cause of that bump on your head..." Carrie's sentence trailed off.

"You must not think that way. Things have a way of working out for the best. You still have the letter and I'm fine. But I do want you to be extremely careful. Those men frightened me." Simpson reached into his desk and took out a card. "Let me give you my business card. I'll put my home number on the back." He uncapped his fountain pen and wrote the number. "Keep the card with you and know that you can call me any time, day or night."

Carrie accepted the card. "I appreciate this. I feel better knowing there's someone I can call."

"I've one more suggestion for you."

"What's that?" she asked.

"I would suggest that you make notes of some sort. Then I suggest that you send your notes to someone for safekeeping. If you want to send your notes here, I promise not to open the envelopes. As you said, James left us with no clues. We have no idea what he was doing. If something unexpected…" He trailed off.

"You mean if something unexpected happens to me? At least you'll know what I was doing."

"Let's not go there. Let's assume you will have the best of luck in bringing this matter to a conclusion."

"That's a good suggestion." Carrie didn't mention that she had already mailed Jamie's letter to her parents for safe-keeping. "Well, thank you for your help and honesty. And I'm really am sorry about last night."

"Don't give it any more thought." Simpson stood and shook hands with Carrie.

11

arrie left Simpson's office with several business cards, a key to Jamie's studio, and more questions than answers. Would Jamie's files help her solve his death? What if the materials led her down the same trail as Jamie? Would she be in the same danger? Had Simpson made the same connection she made that only someone from the wake would have known he had Jamie's letter? These questions occupied her mind during the twenty minutes it took her to travel from Simpson's office to meet Joel for lunch.

Carrie took Joel's suggestion and parked in the garage across from his office. When she arrived at his office, Joel was waiting for her, and within minutes they were seated at a window table at the Harbor Net Restaurant overlooking the harbor waters of Tri-City. It was obvious Joel was a regular at the restaurant when both the management and staff acknowledged him by name. It was a beautiful and peaceful setting, and as they sipped a chilled glass of white Zinfandel, it seemed only natural to reminisce.

"Do you remember the editorial we wrote about the unnamed professor who showed up late for class?" Joel asked.

"Oh, yes, I remember. I especially remember the dozen professors who came forward and were indignant that our editorial singled them out." She laughed out loud.

"Then there was the review we wrote of that awful first play by the theater group," Joel said. "The actors wouldn't speak to us, and the drama department asked the entire newspaper staff not to attend any plays for the rest of the year."

"But looking back, I must say our reviewer was honest. It was the worst play, even to this day, I've ever seen."

There was silence while they enjoyed the moment, and then Joel asked, "You did so much writing in school, how come you ended up as a photographer? We all thought you would be the next Pulitzer Prize-winning journalist or an editor for a top publication."

"Sheer opportunity and the need to make a living. I was trying to get a newspaper job with my state college degree, but I was up against the Jamies of the world, with master's degrees from top journalism schools. I was interviewing for a writing job and had my camera equipment with me. I was being turned down for the millionth time for the writing job when a camera emergency arose. The editor saw my camera, asked if I knew how to use it, and off I went on my first assignment. After the paper saw my photos, I was hired, and the next thing I knew, I was making my living as a photographer. I just happened to be in the right place at the right time. Lately, I've had several opportunities to write copy to go along with my pictures, and that's been nice, plus I'm currently writing a mystery book that I hope to publish someday."

"Then Jamie made a good choice. He picked a mystery writer to solve a real-life mystery."

Carrie laughed. "That sounds good, but I'm quite sure Jamie never knew I was writing a mystery."

The waiter arrived with their chicken Caesar salads and a loaf of warm bread with whipped butter. Joel reached for the wine to refill their glasses, but caught his finger in the wire wine stand.

"Ouch, that hurt. I've torn my nail."

"I've a nail file here in my bag," Carrie offered. "Let me see if I can find it."

"No need, I've a handy little tool that will fix this dilemma." Joel pulled out a silver pocketknife with all the fancy attachments and clipped the broken nail.

"That's quite a fancy version of that knife. May I see?" Carrie held out her hand.

Joel handed Carrie the knife, and she found it was even heavier than it appeared. It must be solid silver. She turned it over in the palm of her hand and saw the initials J.W. engraved on one side.

"Very nice," she said as she handed it back to Joel.

"Let me just say, although the circumstances are not the best, I'm glad you're here. I toast to a good meal, good memories, and you." Joel raised his glass, and they touched their glasses together.

"Thanks, Joel, and thanks for lunch. It's a nice break from all the other issues."

Carrie meant what she said. She was glad for lunch away from the Faradays. She enjoyed the food, the company, and the small talk about the past.

Joel reached over and touched her hand gently, held it for a moment, and then said, "Tell me about the mystery book you're writing."

"It's more of a thriller, but it's not at the top of my priority list. Right now the only mystery I'm working on is this little problem Jamie has left for me." Carrie wanted to get to the subject of Jamie. "Is Simpson a good lawyer?"

A small grin formed at the corner of Joel's mouth as he answered Carrie's question. "Simpson is a very good lawyer, although he's from that old-school mentality we talked about earlier. He comes from a good family, has impeccable law credentials, and a client list that includes the best families in Tri-County. He is also totally dedicated to the Faradays and has been their lawyer for as long as I can remember. That's why if you want someone outside the family to help you with your work, please remember I'm here for you."

"Thanks. In fact, that's one of the reasons I decided to have lunch with you. I need a fresh approach to the situation. What's your take on Simpson being mugged?"

"Whoa, easy does it. What happened to our quiet lunch?"

Before Carrie could answer, their lunch was interrupted by the sound of a boat horn warning people on the dock that a large fishing boat was approaching. After watching the boat slowly ease into its slip, Carrie returned to the conversation.

"It's all right, Joel. I know that one of the reasons for the lunch is to discuss Jamie's letter. I'm willing to trade a nice lunch in a beautiful location for some serious talk."

"All right then, back to more serious subjects. I'm not sure the mugging has anything to do with Jamie. In fact, according to Simpson, nothing was taken. It was probably a prank from a couple of teenagers."

"I think it is a little more than a prank when someone gets clubbed over the head," offered Carrie. She didn't want to share with Joel that Simpson just confirmed the muggers were after the letter.

"Wait a minute. You think Simpson was mugged for Jamie's letter?" He paused for a moment to mull over what she just said. "Is the letter missing?"

"Simpson didn't have the letter. I took it back from him just before he left the house. But only Simpson and I were aware of this fact. Everyone else thought Simpson walked out of the Faraday house with the letter in his pocket."

"Why did you take the letter back?" Joel asked.

"It's quite simple. Everyone seemed so interested in the existence of the letter I decided that I better read it before the meeting in Simpson's office. And before you ask, the letter provided no information about what Jamie was doing."

"Surely Jamie's letter must have provided some information, or why write the letter?" Joel cocked an eyebrow at Carrie.

"The letter started out as we did today, reminiscing about the past. Jamie acknowledged that if I was reading the letter, he was dead. He told me I'd have access to his papers, but mentioned nothing about anything that might have led to his untimely death."

"That's our Jamie." He paused for a moment and then added, "Seems odd the letter didn't mention anything about a story."

"Why…did you think he was working on a story?"

At that moment the waiter came by and cleared the table. They refused dessert, but each ordered a cappuccino to end the meal.

"You were saying you thought he might be working on a story?"

He grinned. "That's not quite what I said. I was asking you if Jamie's letter indicated he was working on a story. For me, it's hard to know. When Jamie came back from overseas we had lunch. In fact, it was in this restaurant. You know Jamie. Even when he was out relaxing with friends, he would ask everyone around him a thousand questions. That's how it was with our meeting. He asked how I was doing, what type of law I practiced, how my import/export business was faring, what type of items were being imported through the Tri-City docks, did I see any of the old gang, on and on. I really don't know if he was gathering information or just being Jamie. I guess I'll never know if his questions had anything to do with writing a story."

The waiter returned with their cappuccinos. They took a moment to enjoy the taste of the frothy liquid.

"How is your law practice doing, and what's this about an import/export business?" Carrie asked.

"My practice is doing well, and my import/export business started quite by accident. I was doing some legal work for one of the many import/export businesses in Tri-City, and my research allowed me to become a bit of an expert. Soon I had a thriving practice, with one import client recommending another. You know, being a harbor city, we have quite a lot of business in this area. I've taken on three additional associates and at least for right now, we have more legal business than we can handle. As far as my own import/export business, it's really quite small. It's more of a hobby as a result of all the legal work I do."

"It sounds wonderful. I'm glad your practice is doing well, and there's nothing wrong with having a hobby." Carrie paused again as she looked around the restaurant. "Joel, what do you think about Jamie's death? Do you think it was an accident?"

"His death was certainly unexpected. As for the details, I really don't know anything more than what I read in the papers."

Carrie sensed that Joel wanted to leave the subject of Jamie, but she asked her question anyway. "Do you think he was meeting someone that night and that's why he was on the pier?"

"I just don't know. However, if there's no indication that Jamie was working a story, I can't imagine why he would be meeting anyone. Besides, the real point of this luncheon is to find out what you're going to do."

"I'm going to go through Jamie's materials like he asked. Get his papers separated so they can be given to Christopher and others. Stone thinks there may be some works that could be published, and then I was thinking about giving the rest of the materials to the Tri-City College."

"Not his journalism school?"

"That school is large enough to receive lots of donations. However, the college here in Tri-County could use the donation. He's probably the most famous student that went through the place. I thought they might want some of his original drafts, along with the published documents for the library."

"You're famous in your field."

"Thanks for the compliment. I'm also still alive and I'm stingy. I'm keeping my papers for now."

"Carrie, I'm going to be perfectly frank. No one seems to know what Jamie's death is all about. Let's assume for a minute it was murder. What will the murderer do to the person who starts to meddle in something they thought was closed? Please don't get curious the way you used to."

"I'm not planning on doing anything other than sorting Jamie's papers. If I find something in the papers that looks like it could be related to Jamie's death, I'm turning it over to the police."

"Good. I'm glad to hear it, and my offer still goes. If you need a place to work, I've an empty office. My secretarial staff would be available to help you do any cataloging. You could ship the whole studio lock, stock, and barrel to my office, and we could help you cut your sorting time." He seemed excited with his plan.

"Thanks, Joel. I do appreciate the offer, and I may take you up on it. I'm not looking forward to spending any more time than necessary in the Faraday house. I'm going to start this afternoon and get some idea about the size of the job. Then I'll let you know."

"Great." Joel seemed satisfied with her answer and insisted on paying for lunch.

After leaving the restaurant, Joel wanted to walk Carrie back to her car. But she convinced him she wanted to window shop before returning to her car. He kissed her on the cheek and she waved goodbye.

12

arrie really didn't want to window shop. She wanted to clear her head from the morning's events. Both Joel and Simpson felt Jamie's death may not have been accidental. Why didn't the Faradays insist on finding out what really happened? With the Faraday money and influence, they could have demanded a thorough investigation from the authorities. No one was doing anything, but everyone was concerned about what would happen to her if she started an investigation into what Jamie was doing. Well, like it or not, she was going to follow Jamie's trail and see where it led. And if she was going to accomplish anything, it would start back at the Faradays, going through Jamie's papers. She ended her wandering and headed toward the parking garage.

On the way to the garage, she spotted a stationery store and decided to pick up some supplies for her cataloging. She purchased spiral notebooks, index cards, and pens in different colors. Even though she brought her laptop, she decided it might be easier to catalog the old-fashioned way with pen and paper. Later she could transfer the written information to her computer. This method would provide backup for her paper notes, which she was planning on mailing to her parents.

She left the store with her purchases and crossed the street to the garage. She waited with a group of people for the garage elevator to slowly make its way to the street level. After waiting what seemed an eternity, the elevator arrived. By the time the people in front of her entered, including a mother with a stroller, there was no room for her and several others. She looked around, saw the door for the stairs, and decided it would be quicker to take the steps to the fourth level, where she parked.

As Carrie was turning the corner to the fourth level, she heard the voices of two men. They didn't seem to be moving but talking in the stairwell at the fourth floor. Carrie stopped in her tracks as she began to understand their words.

"Where is she now?"

"Don't know. Followed her from the restaurant, and then she went in that store." The man answering the questions had a slight accent. Carrie thought it might be Russian or Eastern European.

"Did she buy anything?" The other man's voice was very soft and almost feminine.

"Pens and paper. Then I followed her back here and left her at the elevator. Lots of people waiting. Maybe she didn't get the first car."

These men are talking about me! Carrie thought. She stood frozen afraid to move for fear the men would hear her.

"Maybe she forgot something at the store," offered the man with the soft voice. "Let's find out. You go down the steps. I'll take the elevator down and then back up."

Carrie knew she had only seconds. She forced her body to move. As quietly as she could, she went back down the few steps to the third-floor door. When she reached the third-floor door, luck was with her. There was a group of business people who also took the steps rather than wait for the elevator. They flung open the door to the third level, and Carrie walked through with them. She immediately veered to the left and hopped the low wall of the ramp to the fourth level. Carrie used the ramp wall as cover and ducked when she heard the door open. She carefully peered over the wall, but could see only the back of the door and not the man opening it. The man's attention was drawn by the group of people who entered the third floor with her, and he wasted little time before retreating back into the stairwell.

This was Carrie's chance. She sprinted up the ramp to the fourth floor. Fortunately her car was parked at the end closest to the down ramp and farthest from the elevator. She had her keys in her hand and punched the unlock button on the electronic keypad. Carrie jumped in her car, locked the doors, started the car, and headed toward the exit, all within seconds. When she looked in her rearview mirror, she saw a very thin, short man standing in the middle of the ramp. She had only a brief glance before another exiting car honked him out of position.

Carrie was still feeling an adrenaline rush after her escape, but she breathed a sigh of relief as she pulled her car out of the parking garage. What was happening? She was experiencing events and emotions similar to those Ascot had in the book she was writing.

All the way back to the Faraday house, she kept checking her rearview mirror to see if she was being followed. She spotted no one. However, the more she thought about it, the more she realized these two men didn't need to follow her. They seemed to know how to find her, so they probably also knew she was staying with the Faradays.

Who were these men? She didn't think she was followed from Simpson's office. But if they hadn't followed her, how did they know where she would be? A nagging little voice told her that Joel suggested the parking garage. Then she shook off the little voice when she realized any one of the attendees at Simpson's could have overheard Joel's instructions. Carrie didn't want to face another thought. What were these two men planning to do if they came face to face with her in the garage?

13

arrie parked her car, grabbed her bag of supplies, and was locking her car when she became aware of someone behind her. She spun around

"So, how was lunch?" Charles greeted Carrie as if nothing happened between them at Simpson's office. He had changed from his dark blue suit into brown slacks, a cream shirt, and brown leather jacket. Carrie couldn't stop herself from thinking how good-looking he was.

"Did you go to the Harbor Net Restaurant?"

"What…oh, yes, we did. How did you know?" Carrie was taken aback that Charles knew where she ate lunch in light of her adventure after lunch.

"It's Joel's favorite restaurant, and he eats there almost every day. How was the food?"

"It was fine, although the food wasn't our focus. We spent most of the time reminiscing about college and remembering Jamie." Carrie was actually thinking about her experience after lunch, but decided not to say anything to Charles. After all she still wasn't sure who told those men where she would be. She added, "You know, we did have some good times with your brother."

"I know you did," he said quietly. "Jamie shared many of the stories and even some of your newspaper staff antics with me. Even though I was six years older, we were very close as brothers. I miss him very much." Charles stopped for a moment and then added, "Look, I'm sorry about my comments at Simpson's office."

"It's all right," Carrie responded.

"No, let me finish." His blue-gray eyes focused on Carrie. "You've every right to go out to lunch with whomever you want and whenever you want. We offered you a place to stay, but there are no restrictions on that offer. Come and go as you please. I just ask one thing."

"What's that?"

"I want you to be very careful. I know there's no evidence to support this theory, but I believe my brother was murdered. So until we know for sure, I don't want anyone else to be hurt or..."

"Murdered! Charles, were you about to say 'murdered'? Do you think I'm in danger of being killed?"

"Look, Carrie, I'm not trying to frighten you, but I don't know what is happening. Every time I try to find out information from the police, I'm told the case is still under investigation."

"That explains why nothing seems to be happening, if you aren't getting any help from the police."

"They have been of no help whatsoever. I even tried assigning one of our reporters to the story, and he can't find anything out from his sources in the department. The police have completely shut us out from the investigation. Maybe I'm on the list of suspects, and that's why they don't want to share."

Carrie wondered if something had happened between the brothers that would make the police think of Charles as a potential suspect. She decided to ask, "Why would the police think you could be a suspect?"

"They have this wild theory that with Jamie returning home, there was a power struggle for control of the company." Carrie said nothing, but Charles guessed what she was thinking. "And, no, there was no power struggle. The management of the company was left to me through my father's will, not to mention Jamie wanted nothing to do with management. He wanted to write. Anyway, that's why I'm hoping you'll find some clue in Jamie's papers."

"Apparently everyone else is hoping the same thing. I just hope we aren't all disappointed when everything is cataloged. I know Suzanne is already disappointed because she wasn't given the cataloging job. Charles, I have to ask. How much do you know about Suzanne?"

"Just between us, I know very little about Suzanne. Christopher doesn't seem to know much about her either. She simply showed up in Europe, latched on to his father, and seemed content to be part of their lives. Christopher says she never spoke much about her past. She did tell them she was left an inheritance and was using it to travel in Europe. That's as much as I know about Suzanne."

"There must be some way of finding out more about her?" Carrie added.

Charles looked a little sheepish and then said, "I did ask Jonathan Stone to see what he could find out. He has many contacts including some in Europe so I think it's only a matter of time before we find out more about Suzanne."

"I guess it could all be innocent but it would be nice to have more facts."

And as long as we are being honest with each other and discussing people related to this case, there's someone else I'm not sure about."

"Who's that?" asked Carrie.

"I've never trusted or, for that matter, liked Joel. I look at it this way. If Joel and Jamie were such good friends, how come Jamie went to Simpson to prepare his will and handle your letter?"

"I don't know, but one could ask the same question about the family. How come Jamie didn't have someone in the family go through the papers?" Carrie regretted the question almost the minute she asked it.

"Like me?" Charles took the question in stride. "That's a fair question. I like to think that Jamie thought it might be too difficult for us to deal with his writings after his death. He thought we would either pack his work away without reviewing it, or let the work sit until we felt we could deal with the memories. As a result, any trail related to his death would be cold." He paused for a moment and then looked directly at Carrie. "I also think that my brother might have been afraid that we, especially Mother, wouldn't want to stir things up. But he was wrong. I want to know the truth. And, hopefully, with your help, I'll find out the truth."

Carrie wasn't sure what to say after Charles's revelations about his feelings. Then he added, "Are you planning on getting started this afternoon?"

"Yes. I think the sooner I get started, the better. I've got my office supplies and I'm ready to go."

Carrie held up her plastic bag of recently purchased materials.

"Hey, you don't need to buy anything. If you need any supplies, just charge them to Faraday Press. We have an account at that store." Charles glanced at his watch. "Look, I've got to run to the office for a few hours, but hopefully we can talk more when I get back."

Charles turned and went into the garage. He entered through the side door, and the first garage door began to open automatically. Carrie stood and watched as Charles guided the car out of the driveway. Then she headed into the house to change her clothes to something more comfortable for her task of cataloging. Hopefully, just as Charles suggested, she would find a clue to Jamie's murder in his work.

14

When Carrie opened the door to Jamie's studio above the Faraday garage, she was stunned. It was as if she had traveled back in time. The room looked exactly like the office they shared at the college newspaper. The desk, filing cabinets, and even the desk chair were made of a heavy light-oak wood that was typical of older offices. *Could it be the same desk from our old newspaper office?* She asked herself. There was one sure way to find out. She tried the desk drawer, but it was locked. She took the set of keys that Simpson gave her and tried the one that looked like a desk key. The key worked and Carrie slid open the top drawer. Then she pulled out the second drawer. Inside was a wooden divider that cut the drawer into two sections: a smaller section for envelopes and a larger one for letterhead. She lifted the divider straight up and flipped it over. There it was on the back of the divider— an inscription in the wood! Carrie put on her glasses and read the inscription aloud.

*"For all those who follow, let it be known that the cur-
rent editorial staff of Carolyn Kingsford, Joel Wheeler,
James Faraday, and Stephen Beeker give their blood,
their sweat, and even their tears to bring the truth to this
campus through the written words and photographs of the
student* Courier *newspaper."*

*We were all so young and even silly, but we did believe we were
doing important work on that newspaper*, Carrie thought. *I wonder how on earth Jamie acquired the original desk.*

She ran her fingers over the words that were written with
a non-washable black pen in that tiny draftsman script of
Stephen Beeker. She wondered where Stephen was. The next
time she saw Joel, she would ask. She slid the wooden divider
back into place and sat for a few moments thinking about all
the conversations exchanged while sitting around this desk.
Enough already, you need to get started, Carrie admonished herself. She looked around the room to get a feel for Jamie's
workspace.

The desk was placed to the left of the door and sat out from
the wall facing a large bay window across the room. On each
side of the window were several wooden four-drawer files. To
the right of the desk was another window that looked toward
the back of the Faraday house. Because the desk wasn't close
to either window, Jamie would see only the trees and open
space surrounding the buildings. *What a great setup*, Carrie
thought. *You have the windows, so you don't feel closed in, but not
the distraction of seeing the comings and goings in the neighborhood.*
She continued surveying the room. To the right, against the
far wall, was their old newspaper worktable. Jamie would

have used the table to look at galleys or layouts, but of course now there would be no new layouts. Next to the table were an overstuffed chair, a lamp, and an end table piled with magazines. Carrie knew Jamie spent time reading in this chair and was half-tempted to go and relax in it, but she knew that would only delay her main task.

The top of the desk was clear, with no notebooks or papers. This was unusual. If Jamie was working on a story, reference materials and papers should have been visible on the desk and table. Had someone already straightened the office, or had Jamie deliberately kept everything hidden? Carrie checked the drawers of the desk. The bottom two drawers were empty. The remaining drawers held notepaper and envelopes, stamps, pens, pencils, but nothing of any significance. She wondered if Jamie kept a journal or a diary that he used for notes. She would ask Christopher.

Off to one side of the desk sat a laptop computer and printer. Maybe in this day and age, Jamie did all his work on the computer, but she decided to leave it for later.

Next Carrie went to the file cabinets. They were also locked, but she tried another key from Simpson's ring and unlocked them. The file drawers were stuffed with writings, story ideas, articles, research notes, and photos all filed together and set up alphabetically. One file cabinet was labeled published works. She would leave sorting that cabinet to the end. She grabbed a notebook and started with the first file drawer. If Jamie was working a story, maybe his research materials were somewhere in these drawers. She decided to take each file drawer in order and record the contents in her notebooks. While she knew this would be time-consuming, she also knew it was the only way she would have a complete record of the contents.

She started her work by standing at the files. Then she discovered it would be easier if she took the folders out of the drawer and sorted them on the work table. Carrie sat in the overstuffed chair with her jean-clad legs draped over the side, and began sorting the files and making her notes. Although she had read many of Jamie's published articles, she forgot what a good writer he was. Many of the folders contained multiple drafts of his published article, and she remembered what a stickler Jamie was for perfection. He would always push the newspaper's deadline as he continued to edit to the last moment.

She picked up another stack of folders from the table. As she settled back in the chair with the folders, a three-by-five card drifted to the floor. Carrie picked it up and saw the title at the top: "Getting Exports out of Europe Avoiding the Normal Channels." Carrie recognized that the notes were in Jamie's small, tight script. The rest of the card listed a series of thoughts that Jamie might use in a story, including how to hide an item, how to make contacts, how much money can be made, and how to retrieve items on the other end. Carrie turned the card over. Nothing was written on the back. She went back to the file cabinets and looked in the section of *E* folders. She found no folder on exporting. There was one on elephants, escape artists and many folders on Europe, and then the *F* folders started. She checked under *I* for importing, but again found nothing. She folded the card and slipped it into her jeans pocket. Maybe later she would find other materials on this subject, or maybe this was the beginning of the notes Jamie made from his lunch with Joel. As she continued her work, she noticed that most of the folders contained similar cards with notes like the one that fell on the floor.

Carrie lost track of time as she continued logging the contents of the folders. Dusk was beginning to darken the room, but she didn't take the time to turn on the lights. Unexpectedly, she thought she heard a sound on the steps outside. Then she saw a shadow pass in front of the window that faced the side steps. She was frozen until she heard a key in the door lock. She jumped up and stood behind the chair. She watched as the key engaged the lock and the door handle slowly turned. As the door opened, Carrie was about to duck behind the chair. But before she made her move, a head poked around the corner of the door and Suzanne came into view. Carrie breathed a sigh of relief.

Suzanne saw Carrie and was also startled, "Oh, oh, hello. I didn't know anyone was here. I didn't see any lights," she said, smoothing out an imaginary wrinkle from her brightly flowered top.

"I've been working and didn't bother to turn them on yet," Carrie answered.

"How can you work in the dark?"

Carrie didn't answer Suzanne's question, but instead asked, "Suzanne, what are you doing here?"

"I often kept Jamie company while he was writing," she said defensively.

"I thought you said Jamie wasn't working on a story?"

97

Carrie could tell Suzanne was flustered, but she quickly answered, "I mean I was helping him get the place ready in case he decided to start a story."

"You really shouldn't come up here now that Jamie is... isn't here, until I have all the papers and materials cataloged."

"I'm not going to touch anything. I was just going to sit in the chair."

"I understand that, but this is no longer a place for you to visit. You see, it will take twice as long if my work is interrupted."

"Well, I'm sorry, but I think you're just jealous of my relationship with Jamie." Suzanne sounded like a teenage girl. "From what I understand, you were Jamie's girl in the past. I think you're just pissed that I'm even around." Suzanne paused for a moment and then added, "I was Jamie's assistant, and I could help you. But, no, you just want to sit up here and dream about what could have been." Her voice was now sharp.

Suzanne's outburst stunned Carrie, and she wasn't quite sure how to answer her. She decided on a softer approach. "Suzanne, I know that you're feeling left out. You were Jamie's assistant, and now I've been assigned to handle those things you once did. That's just the way things work out sometimes. I also know you took care of Jamie and Christopher, and I'm sure they appreciated that."

"Yes, they did. I was a big help to both of them," she agreed.

"Exactly, and Christopher still needs your help to get him get through this difficult time. I assure you, all I want to do is to get everything cataloged and be on my way. Don't you think that's the best plan?"

Suzanne looked away as she nodded her head.

"I know you will also understand why I have to do this alone in order to do it quickly."

"I do. I'm sorry. It's just that I miss him."

"I know you do." Carrie waited a moment and then asked, "Since you know about Jamie's work, do you mind if I ask you a question?"

"Sure, go ahead." Suzanne brightened.

"Did Jamie keep a journal?"

"A journal?" She seemed surprised by the question.

"You know a notebook or a diary where he kept ideas for stories or notes from interviews and research."

"Nope, nothing like that." Her answer seemed a little quick to Carrie. Then she added, "He did most of his writing on the computer."

"I guess most people use computers these days," agreed Carrie.

"I'm considered an expert on the computer. That's where I was the most help to Jamie. If you want, I could take the laptop into the house and print out all the files. That would probably save you some time."

"You know, that's really sweet of you to offer. However, I'm going to systematically work my way through the files and then copy my work on the computer. So I really need to keep the laptop here." Carrie knew she was telling a little white lie since she had her own computer.

Suzanne looked dejected again, but before she could respond, Carrie offered, "When I get around to typing my notes, perhaps you could help me at that time. I've never been very good with computers."

"I'll be glad to help." She smiled broadly. "Do you want me to wait?"

"No, I didn't mean today. I won't be ready to type my notes for several days. But if you're going to be around in the next few days, I'm sure you could help me."

"Oh, yeah, I'll be around. Just let me know when you're ready for me to enter items."

Carrie walked Suzanne to the door and watched as Suzanne went down the steps. Suzanne turned and waived to Carrie and hurried across the lawn to the kitchen door. Carrie was sure if Suzanne had been a small child, she would have skipped across the lawn. But Carrie did not buy the sweet little girl persona of Suzanne.

It was getting late, so Carrie decided to stop work for the day. She placed all the folders back inside the file drawers and locked them. However, before she left the studio, she decided to check Jamie's computer. She turned it on and once it booted up, a password screen appeared.

I was afraid of that, she thought. She tried "Jamie," "Faraday," "Christopher," "Suzanne," and even her name. Nothing got her past the password screen. Then she remembered at school they used to refer to the old typewriter as "good old Bessie." She tried "Bessie," and the computer accepted the password and proceeded to the opening screen.

Carrie saw only a few software applications were loaded: a word program, a spreadsheet program, and a few games. She searched the computer's documents and found just a couple of files. She took a blank DVD from her supply bag and loaded all the files she found onto it. Then she shut the computer down. She checked again to make sure everything was locked and returned to the house.

15

That evening, Carrie ate dinner in the kitchen with Christopher, Mary, and Mrs. Cavanaugh. Charles called to say he would be working late, Suzanne was out for the evening, and Mrs. Faraday chose to eat in her room. Carrie and Christopher decided they preferred eating in the kitchen with Mary and Mrs. Cavanaugh rather than being served in the formal dining room.

Even though dinner was held in the kitchen, Christopher was expected to change into clean clothes for the meal. Christopher, being a typical kid, selected khaki pants and a checked cotton shirt for his dining attire. Carrie followed protocol and changed her blouse and traded her jeans for slacks.

Conversation was light during dinner as the two enjoyed Mrs. Cavanaugh's delicious homemade meat loaf. Carrie liked Christopher and focused the conversation on him and how he liked his new school and how he was spending his free time in Tri-City. It wasn't until the end of the meal, when Mary and Mrs. Cavanaugh were clearing the table, that Christopher changed the topic.

"Were you working in my dad's studio today?"

"Yes, I decided I better get started on cataloging all your dad's materials. There's quite a bit of paper to go through, although it seems well organized."

"Yeah, Dad is very...I mean, he was very good about keeping everything organized." He stopped for a moment and then resumed his thought. "I think it was because we moved around a lot. Dad was forced to keep his papers tidy. Sometimes he would send home boxes full of papers. Then when we came home during vacations, he would get everything filed."

"I thought your dad just finished building the studio?" asked Carrie.

"Oh, he did, but before he fixed the studio up, he bought the file cabinets and the other furniture and stored them in the basement. Hey, if everything is so well organized, what are you doing?"

Christopher so reminded Carrie of Jamie. Just like his father, he cut right to the point, but didn't speak with any intended ill will.

"The work is organized, but there's no record of what papers are in the files. I've bought a couple of notebooks, and I'm going through each drawer, listing the items I find."

"Dad used a small notebook when he was working on a story. Then when he was ready to write the story he used graph paper," offered Christopher.

"Graph paper…huh!" responded Carrie.

"Yeah, I know most people don't write that way, but he liked the method.'

"I like graph paper, too. That's exactly how I write."

"I thought you were a photographer?"

"I am, but even photographers have to write. I have to write captions, or sometimes I write a little mini story for the pictures I take. I'm also writing a book."

"You are! What's it about?" Christopher asked excitedly.

"Oh, it's just a little mystery," Carrie said modestly.

"I like to read mysteries. I'm a big reader of the Hardy Boys."

"In that case, when it gets published, I'll be sure you get one of the first copies." Carrie didn't want to admit that she was struggling with the book, not to mention if it ever got published it would never be as popular as the Hardy Boys. "You know, when I was your age, I was a big fan of Nancy Drew. I even read a couple of Hardy Boys when I could sneak them away from my brother."

"Really?" Christopher looked around to make sure Mary and Mrs. Cavanaugh weren't listening. "I've read Nancy Drew, too, but don't tell anyone. I don't want my friends to know that I read a girls' book." Christopher realized that Carrie's book might be a girls' book. He tried to recover by adding, "But I'd read your book even if it's for girls."

Carrie smiled and then asked, "As long as we are talking about writing, I did want to ask you a question. Did your father ever keep a journal or a diary, or did he just write on graph paper and then transfer everything to the computer?"

Christopher pondered the question and then said, "I guess you would call that notebook I mentioned a journal. It was a small leather book that he received as a Christmas gift from Uncle Charles. It was green leather and had a replaceable tablet on one side and card inserts on the other side. Dad always made notes in the journal, and then he would refer to them when he wrote his drafts."

"Interesting," Carrie responded. "Do you know what happened to it?"

"No, I've kinda been wondering what happened to it," he said slowly and then paused.

Carrie thought he was going to add something, but then he changed the subject.

"Did you look at Dad's computer?"

"I turned it on, but I didn't see many files."

"You mean you got in? What about the password?" Christopher looked at Carrie in amazement. "How did you know it was..." he stopped. He realized he was about to give away the password.

"I figured it out." Carrie leaned over and whispered the name "Bessie" in Christopher's ear. "The computer password was the same as the name we gave the old typewriter at our college newspaper office."

"Wow, that's still clever of you to figure it out."

"I assume your dad captured all of his work on his computer?" Carrie asked.

"Not really, Dad only used the computer for the final draft of stories."

"Really, he didn't use it for his notes and rough drafts?"

106

"Nope, as I said, he wrote his notes and even his interviews in the journal and then wrote the draft on graph paper. Only when he was ready to prepare the final piece would he switch to the computer. Why do you ask?"

"I was just wondering. Some people use the computer for all their writing."

Based on what Christopher said, Carrie knew Suzanne lied: first, when she denied the existence of a journal, and, second, when she said Jamie used the computer for all his writing. Carrie wanted to ask Christopher one more question.

"Christopher, did Suzanne type the final story into the computer for your father? I understand she's quite good on the computer."

"Suzanne offered to help on several occasions, but Dad always refused. My dad always worked alone." He fell silent again. "I know what you're thinking. Why did he have her around? I know I'm a kid, but the two of them didn't act like girlfriend and boyfriend. My dad dated after my mom died, but this time it was different. Oh, sure, they did things together, but...well...Suzanne wanted more. She wanted to go out on dates, but she also wanted to live with us and help him with his work, help make decisions."

"What kind of decisions—decisions about you?"

"She wanted to, but my dad wouldn't put up with that. Only Dad and I made decisions concerning me," he said proudly.

Mary brought dishes of ice cream with fresh berries to the table, and the conversation stopped for a moment. Mary and Mrs. Cavanaugh went into the sunroom to eat their desserts, sensing a serious conversation between Carrie and Christopher.

Christopher started talking again about Suzanne. "I remember they had a big fight the night Dad said we were coming home. He said his research was done in Europe, and he needed to come home to follow a story. She wanted to stay in Europe, and she knew the magazine would continue to pay for us to stay there. She said she was sure no story was that important. Dad said she didn't know anything about the story and that he was coming home to finish it. After that fight, I thought she would have drifted away, but she came home with us."

"Do you know what story your dad was investigating?"

"Not really, but I'm not sure that's important."

"Not important! Why do you say that, if the story is what brought him home?"

"Because I don't think the story brought him home. I think it was because of me we came home. And if we hadn't... well, he might still be alive."

"Oh, Christopher, you mustn't feel that way. You aren't responsible for your father's death."

"I'm not so sure. Remember when I said we made decisions about me together? My dad and I decided that I'd attend the Henriton School here in Tri-City. I wanted to go there because most of my friends from Tri-City went there. Dad and Grandma wanted me to go there, too. When Suzanne realized coming home was about me, she suggested that I come home alone. Then she and Dad could stay in Europe and come home in the summer after the school year. But Dad liked to spend time with me, and that's why I think he told Suzanne he was working on a story." Christopher's eyes filled with tears.

Carrie moved her chair next to Christopher, took his hands in hers, and looked him straight in the eyes. "Christopher, you're now old enough to face this head-on. You're not responsible for your father's death. If his death turns out to be an accident, the accident would have happened because it was his time. If your father was murdered because of a story, then the murderer would have tracked him down wherever he was working. Besides, did you ever think maybe your father told Suzanne something different to mislead her? Maybe your dad was suspicious of Suzanne."

"I never thought of it that way," he responded quietly.

Carrie could see he was shaking off the tears, so she continued. "I know you miss your father, but from this moment on, you have to hang onto the good memories. Time spent with memories is much more rewarding than time spent blaming yourself. And now I've a favor to ask. Since I didn't get a chance to see your father to do this…would you mind terribly if I gave you a hug? I really needed to give your father a hug one more time."

Christopher couldn't speak, but he nodded his head. Carrie brought him close to her and held him for a long time, until she felt a calm settle over him. Then she pulled away and kissed him on the forehead. "Hey, you've caused my ice cream to melt," she teased.

"I thought someone as old as you would have learned it's the only way to eat ice cream," he said, and his face filled with a grin.

She bopped him lightly on the head and grabbed the spoon for her ice cream.

16

After the dinner with Christopher, Carrie spent several restless hours in her room. The task of cataloging Jamie's papers was going to take longer than she originally thought. What if she discovered information about Jamie's murder? Whom could she trust? Not Suzanne. Suzanne lied to her. She didn't tell the truth about the journal or the computer, but that didn't mean she was involved with Jamie's death. Then there was Joel, who suggested that all of Jamie's papers should be sent to his office. Did he want to help or have access Jamie's work? Stone also offered his editing skills to help her review Jamie's papers. Maybe he was hoping to find more of Jamie's work to publish. Then there were Charles and Mrs. Faraday, who clearly wanted to keep the papers and Carrie close to them. Christopher was the only person she felt she could trust, but he was only twelve years old.

Then she remembered the advice Simpson gave her. With so many people and pieces to this puzzle, she needed to make notes. Carrie took out several sheets of graph paper and wrote headers on each sheet: "Story Possibilities," "Known Facts about Jamie's Death," "Murder Scene Description," and "Next Steps." Then she started a character sheet on each of the players. She listed who they were, their relationship to Jamie, where they were when Jamie was murdered, and anything else she had discovered so far. When she was finished, she realized the sheets contained very little information.

In her frustration, Carrie looked at the sheet she labeled "Next Steps." The one item that caught her eye was "find Jamie's journal." Jamie's journal could be a key element to providing the missing information.

Did Jamie hide his journal for safekeeping? *I wonder*, she thought as she remembered a hiding place they used in their newspaper days. If the editorial team wanted to leave a message for one another, they would hide it in a pocket folder that was taped to the back of one of the file cabinets. Could Jamie have used this same method to hide his journal? After all, he had all the same furniture from their newspaper office. Carrie decided to slip out and take one more look at the studio filing cabinets before she retired for the night.

෴

Carrie crept down the stairway and moved quietly along the hallway. Just as she was feeling comfortable with the silence of the house, the hall clock struck midnight. She jumped what felt like several feet and muffled a scream with her hand.

Some detective you are. You haven't even left the house yet, and you're jumpy, she admonished herself. Carrie regained her composure and listened to see if she had alerted anyone in the house. When she heard nothing, she continued her journey down the hallway, through the kitchen, and out into the cool night air. She stood listening in the shadows of the house before crossing the driveway. She moved across to the studio steps.

Carrie climbed the steps to the studio and used her key to open the door. She snapped on the small flashlight she brought with her and went directly to the file cabinets. She tried maneuvering her flashlight, but she couldn't quite see behind the cabinet. She extended her arm until her hand felt the edge of something. She pushed her body against the file until her hand could just reach inside the folder. The folder was empty.

Her disappointment was short lived because she thought she heard something on the steps outside. She quickly flicked off her light and flattened herself against the wall, between the file cabinet and the window. Carrie was sure she saw a shadow moving along the outside window. She tried desperately to remember whether she had locked the door, but it didn't matter because she heard a key being inserted into the lock. She was backing further against the drape of the window when suddenly a hand reached out from the curtain and covered her mouth. She reacted quickly by trying to push the hand away, but an arm went across her shoulders and kept her from moving.

17

A voice whispered forcefully in her ear, "Carrie, be quiet! It's Charles! You'll scare our intruder away. I'm going to move my hand away from your mouth. Do you understand?"

Carrie nodded her head in agreement.

"Charles? What are you doing here? You nearly scared me to death," Carrie whispered, trying to catch her breath.

"I'm trying to trap an intruder. Now stay put. I'm going over closer to the door."

Charles headed to the door by cutting straight across the floor. Just at that moment the moon emerged from behind the clouds, and Charles was caught in the glow coming through the back window. As the intruder opened the door, he spotted Charles in the light. The intruder grabbed the trash can by the desk and tossed it in Charles's path and then quickly exited and went back down the steps. The next thing Carrie heard was a crash and a thud as Charles tripped over the trash can and hit the floor. Carrie first went to the door and looked cautiously down the steps, but saw no one. She closed and locked the door and then flipped on the light switch. The studio was now illuminated, and Charles was rolling on the floor, clutching his knee.

"Are you all right?" she asked as she knelt down to help him.

"Why did you turn on the lights?" was his first response.

"All the better to see you, my dear. Plus, I didn't think both of us should lose the battle with the trash can."

Charles couldn't help but laugh. "I guess the trash can did win this battle. What about the intruder?"

"He or she is gone, but what about your knee? Should I get some help?"

"I think it's just bruised. Can you help me to a chair?"

Carrie grabbed the desk chair and rolled it over to Charles. With her help, he used the chair to lift himself from the floor. He sat in the chair for a few minutes, rubbing his knee.

"What brought you to the studio tonight? I thought you worked in here this afternoon."

"I did, but I remembered something and wanted to check it out before going to bed. What about you? It seems everyone has a key to this place."

"What do you mean by that?" he snapped, assuming she was referring to him.

"Suzanne used her key this afternoon to enter the studio, and unless my ears deceived me, our intruder also used a key to open the door."

"Hmm, you're right. Our intruder did use a key. As for me, just in case you were wondering, Jamie gave me a key." He waited for a reaction, but Carrie said nothing. "I've had the feeling since Jamie's death that someone was searching the studio. Two nights ago I was sure I saw a light out here. As a result, I thought I'd hide out tonight and see if anyone showed up. I didn't want you to be in danger when you were working alone in here."

"Charles, that's sweet. It's also..." She hesitated.

"You were about to say 'stupid.'"

"Actually, I was going to say mighty brave. Since both of us agree there's a chance Jamie's death was murder, surprising an intruder could be very dangerous. Next time he might toss more than a trash can at you."

"I might do more than just surprise him."

"Charles, are you carrying a gun?" she asked with surprise.

"I figured it was either carry a gun or have someone accuse me of being stupid."

Carrie chuckled. She never met someone so direct in his approach...except maybe Jamie.

Charles continued, "Could you get whatever you wanted in here so we can go? I think I should get some ice on this knee before it swells up."

"We can go now. What I came to get isn't here."

"Isn't here? When did you have a chance to look?"

"When I first came in," said Carrie.

"But all you did was reach around the back... Oh, I get it, the secret hiding place on the back of the filing cabinet."

"How did you know about that?" Carrie asked, surprised.

"When Jamie was recreating the newspaper office in the studio, he told me how the staff would leave messages for one another. I checked the pouch shortly after his death, hoping all the answers would be laid out for me in some secret message, but..."

"But..." Carrie prompted.

"No such luck. It was empty."

"Do you think there was something in it?" asked Carrie.

"I don't know if Jamie ever used it or just had it as a reminder of the past." Charles started to stand.

"One more question," Carrie asked, as she helped Charles to his feet. "Did Jamie keep a journal?"

"He did. In fact, he used a journal that I gave him as a Christmas present. It was a small, dark-green leather notebook, a little bigger than the three-by-five cards it holds. Is that what you thought might be in the pouch?"

"I wasn't sure, but both you and Christopher have now confirmed that Jamie used this notebook. It might interest you to know that Suzanne denied the existence of the journal and said Jamie typed everything directly into the computer."

They were on the landing, and even in the low light, Carrie could see the look on Charles's face.

"I saw Jamie using the journal just a few days before his death, and Suzanne was in the room," Charles said. "When I first met her, I just thought she was stupid. Now I'm beginning to wonder if Suzanne is stupid like a fox."

They were working their way slowly down the steps. "Sounds like we need to concentrate more on Suzanne. Jamie didn't talk about her to you?" Carrie asked.

"Very little. He said they were good friends and he would like her to stay with us. Mother allowed Suzanne to stay, but in her own room, of course."

"What did Jamie think of those arrangements?"

"Actually, much to everyone's surprise, he was just fine with it. Somehow, it didn't seem to be a close relationship. It was hard for us to understand what Jamie's fascination was with Suzanne. She sure wasn't like Emma, Jamie's wife. With Emma, it was obvious from the beginning that they were meant for each other." Charles realized he had slipped, and then he remembered something Jamie always said, *"Carrie is easy to talk to and very sharp. You find yourself telling her things you want to keep secret."*

When Charles mentioned the closeness of Jamie and Emma, Carrie felt a bit of sadness in her heart for what might have been. She shook off the feeling, knowing that Charles wasn't being insensitive, but just stating the facts. She took a deep breath and said, "To hear Suzanne tell it, she and Jamie were inseparable."

"Suzanne tells quite a few things differently from the world of reality. That's why I'm glad she accepted our offer to stay after Jamie's death. It gives me more time to find out why she attached herself to my brother. I told you I had Jonathan checking on her and I'm thinking I should check in with Jonathan tomorrow and see if he has any updates. I want to know what Suzanne did before Europe, what took her to Europe, and what she was doing before she met Jamie. It doesn't seem logical that she conveniently appears in Europe and inserts herself into Jamie's life."

"'Insert' is an unusual way of putting it, but certainly an accurate way of describing what happened," added Carrie.

They reached the bottom step when Carrie's foot kicked something. She had Charles lean against the wall of the garage while she turned on her flashlight to search the ground. On the grass was a Swiss Army knife. She picked it up and turned it over. The initials J.W. were engraved in the silver metal.

"What is it?" asked Charles.

"It's a fancy knife. Come on, let's get you inside, and I'll show you."

Carrie helped Charles inside the house. She felt comfortable as he leaned his weight against her. He was so close to her, she could smell his shaving lotion.

They stopped and got ice from the kitchen, and Carrie guided him through the hallway toward the staircase. She was wondering how he would navigate the steps when Charles stopped midway down the hallway. He opened a door, revealing a small elevator.

Charles saw Carrie's surprise. "The elevator was installed for Mother. She refuses to give up her room on the upper level, but all those steps were getting to be too much for her." They entered and he pushed the button. The elevator was extremely quiet as it sailed to the second floor. When the elevator stopped, they were opposite Charles's room. He hobbled across to the door and flung the bedroom door open.

His room was large, with a sleigh bed dominating the center of the room. An alcove in the corner provided a sitting area with a large bay window that faced the grounds at the back of the house. Carrie helped him across the room to a chair in front of the window.

"I'm fine now. I think I'm more bruised than injured. I'll put this ice pack on my knee and take a couple of aspirins. I'll be fine in the morning. Hey, before you leave, can I see what you found?" Carrie showed Charles her discovery. Charles turned it over and saw the initials. "J.W. hmm…could this belong to our friend Joel?"

"It could and does. He showed it to me when we ate lunch. It looks like one mystery has been solved. Joel paid Jamie's studio a visit tonight. Maybe it's time you and I have a discussion with Joel," Carrie offered.

"I like that idea, plus I like the idea we'll be working together."

"I have to admit we would have been more effective tonight if we went to the studio together. Agreed?"

"Agreed," said Charles. Carrie had turned to leave when Charles added, "I think Jamie made the right decision when he selected you to handle his affairs. I'm glad you're here."

Carrie smiled and said, "Feel better in the morning."

18

The next morning Carrie decided to visit the main branch of the public library and read the newspaper accounts of Jamie's death. It was obvious from the first article she read that the papers couldn't decide if the death was accidental. One of the dailies took the angle that alcohol played a part. The other daily thought it might have been a botched robbery and wrote a sidebar about increased robberies in the city. Carrie found only one of the smaller weekly papers that thought Jamie was deliberately murdered. The reporter discovered what Carrie knew—Jamie was a champion swimmer, and therefore drowning didn't make sense. The reporter also noted that Jamie worked for *News World* and suggested Jamie might have been researching a story. While Carrie agreed with the reporter's theory, he provided no evidence to support his conclusions. Carrie continued to read the details.

Son of Prominent Publishing Family Found
Floating in Harbor

The body of James Wesley Faraday, son of the prominent Faraday publishing family, was found floating in the water near Pier Seven in the harbor early this morning. The body was discovered around 2:00 a.m. by employees from the Admiral's Saloon as they left work.

Preliminary results indicate that the cause of death was due to drowning. It was reported that Mr. Faraday was seen earlier in the evening at the bar in the Admiral's Saloon. Alcohol has not been ruled out as a factor in his death.

The manager from the Admiral's Saloon, Mr. John Kensington, stated that one of his bartenders engaged in a discussion with Mr. Faraday about his swimming. Several of Mr. Faraday's swimming records remain unbroken at Tri-City College, and Mr. Kensington offered this possibility: "Perhaps he jumped in the water to see if he could still swim the distance and hit his head by accident."

Heavy rains earlier in the day soaked the piers at the harbor, which also led to speculation that Mr. Faraday may have slipped on the pier.

James Faraday attended…

The article went on to give details of Jamie's background and education. Carrie skipped through the next several paragraphs until she found the autopsy results.

Mr. Stephen Beeker, deputy medical examiner, stated, "Results of the autopsy indicate alcohol was present in his system, which may have been a factor. While the amount in his system was not over the legal limit, it is possible the alcohol contributed to Mr. Faraday losing his balance. If Mr. Faraday was unconscious when he hit the water, this would explain why an expert swimmer drowned." Mr. Beeker ended his formal statement by indicating that the coroner's office was classifying the death as "suspicious" at this time.

I guess I don't have to ask Joel what happened to Stephen, thought Carrie. *He's right here in Tri-City working in the coroner's office.* Carrie left her table and asked the librarian for a phone book. Once she found the number, she stepped outside the building and used her cell phone to dial the morgue. She asked to speak to Stephen Beeker, and to her surprise was put right through.

"Hello, Beeker here." The voice sounded professional but friendly, exactly the same as she remembered from college.

"Hello, Stephen. It's Carrie Kingsford."

"Well, hello, Carrie, I wondered when I'd hear from you. Joel said you were coming back for Jamie's funeral. I hoped I'd see you at the funeral, but then I had to miss it because of a case. Of course I already said my goodbyes to Jamie when he was here on the..." He was about to say "table," but then quickly changed it to "in the office."

"Stephen, the reason I'm calling is Jamie wrote me a letter before his death. He asked me to investigate, if his death was classified as anything other than by natural causes."

"Good old Jamie, still controlling the story even from the great beyond. I guess you want me to tell you everything I know?"

"I've been reading the newspaper accounts, but anything you can add would be appreciated," Carrie said. "I need more information in order to decide if there's anything to investigate."

"Officially, I can't tell you much more than what you saw in the papers. I can tell you as a friend that there are different ways to weigh the facts. Here's the problem as I see it. There are three elements to Jamie's death: the drowning, the alcohol, and the bump on the head."

"I agree the papers all mention this same information, but are you saying there are different interpretations?"

"You got it. The reporters and even the police like a nice, neat package."

Carrie remembered Jamie's wake. Simpson used the same phrase about nice, neat packages.

Stephen continued, "One package is Jamie drank too much, lost his balance, hit his head on the pier, fell in the water, and drowned."

"And how would you wrap the package?" Carrie asked.

"You and I know Jamie could always handle liquor. He could out-drink anyone and then proceed to write a perfectly coherent story. Knowing this, I don't believe the amount of alcohol in his system was sufficient to cause him to lose his balance. Did he hit his head on the pier diving in? I don't think so. Have you seen Pier Seven, where he was found?"

"I'll be checking out the pier next," Carrie responded.

"When you see it, I think you'll agree it's not that easy to hit your head on the piling. It means the bump occurred first, and then he fell, or he was…"

"Pushed," Carrie finished the sentence for him. "And that would make it murder or, at the very least, manslaughter."

"What I've told you is purely subjective because I knew the victim. It may be what I think, but I can't prove it based on medical findings."

"Knowing the victim and their habits often solves the crime. Stephen, I appreciate everything you've shared with me, and I promise before I leave Tri-City, you and I will get together."

"Sounds good to me. And, Carrie…be careful. Make sure you have a backup for whatever you do, just in case Jamie's death was a murder."

Carrie returned to her table in the library and continued checking later editions of the papers, but there was no additional information. No witnesses came forward, no new pieces of evidence were discovered, and no reporter decided to do a follow-up. The story was front page for a couple of days, and then Jamie's death not only disappeared from the front page, but entirely from the papers. Jamie's killer was probably feeling confident that he had gotten away with murder.

Carrie pushed herself away from the table and removed her glasses. She felt dissatisfied. There was too little information, but too many possibilities—the possibility of a robbery, the possibility of a swimming accident, the possibility of too much alcohol, the possibility that Jamie hit his head, the possibility that Jamie was pushed, and the possibility that Jamie was writing a story.

All these possibilities did clarify one thing for Carrie. She needed to see Pier Seven. She would return to the house and inform Mrs. Cavanaugh that she would be eating with friends. Hopefully, by the time Carrie finished talking with John Kensington and the other workers from the Admiral's Saloon she would have some new friends.

19

Carrie parked her car on the lot at Pier Eight. She figured this would put her midway between the Admiral's Saloon and Pier Seven. She also parked at Pier Eight because she wanted her first impressions of Pier Seven to be in the dark, the way Jamie would have viewed it the night he went into the water.

It had rained earlier in the day, which would make the pier and the harbor area also resemble the night that Jamie was murdered. The rain left the night feeling cold and damp, and Carrie was glad she wore a black turtleneck and a matching black crew neck sweater with her black slacks. The night air also made her realize how hungry she was. She had not eaten since breakfast, so the Admiral's Saloon would serve two purposes for her.

The saloon was located in an old warehouse, which at the turn of the century housed ships' cargo. The outside of the building was highlighted by a neon sign featuring a ship's admiral with a tri-corner hat and an eye patch that changed colors from blue to orange to green. Inside the front door was a large waiting area with high-back wooden benches for the crowds waiting for tables. That night the seats in the waiting area were empty, as patrons were being handled as they arrived. To the left of the waiting area, through wooden French doors, was a long U-shaped bar. On the one side of the bar was a movable glass wall that enlarged the bar space into the main eating area for the late-night drinking crowds.

In the center of the first floor was a huge circular salad bar, with a vast assortment of hot and cold selections. Surrounding the salad bar were tables of various sizes and hugging the outer walls were booths.

Carrie was seated at a table on the loft level overlooking the eating area and the massive salad bar below. The surrounding walls displayed paintings of sailing ships and harbor scenes. Carrie was looking at the picture nearest her table when a young lanky waiter in his early twenties, with long, dark hair, approached her table.

"Hi, my name is Ben, and I'll be your waiter tonight." His voice was friendly and upbeat as he presented her with a plank of wood listing the restaurant's entrées.

Keeping with the spirit of the place, Carrie said, "Hello, Ben. My name is Carrie, and I'll be your diner for tonight. Got anything to drink around here?" Carrie gave Ben her best smile.

Ben smiled back, knowing he had someone who would be fun to serve. "I doubt there's a drink on this earth we can't make. What's your pleasure?"

"I don't want anything too exotic. How about a glass of white zinfandel?"

"Let me get your drink while you review the menu."

When Ben returned with her drink, he bumped into her table, almost spilling the wine.

"Ouch, that hurts," he said. "I go home most nights with bruises. I'm constantly bumping into these tables, and they are very heavy."

"They are incredibly solid. Why don't you sit for a minute until the pain eases?" Carrie offered.

Ben looked around for signs of management and then accepted her offer. He sat down and began rubbing his leg as he gave Carrie some history about the restaurant.

"Before this place became a restaurant, it was a bar for sailors. There was a tendency for bar room brawls and the furniture would get broken. To solve the problem, the saloon owners made the tables extra heavy."

"That was thoughtful of them," she said, smiling. "I can't imagine trying to pick one of these wooden tables up to throw at someone." Carrie realized she had left her glasses back at the Faraday home and would never be able to see the fine print on the menu. "Speaking of wood, what would you recommend from this menu?"

Ben looked her over. "Do you eat meat?"

"Absolutely! Why do you ask?"

"These days, with all the diets and cholesterol concerns, some people want to avoid meat and just eat from the salad bar. But if you like meat, I'd recommend the petite filet and a trip to the salad bar. The meat is so tender it rivals the best steakhouses in Tri-City. And if you can't find side dishes you like on our salad bar then you probably shouldn't be eating out at a restaurant," He said with the authority of someone who had made this comment many times.

"Then that's what I'll have."

Ben smiled and seemed pleased that she accepted his recommendation.

"Before you get my order, I've another question. Were you working the night that Jamie Faraday died?"

He looked at her suspiciously and asked, "Hey, you a cop?"

"Do I look like a cop? Actually, I'm an old friend of the victim. He asked me to investigate his death if it was in any way suspicious."

"You're saying, like, he knew he was going to die?" asked Ben. "Wow, that's creepy."

"It would seem that way, but so far all the evidence seems to point to accidental drowning. That's why I thought I'd check out the scene myself. Did the police interview you? I saw in the newspaper that several people from the saloon were interviewed."

"No, I wasn't interviewed." He sounded annoyed. "I'm not a manager who likes to get his name in the paper, if you know what I mean." Ben saw the disappointment in Carrie's face and quickly added, "But that doesn't mean I don't know things. I served Mr. Faraday dinner the night that he drowned."

Ben looked around and suddenly jumped up. The manager was approaching the table.

"Is there a problem, Ben?"

Carrie piped in. "Not at all. Ben bumped his knee on the table, and I suggested he sit for a moment to ease the pain. He has been telling me about the history of the restaurant, plus making some wonderful menu suggestions."

"Thanks for letting me sit, ma'am. I'll get your order started," Ben responded with a wink as he moved away.

"What a nice young man," Carrie said. "Friendly service, that's what makes a good restaurant, not just good food."

"Yes, Ben is one of our best. If you need anything, just let me know. I'm Mr. Kensington, the manager. Enjoy your meal."

Carrie saw what Ben meant by Kensington wanting to be the center of attention. He wandered around the loft, letting every table know he was the manager.

She made two trips to the salad bar, and when her steak arrived, she ate her meal alone without the opportunity to talk further with Ben. At the end of the meal, when Carrie was enjoying her coffee, Mr. Kensington finally went downstairs to open the glass wall to enlarge the bar. The minute Kensington was downstairs, Ben slipped back to her table.

"So where were we?" Ben asked brightly, as if no time had elapsed in their conversation.

"You were telling me you served Jamie Faraday the night he died."

"Yes. In fact, he ate the same thing you did." Carrie imagined quite a few of Ben's customers enjoyed his recommended selection.

"Did you talk with him?" prodded Carrie.

"Just polite chit-chat, but he seemed to be a real nice guy, and he was a good tipper. That's why I remember him."

"That sounds very uneventful. Is there anything else you remember that was out of the ordinary?"

Ben looked over his shoulder for the second time that night to see if anyone was listening. "I think he was planning on meeting someone. I can tell when people are deliberately lingering, and toward the end of the meal, he was definitely delaying his departure. Finally, when we were closing off the loft, he went down to the bar. That's when he had the conversation with the bartender about swimming. You know, the one quoted in the paper."

Carrie nodded her head. "Aside from the bartender, was he talking to anyone else at the bar?"

"Not that I saw, but I noticed one more thing. After I finished serving dinners on the loft, I went down to help with the bar crowd. A couple of times when I picked drinks up from the bar, I noticed Mr. Faraday looking at his watch. Then around eleven-thirty, he suddenly paid his bar bill and left. I thought that was unusual because he had just ordered a fresh drink."

"Did you see anyone?"

"A man was on the pay phone by the door. Just as Mr. Faraday was leaving, that man left, too, but that could have been a coincidence."

"Can you describe the man on the phone?"

"He was a small man dressed in jeans and a dark jacket, but I only saw his back. That's why I didn't say anything to the police. What I saw may not have been related to Mr.

Faraday, and, besides, I couldn't identify this guy. Do you think it was important?"

"I don't know, but the fact you're telling me means you thought it was worth remembering."

"Maybe Mr. Faraday just decided he had enough to drink and it was time to go. Or maybe based on the conversation with the bartender, he got the urge to go for a swim."

"Or maybe he spotted the person he came to meet," suggested Carrie. "Ben, you've been a great help. I appreciate the meal, the good service, and the information."

"Where are you going now?" Ben stopped, a little embarrassed by his abrupt question. "I mean, you ought to stick around. We have a nice crowd—not the kids, but an older group that comes in at this hour for drinks, with lots of singles."

Carrie wasn't sure if being associated with an older group was a compliment, but she wondered something else. "How do you know I'm single?"

"The obvious answer is you're not wearing a ring, but there are other things. You dress very classy, and you're too relaxed to be worrying about kids or a husband."

"You are very observant. Thanks for the offer to stay, but I think I'm going to take a look at Pier Seven."

"You want to go out the main door and head straight for about five hundred yards. Then make a left. His shoes were found at the end of the pier."

Carrie left a very generous tip for Ben and left the Admiral's Saloon.

❧

Ben watched Carrie leave and then went to the employee pay phone inside the kitchen. He dialed a number from a slip of paper he kept in his wallet.

"Yeah, it's Ben from the Admiral's Saloon. You know how you asked me to call if anyone asked about Faraday? This lady came in tonight, said her name was Carrie. Says Faraday asked her to investigate his death if it was suspicious... Yeah, sounded kind of spooky. Sure, I can describe her. She's around five-eight, brown, curly hair, attractive, late forties... No, she's gone now. Said she's going out to look at Pier Seven. You're welcome. Glad I could help. Can I expect a payment like you promised? Great, I'll pick it up at the bar tomorrow! Thanks a lot."

Ben felt no guilt about his phone call. After all, he was a struggling college student and needed the money. He didn't mind if he earned it from his customers as a tip, or from selling a little information on the side. After all, Carrie got the information she wanted, and so did the caller. Simply sell the truth to anyone who would pay. That was his motto.

20

arrie stopped by her car and got her digital camera from the trunk, put her credit card wallet in her pocket, and locked her purse in the car before continuing to Pier Seven. Pier Seven was part of the Tri-City harbor reconstruction that was started about fifteen years before. The construction contract was awarded to two different firms who began building simultaneously at opposite ends of the old wharf. Piers One through Five were adjacent to many of the harbor hotels and contained two pavilions of boutiques, specialty stores, restaurants, and souvenir shops. Piers Six through Ten were located in the Federal Point residential area and combined restaurants, stores, and parking with office buildings. Behind these businesses was a neighborhood of turn-of-the-century, renovated townhouses that added a quaint atmosphere to the area. The renewal brought lots of new visitors and residents to the harbor, and business was booming.

The shipyard for merchant vessels that used to be on the Federal Point side of the harbor was moved to the other side of the water. Occasionally sailors would venture over to the tourist side, but the barroom brawls and rowdy behavior of the past were no longer a problem for the city.

Pier Seven extended a good three hundred yards out from the walkway, and Carrie started her walk to the end. Pier extensions at that end of the harbor provided parking for cars or docks for visiting boats, but this night no boats were moored. The dark water was calm, causing only a gentle slapping sound as it lapped against the wooden pier. Toward the end of the pier were two pilings, with the remains of a sagging yellow police tape.

This is the spot, Carrie thought.

She tried to imagine Jamie standing on this pier his last night on earth. Suddenly Carrie saw what Stephen Beeker meant: an experienced swimmer like Jamie would have walked out to the end of the pier, not jumped in the water between two pilings. Carrie set her camera and started snapping pictures. She was concentrating on her picture-taking and thinking about the implications of her discovery when she became aware of a figure behind her.

"Morbid curiosity or do you have some reason for being on this pier, in this spot?"

Carrie spun around and faced one of Tri-City's beat cops. He looked to be in his late forties, a little pudgy in the middle, wearing a uniform shiny in spots from too much wear and probably known by every business owner in the area.

"Good evening…" Carrie paused while she read his name tag and then added, "Officer Reynolds. I guess a little of both. I'm a friend of the Faraday family, and I was asked to take a look at facts surrounding Jamie Faraday's death. So I thought I'd check out the pier."

"Don't tell me you're a detective? I saw you taking pictures. You look more like a tourist."

She laughed out loud. "No, I'm not a detective. Actually, I'm a photographer by profession. Since photography is what I know, I thought I'd take some pictures of this spot."

"And as a friend who's looking into this case, what makes you think you will come to a different conclusion than the police? No doubt you believe you'll find some undiscovered evidence and bust the case wide open," he said with a bit of sarcasm in his voice.

"At this point, I don't believe anything. I'm a big supporter of the police and even went to school with the coroner on this case. In fact, I'm sure my conclusion will be that the death was an unfortunate accident. However, I did promise the family I'd look at all the possibilities." Carrie spoke in a low, calm tone and then gave Officer Reynolds a gentle smile.

Carrie could see that her answer was the right one, as Officer Reynolds visibly relaxed, and then she asked, "Were you on duty the night of Jamie Faraday's death?"

"Not only on duty, but I was walking only a five-block beat. There was a big convention in town that night, and we had extra police in the area. We want the tourist experience to be pleasant and safe so they come back."

"Hey, what about us local folk?" Carrie asked lightly. "We like to be safe."

"We all benefit if the tourists feel safe. They spend money. That gives the city money for more police, and the locals are protected year-round. It's a lovely circle."

"Officer Reynolds, I like your approach."

He smiled. "Now I guess you want to know if I saw anything unusual that night."

"I do, but I wanted to ask you a question first. I see the remains of the yellow police tape. How do the police know that's the spot where Jamie went into the water?"

"See those two pilings?" Officer Reynolds said as he pointed at the wooden structures. "Faraday's shoes were sitting neatly between the pilings, with a sock draped over each shoe. The investigators believe Faraday sat on the smaller piling and took off his shoes and socks. Then they assumed he most likely dived into the water next to where he placed his shoes."

"Makes sense to me." Carrie also realized that the neat placement of the shoes dispelled the alcohol theory. Someone with too much to drink would probably have dumped their shoes haphazardly and not taken their socks off before they went in the water. "What else was happening that night?" prodded Carrie.

"I hate to disappoint you, but about the only thing I saw were people. It had been a dark and stormy afternoon, and no one was around. And then just as quickly as the storm arrived, it was over, and a flood of people appeared on the boardwalk enjoying the shops, restaurants, and bars."

"What about after the stores and restaurants started to close?"

"People want to get to their cars and go home or get back to their hotels. The crowds disperse just as quickly."

"How about out on the main streets?"

"The avenues are patrolled by car, and then the cars drive down each of the side streets to the edge of the dock. Foot patrolmen like me walk the docks. Believe it or not, with all those people from the convention, there wasn't a single incident, not even a drunk and disorderly. That was, until the body of your friend was discovered."

"Based on what you've said about the large crowds, it does seem unbelievable that no one saw anything."

"Well, fog was coming off the water that night. I walked back and forth many times, and I'll admit it was difficult to see anything way out..." Officer Reynolds hesitated.

Carrie heard his hesitation. "The fog made it tough to see, but did you hear something?"

Officer Reynolds rubbed his chin as if he was remembering something. He chose his words carefully. "Talking to you reminded me of something I had forgotten." He looked straight at Carrie. "You seem to be levelheaded, so I hope you won't blow this little piece of information out of proportion. I did hear something around the time when your friend may have been on the pier. I may have heard a splash."

"A splash loud enough to be someone diving in the water?"

"I'm not sure about that. I was several hundred feet down the boardwalk. When I got to Pier Seven, I stopped and listened, but I saw nothing, absolutely nothing."

"You didn't see the shoes and socks?"

"I didn't see the shoes and socks because I didn't come this far out. At that moment one of the shopkeepers called to me. She had the night's receipts and wanted me to watch as she went to her car. So it was a few minutes before I returned to Pier Seven."

"You didn't see anybody in the area?"

"I did see three men about a hundred feet in front of me heading toward the hotel district. They appeared to be overly saturated and helping one another, if you know what I mean. You know, singing a bit and steadying each other as they walked. I think at the time I thought they might have thrown a bottle in the water, causing the splash."

"Do you remember what they looked like?"

"The man being helped was well dressed. I remember him because most people who come down here are not in suits with white shirts. Even if they are in town on business, they dress casual for the evening. He had gray hair and was about five-foot-ten. The other two looked like Mutt and Jeff. The one guy was tall about six-foot-three, heavy, and looked like a football player. He was wearing khakis with a dark pullover. The third man was small, about five-foot-six and slight of build. He was dressed in jeans and a dark jacket. Unfortunately, I only saw them from the back and didn't see their faces."

Carrie remembered Ben's description of the man on the phone at the Admiral's Saloon. Then she turned back to Reynolds. "That's still a good description. Want a good description, ask a cop." Reynolds smiled at the compliment.

"Were these guys heading toward the hotels?" Carrie pointed with her hand.

"Correct, but that doesn't mean they were tourists. They could have been locals, heading for one of the uptown parking lots."

"You haven't seen them around since that night?"

"I haven't seen a group of three men helping one another, but, like I said, I never saw their faces. I might be passing them every day, and I wouldn't know."

A silence fell between them, and then Reynolds asked, "Are you planning on telling anyone about what I told you?"

Carrie took his arm as they headed back from the end of the pier to the walkway. "Nothing to tell—probably three tourists who drank too much," she said.

"I can't believe I forgot about that incident until now. I'm really good about reporting everything. I mean, I even report when a light is out on the pier." He stopped and pointed to the one they were passing under. "The night of the Faraday incident, that light was out."

"This section of the pier was dark that night?" Carrie looked up at a light, which was now burning brightly.

"The light was broken, but with the fog, I'm not sure it would have mattered. I called it in, and maintenance fixed it within a day." They had reached the end of the pier and were on the walkway.

"It's been a pleasure talking to you, miss. May I ask your name?"

"Of course. My name is Carrie Kingsford." She offered her hand and they shook.

"It's been a pleasure meeting you, Miss Kingsford. Up until this minute, I believed that Mr. Faraday decided to go for a swim and maybe didn't realize the water was cold. Or maybe he had too much alcohol for a swim, but in any case it was an unfortunate accident. Now, talking with you, perhaps—and, mind you, just *perhaps*—there are some other possibilities."

"That's why I'm rechecking all the facts. I'm looking at all those other possibilities."

"I should caution you to be careful. If Mr. Faraday's death wasn't an accident, then poking around could put you in danger. If you need anything, you have my name. You call the precinct and ask for me. I'll get you help. Where are you heading now, Miss Kingsford?"

"I'm done for the night. I'm heading home."

"Good. I'm glad to hear that. Should I walk you to your car?"

"No, I'm fine. I'm just in the parking lot at Pier Eight. Officer Reynolds, I'm glad Tri-City has officers like you on duty." She squeezed his arm.

Reynolds watched Carrie Kingsford head for the Pier Eight parking lot. He turned and walked in the direction of the hotels. Carrie was deep in thought as she walked slowly back to her car, mulling over what she just learned from Officer Reynolds.

She didn't see the two men until she was almost upon them. They were standing by her car, facing away from her. One man was tall and looked like a football player. The other man was short and slight of build.

She cut over quickly to another row of cars. As she walked between two cars, she lost her balance on the gravel and bumped against one. The car alarm went off. *Damn alarms*, she said to herself.

The men looked over in her direction. She regained her balance and quickly started back to where she left Officer Reynolds. When she looked over her shoulder, the men started to move toward her. Without a doubt they recognized her.

She broke into a dead run.

21

The night air may have been cool, but Carrie was sweating inside her clothing as she ran. *What to do now? Think!* She demanded of her brain. She checked once more over her shoulder. The men must have split up. One man was directly behind her, but where was the other man? *Good grief*, she thought, *is this art imitating life? I seem to be reliving a chapter from my book.*

She decided to try to head back toward the Admiral's Saloon, where there would be people. The minute she made the turn from the walkway, she got the answer to her earlier question. The other man was at the far end of the street, blocking her path back to the saloon.

Then she remembered what Officer Reynolds said about police cars patrolling the main avenues. She headed straight for Harbor Avenue. Behind her she could hear the sound of both men running after her. She reached Harbor Avenue and looked for a patrol car. No such luck.

Carrie turned onto Harbor Avenue at Olympic speed. She cut across the road to the other side, hoping it would buy her a few extra seconds, while the men's eyes focused on their side of the street. However, she couldn't silence the sound of her leather shoes on a quiet neighborhood sidewalk. She turned the corner and cut across to the opposite side of Water Street, heading toward Fleet Street, the other major thoroughfare. On Fleet she stopped for a minute, leaning against the edge of a building to catch her breath. She instinctively placed her hands in her pants pocket and felt the smooth leather of her card case.

She heard a sound and carefully peeked around the edge of the building. They were coming. She thought of knocking on a door and trying to rouse one of the residents, but then another idea began to take shape.

The answer was right next to her: a Citibank branch with an inside ATM. Carrie took out her ATM card and swiped it through the card reader to unlock the door. There was a buzz as the door released. She hoped the men hadn't heard the door buzz as she entered the branch and pulled the door shut behind her.

Carrie hit the floor and slid under the check-writing desk located below the window of the branch. The cool floor felt good as she wedged herself tight against the brick wall. The view from the only window gave the outsider limited sight into the branch. Carrie heard someone approach and decided this time she was going to get a look at these guys. She edged out from her hiding place to see the back of a man who was small and very thin. As she watched, she heard the second man approaching from the opposite direction. When the second man stood next to his friend, he was huge, over six feet and more than two hundred pounds. Carrie could just make out what they were saying.

The bigger man spoke with a slight accent. "Bill, where she go? She should be here, between us, no."

Carrie realized that had she stayed on the street, she would have been trapped between the two of them. By thinking about being trapped, she almost missed the motion of the men turning. She barely had time to scoot back against the wall. Their jewelry clanked on the glass as they cupped their hands to look through the window. She wondered if either man carried a bank card.

"Now what we do?" asked the larger man.

"I don't know. It's possible she ran into one of those small alleys between the townhouses. What do you think?" said Bill.

"Maybe she hid behind that row of trash bins on other side of street," he offered

"I'm pretty sure she didn't get beyond this street. Let's head back toward her car," Bill suggested.

Carrie heard the sounds of the men moving away from the window. "I don't want to admit we missed her again. This time you call Mr...."

Carrie strained, but the men were out of her hearing range. She missed the name of the person they were going to call.

She waited. Then she relaxed a little and looked at her watch. She forced herself to wait another five minutes. They wouldn't be traveling that fast if they were checking trash cans and alleys. Should she venture out onto the street or use the customer service phone next to the ATM? She chose the phone.

She was relieved when a person answered her call. It took only a few seconds to give her name and convince the bank representative she needed help and to send the police. Then she slid back into her hiding place. As she sat waiting for the police, she suddenly realized she also had a solution for the problem she had created in that alley for her character Ascot. She would have him hide out in the ATM lobby to escape the men chasing him, just as she had escaped her assailants. How strange that her book paralleled something in real life. Oh, well, she was sure she wasn't the first writer who had this happen.

It was only a few minutes before she saw the flashing red and blue police lights reflecting in the window. She opened the door of the bank and looked both ways before she fully emerged onto the sidewalk.

"I can't thank you enough for coming so quickly," she said to the officer holding open the back door of the squad car. She climbed into the back seat, and the officer behind the wheel turned off the flashing lights. The first officer got in next to his partner and turned to look at Carrie through the metal frame of the wire cage.

Carrie didn't wait for the officer to ask her any questions. "I guess you gentlemen would like an explanation," she volunteered.

"We don't, but our captain would like to speak with you."

"Are we going to the police station?" she asked as the car pulled away from the curb.

"No, our captain is waiting a couple of blocks from here." They drove two blocks and pulled alongside a dark blue unmarked car. The officer once more held the door for Carrie as she left the one vehicle and entered the passenger side of the captain's car. Then the officers pulled away.

"Hello, Captain…" She hesitated, not knowing his name.

"I'm Captain Becker," he said, giving her his name. He was a man in his late thirties who displayed a nice smile as he turned to face Carrie. Becker wasn't wearing a uniform, but a dark-blue turtleneck sweater. His head was closely shaved. She could tell, because very little hair showed out from under the dark-blue cap he was wearing. Carrie found herself staring at Captain Becker. She knew she had seen him before. Then she remembered. He was the man standing on the incline at Jamie's funeral.

"Well, Captain Becker, I'm sorry for all this trouble, but I certainly appreciate your officers helping me."

"Can you tell me exactly what happened tonight?" he asked.

"It seems kind of silly now. I was bothered by a couple of men who just wouldn't leave me alone. When I tried to go to my car, they began to chase me."

"So it was just a couple of guys who wouldn't leave you alone," he repeated.

"That's all it was. Now, if you or one of your men could give me a ride to my car at Pier Eight, I'd be most grateful," she said, sounding totally innocent.

"I'll be more than happy to give you a ride," answered Becker. The captain pulled out of the parking spot and headed toward Pier Eight. As they turned the corner onto Harbor Avenue, Carrie was sure she saw a couple of dark figures dart into an alley between two houses.

Becker pulled onto Pier Eight, and Carrie directed him to her car. She thanked the captain again for the courtesy ride and was about to get out when he touched her arm.

"All right, Ms. Kingsford, how about the real story? I've no time for games or your amateur interference in the Jamie Faraday murder case."

22

"How did you know who I was?" Carrie asked, and then she answered her own question. "Ah, I gave my name to the bank representative, and of course there's Officer Reynolds."

"I asked Officer Reynolds to keep his eyes open for any activity or interest in the Faraday case. Reynolds gave me your name and said you were a friend of the family who was looking around the scene. I called Charles Faraday to find out about you."

Carrie could feel her face getting hot. "And what did Mr. Faraday say?"

"He said you and his brother were college friends. The family wasn't sure why his brother contacted you, but he verified that his brother left you a letter requesting you investigate his death. But back to my original question: what were you doing tonight?" Becker was very well spoken which Carrie didn't expect.

"I'm also sorting Jamie's papers and I'm checking to see if he was writing a story." Carrie worked hard to keep her voice calm and even. "So tonight I was doing research to get more of a complete picture of what he was doing the night he died."

"In order to complete my picture of what happened, as you phrase it, I want this letter that Mr. Faraday left you. If James Faraday knew he was in danger and his death should be investigated, then that letter is police evidence," He emphasized the word evidence.

"Unfortunately, Captain, since the letter seemed to be causing problems, after I read it I got rid of it. However, I can assure you his letter left no clues or indicated any danger he might be in. It simply asked me to investigate his death if it wasn't by natural causes."

Carrie hoped her phrasing would lead Captain Becker to believe she destroyed the letter.

Carrie's phrasing worked, as Becker snapped back, "You did what? Didn't you realize the letter was evidence in a death that may not be accidental? See, this is what happens when amateurs decide to play detective. Vital evidence is lost." Becker had lost control. His face was flush and a small vein on the side of his neck was protruding. Carrie thought he was about to continue his rant but instead he refilled his cup of coffee from a thermos he had next to him. He took a big gulp, which seemed to help him regain his composure.

"I have an extra cup. You want some coffee," he offered. Carrie shook her head no. Then the captain asked, "What do you mean the letter was causing problems?"

Carrie sat quietly, trying to decide how much information to tell Becker. She didn't care for his outburst, and the police investigation under his direction was stalled. However, he did admit Jamie's death might not be accidental.

"If you don't want to cooperate, I could run you in for interfering in a police investigation."

Now Carrie was annoyed. "I'm more than happy to share information. I was just gathering my thoughts. How about a little background before I tell you why I think the letter was creating problems. First, I wasn't aware of Jamie's death until I received a call from a mutual friend. He also informed me about the letter."

"Would this mutual friend be Joel Wheeler?"

"Yes, but how did...?"

"Mr. Wheeler has contacted us several times about our progress on the case as an interested friend of Mr. Faraday. So Wheeler called you about the death, not the family?"

Carrie didn't like the inference, but she carefully answered, "I think the family felt that it would be easier for me to hear the news from Joel. You have to understand that while Jamie and I were close friends in college, I was never particularly close with his family."

"I see...the family also thinks you're intruding. Anyway, back to this letter you received."

Carrie gritted her teeth and responded, "I received the letter at the funeral luncheon from Simpson, Faraday's lawyer. That's when I realized there was a great deal of interest in the letter." Carrie told Becker how she asked Simpson to hold the letter and then later changed her mind and asked Simpson to give her back the letter. "Later that night Simpson was mugged."

"You honestly think Simpson was attacked to get the letter?"

"Simpson told me that while his assailants thought he was unconscious, he heard them say they were looking for the letter."

"Interesting. I'll take a look at that report when I get back to the office. Now tell me about these two men who were chasing you."

"All right, I'll level with you, Captain Becker. After talking to Officer Reynolds, I was heading back to the parking lot. Two men were standing by my car. I didn't like their looks, and I decided to head back to the Admiral's Saloon for safety. They spotted me. The next thing I knew, they were chasing me."

"Can you give me a description of the men?" He placed his coffee cup on the dashboard and took out a small notebook.

"The one man's name is Bill."

"How do you know that?"

"When I was stretched out on the bank floor, they both came up and looked in the window. I heard the one man call the other man Bill. Both men wore jeans with dark jackets. One man is about six-foot-three and stocky, like a weight-lifter. The second man is small, about five-foot-six with a slight build. Together they looked like Mutt..." Carrie stopped mid-sentence. She was using the same phrase that Reynolds used to describe two of the three men on the pier the night Jamie was killed.

"You were about to say Jeff? They looked like Mutt and Jeff."

"Yes, exactly," Carrie confirmed.

"And you've never seen these men before? Maybe you saw them at the funeral or earlier tonight at the Admiral's Saloon?"

"No, I never saw them before tonight." Carrie decided not to tell Becker about the garage incident. Although she had no doubt in her mind they were the same two men, she didn't want to tell him they appeared after a lunch with Joel. She still wasn't willing to admit Bill and his friend might have a relationship with Joel.

Becker broke the silence, "I guess that's about it, Ms. Kingsford. I'll follow-up with Simpson about his mugging, and I'll add your adventure tonight to the Faraday file."

"I thought the file on Jamie Faraday's death was closed," said Carrie.

"No, it's not closed because I haven't closed the file. I don't like it when little events like a mugging or your incident tonight occur on what is suppose to be an accidental death. It tells me there might be more to this case. It also tells me that there's still danger associated with this case."

"You mean danger associated with these men?"

"No, I mean you, Ms. Kingsford. You are a danger to this case. You feel you've been given…shall we say a 'mission' from a dead man, and you feel obligated to overturn every stone. Without knowing who or what you're disturbing, you're plowing ahead. Real clues are lost, like the letter. Not to mention you're putting yourself in danger and causing problems for my department. Let's assume James Faraday's death wasn't an accident. What do you think those two men were going to do to you tonight? Ask you some questions, mug you, or murder you?"

Carrie until that moment really hadn't given any thought to the possibility that those men were out to murder her. Her heart started to beat faster.

"Ms. Kingsford, as of tonight I want you to stop your independent investigation! You can continue sorting Faraday's writings, but no more excursions. If the sorting turns up something of interest, you call me."

With that, Becker reached into his coat pocket and pulled out a business card. He then wrote something on the back. "Here is my card with my office and cell phone number. If you discover something, you can call me at any time." He reached across her and opened the door of the car.

Carrie got out of the car, turned back to Becker, and said, "I appreciate your help tonight."

"Right, I'll follow you onto the expressway to make sure those two guys aren't around. But remember what I said: let the police do the investigating. I don't want to be solving two murders."

23

True to his word, Captain Becker followed Carrie onto the expressway and maintained his surveillance for several exits.

As Carrie drove back, her one nagging question was: who alerted those men to her activities? Was she followed when she left the house? No, she checked her rearview mirror regularly and was sure she wasn't followed from the house. Christopher was in the kitchen when she told Mrs. Cavanaugh she was going out for dinner. Would he have told someone, like Charles? Was the Admiral's Saloon under surveillance? What about Officer Reynolds? *No, he's in the clear,* she thought. *The men were already waiting at the car when I walked away from Reynolds. Besides, Reynolds was somewhere alerting Becker that I was on the pier.*

Carrie checked her rearview mirror one more time as she took the freeway exit for the Faradays. She also checked for strange cars as she drove down the street to the house. The street was quiet, with the residents' cars neatly tucked away in their driveways or garages.

Carrie turned her car lights out before entering the driveway so as not to disturb the family. She parked her car on the pad in front and to the left of the garage and entered the house by the kitchen door. A nightlight in the kitchen was sufficient to guide her into the main hallway. She was starting up the steps when the study door opened behind her and Charles came out into the hallway.

"Are you all right? I've been very worried about you. Captain Becker called and said you were in trouble. Then he hung up before giving any details. That man is maddening! I was going to drive down to the harbor to try to find you, but I didn't know where you were. And with my knee…well, I still can't walk long distances." Charles raced through his sentences.

Carrie was still peeved over Charles's explanation to Becker about her, but on the other hand, it was sweet that he waited up for her.

"I'm fine…just a minor incident. A couple of men followed me after I finished my dinner. Did Christopher tell you I was having dinner out?"

"Christopher? I haven't talked to Christopher all night. He went to the movies with some of his friends and then came home and went to bed."

Carrie thought to herself; *Good, I'm glad it wasn't Christopher who told*. Then she said to Charles, "I was at the Admiral's Saloon and the food is very good. Have you ever eaten there?"

"I've eaten there many times, especially since Jamie's death. You didn't happen to wander out onto Pier Seven?"

Guilt must have shown on Carrie's face because before she could answer, Charles added, "I thought so. I wish you had asked me to go along with you."

"I didn't ask you because of your knee. Besides, I only wanted to see the spot where Jamie went into the water. I certainly didn't think just looking at the spot would invite trouble. And while I appreciate your concern, what was this story you told Becker? Something about you have no idea why Jamie selected me to investigate his death?"

"Good old Becker. Look, that's not what I said. Let's go into the study so we don't wake everyone, and I'll tell you what I actually said. Then you can tell me why you called the police for help."

Carrie would have preferred to go to bed. It had been a long day and a tough night, but she obediently followed Charles into the study. He went to a desk and removed a small tan leather notebook and pen. She wondered if this book was similar to one that Jamie used. She took a seat at a round table where a jigsaw puzzle lay partially completed. Charles waited until Carrie was seated, and then sat across from her, displaying a warm smile. Again, Carrie thought what a good-looking man Charles was and wondered why he never married. He had the same strong face as Jamie, with soft blue-gray eyes that could hold you captive and thick, wavy hair. Somehow the silver color didn't make him look old, just distinguished. She snapped back to reality as Charles continued talking.

"First, when Becker called, he gave no information. He said you were snooping around the pier and could I identify who you were. I told him you were a friend of Jamie's from college and that Jamie left you instructions to look into his death. Becker asked if the family knew about Jamie's intentions. I said no, we had no knowledge of Jamie's plan to contact you. Before I could add anything, he said he had to go because you called the police for help. I hope you see the negative slant was Becker's, not mine."

"I'm sorry for my rudeness, but Becker made it sound like I was this intruder the family didn't want around."

"I really don't care for that guy," Charles said. "Every time I ask him for an update, he says it's an open case and he can't discuss details. But nothing seems to happen."

"He told me the same thing that the case is not closed. And he added that he doesn't like when incidents, such as what happened to me tonight occur on an accidental death case."

"That's good to know, but what happened tonight? Why did you call the police?"

Carrie hesitated. From the moment she had arrived in Tri-City, someone was out to stop her from learning about Jamie's death. She felt the need to share her information with someone, but should that someone be Charles?

Charles must have read her thoughts because he asked, "Still not sure if you can trust me?"

Carrie looked at this man who possessed the same quiet charm as Jamie. Was she being lured into trusting Charles because of her past feelings for Jamie? Could this man have been involved with the death of his brother? She decided the answer was no.

"I know I need to trust someone, and despite our differences in the past, I know Jamie trusted you. I'll trust Jamie's judgment. Can I have your promise that what I tell you will not be shared with anyone else?"

"You've my word of honor, as Jamie's brother."

"Okay, this is what I've learned so far. Jamie's letter, contrary to what everyone thinks, didn't reveal any startling facts. It simply stated that if his death was questionable, he would rely on my analytical skill to determine if it was murder."

"Nothing else…no hints of what he was investigating or why he thought he was in danger?" Disappointment showed in Charles's face.

"Nothing. So while you and I think Jamie was murdered, the letter offered no magic bullet for a quick solution. However, the 'bad guys' don't know this, and I think that's why they are trying to find the letter. I know that's why Simpson was mugged, and that's why they were after me."

Carrie told Charles about her trip to the Admiral's Saloon, her discussion with Officer Reynolds, his description of the three men the night of Jamie's murder, and then her chase through the streets, which ended with a rescue by the Tri-City police and Captain Becker.

"That was very clever to hide out in the bank. I'm not sure I'd have the presence of mind to think of that. You know, your adventure tonight has one positive result. It supports our belief my brother was murdered. However, on the negative side, you've placed yourself in danger. No, I can't have this. Starting tonight, I don't want you doing any more investigating!"

Charles was starting to sound like Becker. At that moment, Carrie saw where a piece of the jigsaw puzzle fit. She took the puzzle piece and angled it into position. She looked up at Charles and said, "Charles, you know I'm not going to do that. I'm going to finish what Jamie asked me to do. It just means I have to be more careful."

Charles was silent for a moment and then added, "I remember Jamie telling me that once you're committed to a project there's no stopping you. All right, then, I propose a compromise. Starting tonight, we share all information and we don't do anything alone. No more solo excursions. Deal?"

"Actually, I'd like that. Deal!"

Charles and Carrie shook hands and then Charles looked at the notes he made during Carrie's narration. "You believe 'Bill' and the other man chasing you were two of the three men Officer Reynolds saw the night of the murder."

"You have to admit the descriptions match those two. However, it's the third man that sounds like the boss. That's who we need to find."

"Older with graying hair and dressed in a suit isn't much of a clue. It could be hundreds of men. Most of the men who were at Jamie's funeral have gray hair, including Simpson, Stone, and Joel, staff reporters, editors, and me. That's assuming this third man is someone we know."

"Remember, Reynolds never saw the man's face. Just because he has gray hair doesn't mean he's old. I mean, you have…" Carrie stopped.

"It's all right. I'll take that as a compliment that you no longer see me as old. I think there was a time when you and Jamie thought me ancient. Funny, as people grow older, a six-year difference grows smaller," he said, reflecting back.

Suddenly Carrie bolted to the French windows.

"What is it?" Charles asked.

"I'm sure I saw a light in the studio."

Charles joined her at the window. "Are you sure? Sometimes you can get a reflection from car lights on the street."

"I didn't hear a car, and this was more like a flashlight." She grabbed her keys. "I'm going to check."

"Not without me! Remember the pact we just made."

24

arrie headed for the kitchen door with Charles hob-
bling as fast as he could behind her. She pulled the
white sheer kitchen door curtain back slightly and
peered out while she quietly unlocked the door. As she slowly
pulled the door open, a loud crash behind her caused her to
fall against the door.

"Ouch, damn it," said Charles.

"Charles! Charles, where are you?" She couldn't see clearly
in the darkened kitchen and was forced to turn on the light.
She saw Charles slumped on the floor between several pots
and pans, holding a frying pan. "Good grief," she said as she
rushed to his side. She helped extract him from the pots and
got him to a kitchen chair.

"Thanks. I hope we haven't awakened the entire house,"
he said, rubbing his ankle.

"What do you mean 'we'?" Carrie said laughing and then
added, "What happened?"

"I guess I was moving a little too fast, and my knee gave out. I started to lose my balance and reached out to grab hold of something. Unfortunately, it was the pan rack I grabbed. The next thing I knew, I was on the floor. I'm okay now. Let's go." He stood up and limped toward the door.

Carrie turned the light out and they stood side by side for several moments. There was no sign of a light or any movement near the studio.

"Do you think all that noise alerted the intruder?" asked Charles.

"I'm sure if the noise didn't, my turning on the lights did. We should still probably check, just to be sure."

They both went outside to the steps that led to the studio. Carrie insisted that Charles remain at the bottom step while she went up and took a look. Carrie climbed the steps slowly, listening for sounds. Charles watched for any flickers of light coming from inside the studio. When Carrie's head was level with the window, she peeked through the glass. She saw nothing. She moved up the steps, keeping her head low. She tried the door, but it was locked. She took out her keys and unlocked the door. She listened again. No sounds. She opened the door a fraction, reached in, and flipped on the lights. She flung open the door with such force that it hit the back wall and sprung back toward her. She peeked inside, but saw no movement, no stirrings, nobody. She ventured inside and looked around. The files were closed, the desk drawers shut, and nothing was disturbed. Carrie turned the lights off, locked the door, and left the studio.

"Anything?" asked Charles.

"Nope, maybe it was just a reflection," responded Carrie, now unsure of what she thought she saw.

They went back inside the house. Charles locked the kitchen door and turned the lights off. Carrie was silhouetted in the moonlight coming through the kitchen window. Charles took her by the shoulders, turned her to him, and kissed her gently on the forehead. Carrie was stunned and a little confused, but offered no resistance.

"I've wanted to do that for a long, long time. I've missed you, Carrie Kingsford. Contrary to what Becker said, I'm glad you're here."

"Charles, I don't..."

"Don't say anything. I won't put any pressure on you. We'll wait until all this is behind us. But remember, starting tonight, we're working together."

They left the kitchen. Charles insisted on taking the steps. When they were outside Carrie's bedroom, Charles kissed her again and hobbled off toward his room.

Carrie got ready for bed, but couldn't sleep. She lay in the dark wondering about all the events of the last few days. So much was happening. It was hard to keep everything straight. She couldn't seem to make the connections she needed to solve the puzzle. Now she had a new dilemma. She wanted to remove Charles from her suspect list. Did he stumble on purpose in the kitchen to warn the person in the studio? Were his feelings toward her genuine, or was it... She didn't finish the sentence.

The thoughts kept repeating in her brain without answers until they were interrupted by a slight sound in the hallway.

She quietly arose from her bed and tiptoed to her door. She cracked open her door and looked out.

Christopher was sneaking down the hallway to his bedroom.

The next morning, Carrie decided how to deal with intruders in the studio. She took the phone book from the nightstand next to her bed. It wasn't the newest copy of the massive book, but it served her purpose. She dialed one of the numbers listed, placed her order, and was informed that the job would be completed later that afternoon.

"Yes, I want to make sure these are the type that can't be duplicated. Good, that's what I want... There's one additional piece of information I want noted on the work order. When the workman is finished, he's to speak to no one other than myself. Is that understood? You won't need my credit card number. I'll pay the workman in cash. Great, thanks."

∾

The company was true to its promise. Just before three that afternoon, the green and white Exeter Lock Company van pulled into the Faraday driveway. Charles was at work, Mrs. Faraday had gone to a luncheon, and Christopher was still in school. Carrie was also pretty sure that Suzanne wasn't around, although she had no idea where she was. Carrie was in the study watching out the window. When the van came down the driveway, Carrie went out through the French doors and met the driver.

No one would know the locks were changed until he or she tried to use the old key. This should help eliminate intruders, both the ones Carrie knew about and the intruders she hadn't discovered. Maybe a new lock would give her enough time to go through Jamie's papers undisturbed and find out what Jamie was investigating.

While the locksmith set about his work, Carrie took the opportunity to use Jamie's printer to print out copies of the photos she took at Pier Seven. By the time she finished her prints, the locks were changed.

"Here you are, ma'am, two new keys, just like you asked." The locksmith was a big, bulky man, with a round, pleasant face. His pudgy hands opened to reveal two keys that he dropped into Carrie's palm.

"Now, these are the type of keys that are not easily duplicated?" she asked.

"Yes, ma'am." He took one of the keys back from her open palm. "See this sort of squiggly scratch in the groove here? That means it's a key that someone can't take to the local hardware store and have duplicated."

"Perfect."

"Been having problems? Is that why you wanted the locks changed?"

Carrie didn't want to reveal her real reason for changing the locks. Instead, she said, "The upstairs studio has been here for a long time. Many keys have been given out over the years, and many keys have been lost. It's just smart in this day and age to get the locks changed once in a while. Don't you agree?"

"Absolutely, shame more people don't do this. Especially in older, wealthier neighborhoods like this one. Burglars like these neighborhoods because they know the locks are often old. Let me grab the work order from my truck." He shut the door and then checked both keys to make sure they worked. He and Carrie went down the steps to his truck. Carrie waited while he totaled the bill.

"According to this work order, you're paying with cash?"

"I've got it right here." Carrie counted out the amount showing on the work order and added a nice tip.

"Much appreciated. Have a nice day, ma'am, and if you need any other work, just give us a call. Ask for Bo; that's me," He said using his thumb to point to his chest.

At that moment Charles pulled into the driveway, followed by another car driven by Jonathan Stone. The two men came and stood next to Carrie and watched as the workman got in his truck and headed out the driveway.

"Locked your keys in the car?" asked Charles.

"No, I have my car keys right here." She patted her pants pocket. "I changed the lock on the studio door."

"You should have discussed this with me before making that decision," Charles said, trying to control his anger.

Carrie held up the extra key.

"What's that?" asked Charles.

"I had two keys made, one for you and one for me, since we are working together." She smiled.

"Oh," Charles said as his initial anger quickly deflated.

"Looks like Carrie has everything under control," added Stone. "Charles, it's probably a good idea to have the locks changed. I think Carrie did the right thing."

"Of course you're right, Jonathan." Charles decided he had lost the battle and changed the subject. "Let me get you the folder with the budget numbers." Charles left Stone and Carrie standing in the driveway while he went inside.

"Did you follow Charles all the way home just to get a folder?" asked Carrie, keeping the conversation going.

"I live only a couple of miles away in the new condos over by the lake area, so this is on my way home. I'd much rather work on budget numbers at home, where there are no interruptions. Also, there is nothing like a good wine to make the numbers much easier to understand." Jonathan laughed at his own words.

Carrie remembered seeing the new condos when she returned from the library. They were in one of the revitalized areas of Tri-City. "I passed that area the other day," she said. "The condos look lovely."

"They are both convenient and comfortable, and the nice thing about new construction is the buyer gets all the latest designs and gadgets. You must come and visit me while you're here. We'll share one of those good bottles of wine I mentioned."

"Jonathan. If you don't mind I'd like to ask you a confidential question."

"Of course I don't mind. I'm delighted you feel you can come to me."

"Charles mentioned he asked you to check out Suzanne. Did you have any luck finding out more about her background?"

"Well, keep in mind I'm not the police. I've had to ask our European bureau chief to work with some of his reporters to see if they can find anything out. So it's slow going."

"You haven't found out anything?" Carrie couldn't keep the disappointment out of her voice."

"No, not exactly my dear. We did find the hotel Suzanne was staying in before she met Jamie. They verified she was from New York and had been in Europe for about two weeks before she met Jamie. That matches what Jamie said. He told us she received a small inheritance and used it to travel to Europe. And we did verify that her name did not appear on any of the local police reports in either New York or Europe. So her story seems to be legitimate"

"Oh I see."

"I told Charles that if he wanted more information he should hire a detective, but I think it's a waste to spend money on an investigation that won't produce much. Of course in the meantime we are still poking around so maybe something else will turn up."

At that moment Charles returned with the folder. Carrie didn't ask any more questions and after a few moments Stone said goodbye. After Stone pulled out of the driveway, Carrie turned to Charles.

"I'm sorry, Charles, I should have told you first, but you weren't around to ask. After last night I decided we shouldn't wait another day. We need to try to cut down on the traffic through the studio until you and I can figure out what's happening."

"No, I snapped too quickly before I had all the facts. Please chalk it up to the fact that it's been a rough day at work, and I'm tired. Too many late-night adventures, but you did the right thing by changing the locks."

"Good. I thought you would agree with my decision, otherwise I wouldn't have done it."

"That's not exactly what I meant. I mean I like the fact you're thinking for both of us."

Carrie could feel her face growing hot.

Charles continued, "At one time you only thought of me as Jamie's older brother. Hopefully now you will see me as someone here to help you."

"I'm fine with that," she said.

Charles reached over, put his arms around her, and gave her a quick hug. "So where are we in all this?"

"We have two shiny new keys, but no new leads. How's your knee?"

"It's much better today. It just needs time to heal."

26

A t first there was no smell of smoke. Carrie became aware that something was wrong when bright light started to fill her bedroom. In her dreamy state, she thought it was the sun coming up. She rolled away from the light toward the clock on the nightstand. She opened one eye and saw on the clock dial it was a little after one. "How could I have slept until one in the afternoon?" she mumbled aloud. Then as the functions of her brained kicked in, she realized the numbers "1:00" on the clock had a small "a.m." next to them. *Good heavens, it's one in the morning. What is that light?*

She arose and went to her window, pulled the curtain back, and gasped. "We're on fire!" She naturally drew back from the window, but the flames beckoned her for a closer look. It wasn't the house that was on fire, but Jamie's studio that was shooting bright orange bursts toward the sky. Carrie spotted Charles opening the garage doors and driving the vehicles out of the burning structure.

Carrie knew she had to get downstairs to be with Charles. As she put on her robe, she continued watching the fire. She was just about to leave her room when she saw a movement in the shadows. She opened the curtain a little wider. The figure waited until Charles entered the garage again before making a move. Carrie was glad she was in a corner room and moved to the other window that gave her a side view of the house. The figure darted from a tree and was now standing next to her car. Based on the height of her car, this person wasn't large in stature. The figure crouched on the concrete pad and then reached up and opened the door of Carrie's car. The figure didn't get into the car. In a split second, the car door closed, and the area was once more in darkness.

The first fire engine swung into the driveway, and its headlights illuminated the figure standing by her car. Christopher Faraday stood on the edge of the driveway and waved the engine toward the garage.

Carrie finished tying her robe and headed downstairs. When she arrived in the kitchen, Mary and Mrs. Cavanaugh were standing together, looking out the open door.

"Oh, Ms. Carrie, isn't this awful? The entire garage is in flames," said an emotional Mary.

"Mary, it's more important we account for everyone in the household. I saw Christopher and Charles outside. Is Mrs. Faraday upstairs, and what about Suz..." Carrie didn't finish the sentence as Suzanne wandered into the kitchen.

"Mrs. Faraday is fine and in her room," answered Mrs. Cavanaugh.

"Then that's what's important: everyone is okay," said Carrie.

"Everything is not fine because Jamie's work is burning. Some of it could have been saved if we had a key to get into the studio," accused Suzanne.

It was obvious Suzanne knew that the lock on the studio was changed.

"Actually, Suzanne, Charles and I both have keys. But it would be foolish for anyone to risk their life to save papers." Carrie wanted to change the subject. "Mrs. Cavanaugh, maybe you should let Mrs. Faraday know everyone is safe."

"I'll go to Mrs. Faraday," volunteered Suzanne.

Before Carrie could make a comment, Mrs. Cavanaugh jumped in. "No, Ms. Suzanne, you stay here in the kitchen in case you're needed. I'll go up to Mrs. Faraday."

Carrie didn't wait for Suzanne's response and went out the kitchen door. She was greeted by the flashing lights of the fire engines and the mass of hoses that cut like an abstract painting across the lawn. She spotted Charles and Christopher by the corner of the house and went over to them. Charles put his arm around her shoulders and pulled her close.

"Are you all right?"

"I should be asking you that question. From my window I saw you moving cars out of the garage."

When Carrie said the words "from my window," she stared directly at Christopher. She had a feeling Christopher got her meaning because he averted his eyes and looked toward the ground.

"I thought of trying to extinguish the fire with the garden hose, but realized that wouldn't do anything. It was spreading too quickly. I decided the next best thing to do was get the cars out of the garage."

"When did you discover the fire?"

"I was working late in my office on some galley proofs for the magazine when I heard the sensor and noticed one of the lights on the fire board was blinking."

"Fire board?" asked Carrie.

"With the house being as old as it is, I took some precautions. I had the house rewired a few years ago and had a fire board installed. If there's a fire, a sensor goes off and a light flashes on the board, indicating the location. I could tell by looking at the board the fire was in the studio. So while the system automatically called the fire department, I headed outside."

"The system indicated the studio, not the garage?"

"There are separate sensors for each location. That's why I knew I had time to get the cars out. The fire hadn't set the sensor off in the garage."

"When I looked out my window, the studio seemed to be fully engulfed in flames. Don't you think that was kind of quick?"

"If you're asking do I think the fire was deliberately set, you bet I do."

"How about you, Christopher, what do you think?" Carrie asked.

Christopher still looked guilty as he found his voice and said almost in a whisper, "I'm not sure. Uncle Charles was moving the last car out of the garage. I was directing the fire engines down the driveway. When I looked up the garage was on fire, too."

After several more minutes, Charles said, "It looks like the firemen have it under control. You two better get back inside. I'll wait with the firemen in case they have any questions."

"I'll wait with you, Uncle Charles," added Christopher.

"No need, Christopher. Besides, I want you to go up to Grandma and let her know everyone is all right."

Before Carrie could say another word, Christopher dashed off.

"Mr. Faraday?" A fireman in full gear approached Charles. Behind him was a policeman. "I'm Lieutenant Harriman and this is Officer Kenneth. I'm afraid we couldn't do much to save the studio, but we did save most of the garage and kept the flames from jumping over to the main house. The fire appears to be out, but we'll continue wetting down the building to make sure the fire doesn't reignite."

"Thanks, Lieutenant Harriman, you and your men did an excellent job. Please give them my thanks."

"I'll be sure to do that, Mr. Faraday." Harriman was clearly pleased by Charles's compliment. "Do you have any ideas how the fire got started?" asked Officer Kenneth.

"The first I knew we had a fire was when the sensor on the fire board buzzed. By the time I got out here, I barely had time to get the cars out of the garage."

"The fire appears to have spread rapidly, considering the alarm system and how quickly we responded," offered Harriman.

"Do you suspect it was deliberately set?" Asked Charles.

"Yes that's why I came over. I wanted to let you know that as soon as our cleanup phase is complete, our arson team will start their investigation."

"I'll need to get a more complete statement for the record," said Officer Kenneth. Then he added, "But I don't think it's necessary for you folks to wait out here."

Charles accepted the offer to get out of the way. "I'll be in the kitchen, if you need me," he stated. "I'll also arrange for some coffee and sodas for your men."

27

arrie needed to talk with Christopher, and she didn't want to wait until morning. She left Charles in the kitchen preparing refreshments for the firemen and hurried upstairs.

The upstairs hallway was U-shaped. Carrie and Charles had opposite corner rooms, with another guest room between them on the backside of the house. Mrs. Faraday's suite was down the hallway on the side furthest from the garage. Down the hallway along the driveway side were three rooms. Christopher's room was his father's and faced the front of the house. Suzanne's room was opposite Christopher's and faced the driveway.

Carrie checked the hallway. No one was around. She went swiftly down the hallway to Christopher's door and knocked. She didn't have to knock a second time. Christopher opened the door just a crack.

"I've been expecting you," he said softly. "Come in."

As Carrie entered the room, Christopher peered into the hallway to see if she had been followed.

"Don't worry," said Carrie. "I checked to make sure no one was around."

"Just wanted to be sure, especially with you know who across the hall. I don't want our conversation to be overheard." Christopher led her to the other side of the room.

Carrie sat on the desk chair while Christopher sat on the edge of an old-fashioned double-poster bed. Carrie glanced around the room. It was obvious the decor hadn't been updated since Jamie was a small boy. The wallpaper displayed cowboys on horses in various action shots of riding and roping. The drapes were a heavy hopsack fabric in a combination of colored blocks matching the wallpaper. The room was old-fashioned and didn't reflect the tastes of today's boys, especially a boy about to enter his teens. She made a mental note to suggest to Charles that the room needed some modernizing.

"Christopher, you're acting a little paranoid. I left Suzanne downstairs with your uncle making refreshments for the fire crew."

"I can't help it. I don't trust her, and she has this way of unexpectedly popping up." His brown eyes were big and sparkled with excitement.

"Since you expected me, you must know why I'm here. I saw you sneaking along the driveway just after the fire started."

"You don't think I had anything to do with the fire?" He looked straight at Carrie. "You do! You think I set the fire, don't you?"

Carrie looked him in the eye and said, "I don't think anything until you tell me. But that means you tell me the whole truth, the first time, straight out."

He nodded in agreement. "Okay, here goes. I heard you changed the locks today. I decided I wanted to see if I could pick the new lock."

"You could have asked me for a key. Remember, we decided we were in this together, or did being a detective have more of an appeal?" she asked teasingly.

Christopher smiled sheepishly. "I did sort of want to see if I could pick the lock. Plus, I didn't get the idea to go to the studio until everyone was in bed."

"And did it work? Were you able to pick the lock?"

"Not exactly. I couldn't get through the door, but I was able to get in through the window," he said with a great deal of pride.

"That's very impressive, but it doesn't say much for my changing the locks to curtail traffic in the studio. Why did you feel you needed to break in tonight? You could have tried early in the morning or after school."

"Because of the fire, you'll be glad I broke in when I did." Christopher got up from his perch on the bed and went to the door. He listened for a moment and then snapped the door open. No one was there. Christopher shut the door and returned to the bed. "Anyway, I got to thinkin' about Dad's journal. I figured there were only two choices. Either they got the journal, or it was still hidden."

"Christopher, who is the 'they' you refer to?"

"The ones who murdered my dad." He lowered his voice. "I know he was murdered. No other explanation makes sense." He paused for a moment and then continued, "I figured they hadn't found it. I mean, the studio being broken into and Simpson being mugged."

"You know about the adventure Uncle Charles and I had the other night?" asked Carrie.

"I heard Uncle Charles and Grandmother talking this morning. Anyway, I remembered a story Dad was working on when we were in Poland. His story revealed that the new government people were getting money from the bad guys. While he was writing the story he kept names and important information in his journal like always. But because he had names of people getting money, he kept the journal hidden until he finished the story and the police locked everybody up. Anyway I've been going out at night to the studio looking for the journal."

"You were in the studio last night, weren't you?"

Christopher nodded.

"I thought so," continued Carrie. "Uncle Charles and I thought we saw someone. Then later, I saw you sneaking down the hallway. Christopher, I checked everything in your father's studio, under desk drawers and chairs, behind filing cabinets, even behind the pictures on the wall. I couldn't find anything."

"I bet you didn't look under the floorboards!"

"The floorboards!" she said with surprise. "No, I didn't look under the floorboards. Why did you look there?"

"Because that's where he hid the journal when we were in Poland: in the floorboards beneath his desk. That's what I remembered tonight."

"You found the journal!" Carrie couldn't conceal her excitement. "That's wonderful! Did you get a chance to look inside it?"

"No, I had a bad feeling, so I got out of there."

"Christopher, what do you know about the fire? Did you use a candle for light in the studio?" Carrie asked calmly.

"Get real!" He looked at Carrie the way every child looks at an adult who has lost touch with the real world. He went to his bureau drawer and pulled out a small black rod. "I used one of these new mag lights. It's got a real strong narrow beam of light. I saw this used by burglars on television."

Carries accepted the light from him. "I must say an excellent choice of tools. I should have known you would use something modern. How long were you in the studio looking for the journal?"

"Only about ten minutes because I found the floorboard right away." He paused for a moment and then added, "I also know that the fire wasn't an accident."

"I'm pretty sure the fire department will come to that same conclusion. It spread too quickly not to have been started."

"You don't understand. I'm not making a guess. I saw two men set the fire. Well, I didn't quite see them, but they started it."

"Christopher, slow down and tell me exactly what you saw."

"It's like I said. Once I discovered the journal, I didn't feel comfortable hanging around the studio. I left and was heading back to the French doors at the study. I go in and out that way to avoid the light by the kitchen steps. I was ready to enter the house when I saw two men approaching, so I ducked behind the shrubs by the door. The men went up the steps to the studio, carrying metal cans and a crowbar. When they came back down, they didn't have the cans. Within seconds, the entire studio burst into flames. I think they used whatever was in those cans to start the fire. Then they left the property through the hedges by the back of the garage."

"Can you describe these men?"

"One was very tall, taller than Uncle Charles and he looked strong. The other guy was short and thin. That's about all I remember because I was pretty scared, especially when the fire started."

Carrie sat next to Christopher on the bed. She put her arm around his shoulders and gave him a quick hug. He didn't resist the gesture.

"Sounds like the same two guys that chased me the other night. I'll tell you a secret. I didn't get a real good look at them because I was scared. I think you were pretty brave to get as many details as you did. You've had quite an adventure tonight. However, tomorrow morning you're going to have to tell the fire investigator what you saw."

"I don't want to do that."

"Now, Christopher…"

He interrupted. "I mean, I'll talk to the police or whoever else about those men, but I don't want to tell them about the journal. I'll just say that I go to my father's studio sometimes to hang out. I'm calling in my future option. I didn't tell on you outside the study your first night here, and now I'm asking you not to tell on me."

She looked at Christopher. This was an important moment in their relationship. "All right, I won't say anything. It will be up to you to decide when and who to tell about the journal."

Christopher was visibly pleased with Carrie's decision. Then he said, "I don't want to wait until morning to get the journal. I want to go get it now."

"Go get it! Where is it?"

"You saw me open your car door."

Carrie nodded.

"I hid it under the seat in your car. If you saw me open the car door, someone else may have seen me, too. That's why I want to go get it now."

"Why didn't you get it when the firemen and everyone were running around? With all the excitement, no one would have noticed."

Christopher again looked a little sheepish. "You left your car door unlocked. That's how I was able to hide the journal in the car. After I hid the journal under the seat, I hit the lock button. I need your keys to unlock the car."

"Are you sure you don't want to practice your lock-opening techniques?"

"No, breaking into cars wouldn't be a good habit to start." He grinned.

"Come on, I'll get my keys, and we'll go get the journal."

28

They trotted back down the hallway to Carrie's room to grab her car keys. However, when they were ready to leave, Christopher turned and faced Carrie.

"Look, how about you waiting up here while I get the journal?"

"Christopher, I'm the adult. You should wait here while I go down to the car."

"But this is safer. If the two of us go, we create more of a commotion and the chance that someone will see us. I can go out the French doors like before and hide by the bushes until the coast is clear. You stand at the window and watch. In case anyone stops me, you can yell at them or get help. If you're with me, we're both trapped."

Carrie wasn't quite sure why, but she agreed to Christopher's plan. She turned the lights out and went over to watch out her window. She opened the window just enough to hear. She was immediately hit with the acrid odor of wet burnt wood and other chemical smells resulting from the fire.

After a few minutes, Christopher appeared from the shadows of the house and went straight to Carrie's car. Carrie positioned herself for the best view. Christopher bent down next to the car door. He was very quick. After the car alarm beeped, the car light came on and went out almost immediately as the door was closed. As Christopher stood up, ready to return to the house, a voice called out.

"Hey, what do you think you're doing?"

Christopher didn't run, but stood and waited. Carrie panicked and opened the window wider.

She heard Christopher say, "Oh, hello, I'm Christopher Faraday. I live here. With the fire and all the excitement, I couldn't sleep. I came out to get my library book, so I could read before going to bed. I hope that's okay, Officer."

Carrie lifted the screen, leaned out the window, and said, "It's all right, Officer. I'm watching him to make sure he comes right back." Carrie waved to the policeman.

"No problem mamm, we just want to keep the area clear so no one gets hurt," the officer said, addressing Carrie at the window. Then he turned back to Christopher and said, "Go ahead, young man, back inside."

"Christopher, say goodnight to the officer and come straight inside," Carrie said, still leaning out the window.

"Thanks for all your help tonight and watching over everything." Christopher said in a very polite voice.

Christopher didn't wait for any additional encouragement. He rushed for the door of the house.

Carrie was standing in the hallway waiting for Christopher, who stopped and looked behind him and then scooted into her room.

"Good job," Carrie said as she patted him on the back. "Telling the policeman you were getting a library book was quite clever." She allowed him to bask in the praise for a minute and then asked, "Christopher, I was so busy watching you, I didn't really check out the area. Did anyone else see you?"

"Two other firemen were working at the back of the drive-way. They stopped and looked when the policeman called to me, but went back to work. Uncle Charles wasn't around. I even glanced up at Suzanne's room, but it was dark." He lifted up his shirt, took out a worn green leather journal, and handed it to Carrie. "Here's my dad's journal," he said proudly.

Carrie ran her hand over the worn leather. "You know, it's quite late. Should we find a place to hide the book and wait until morning to look at it?"

Disappointment showed in his face. "We could take a peek, just to see if anything important jumps out. After all, I've been looking for this clue for some time," he added hopefully.

She felt his excitement and responded, "All right, let's take a quick peek."

They sat side by side on the bed. She flipped the journal open to the first entry and saw Jamie's familiar handwriting. She stood staring at the page without really reading what it said.

"Hey, are you okay? You're acting like you're in a trance."

"Sorry, I was just thinking about your father."

"You really liked my dad, didn't you?"

"Yes, your father and I were very good friends at one time."

"Dad often spoke of you, and I know he followed your work. He checked photo credits on every article he read. When he found your name, he would always show me the photographs." He waited a moment and said, "I was wondering why you didn't marry my dad."

"We talked about it, but our careers took us in different directions. Then your father found your mother, and I know he loved her very much. Besides, I hear they had this wonderful son."

"All right, enough mushy stuff," said Christopher. He started slowly turning the pages. "Here, look! These are the notes I was telling you about for the Poland story. I recognize some of the names."

Carrie looked briefly at the notes and then said, "Let's flip to the back of the journal and see the last entries."

Christopher nodded, and they found an entry concerning shipments of merchandise bound for the United States. "Looks like notes for a story on exporting goods to the States," suggested Christopher. "You know, now that I think about it, Dad was spending a lot of time at the docks before we left Poland."

Carrie remembered the slip of paper she'd found in Jamie's studio. She was about to get the paper out of her pants pocket when there was a light tapping at the door. Christopher looked a little frightened as he exchanged glances with

Carrie. She took the journal from the table, slipped it into her robe pocket, and went to answer the door. She opened the door and Charles entered the room.

"What are you two up to? One of the firemen told me Christopher was just outside."

Carrie looked over to Christopher, who seemed to have lost his voice. Carrie helped him out. "In all the excitement, I forgot something from my car. Christopher was kind enough to go downstairs and get it for me."

Charles would have probably asked more questions if it weren't for the wink that Carrie gave him.

"I see. That was nice of you, Christopher, but now it's time for bed. In fact, it is way past time for bed. Let's go." Christopher was going to protest, but Charles added, "No excuses, young man. You'll have plenty of time to talk to Carrie tomorrow. I'm going to let you stay home from school. With all of tonight's excitement, you deserve a day off."

As Christopher passed by Carrie, she stopped him. "Let's continue our discussion first thing in the morning. If we both get some sleep, we can take a fresh approach."

The thought of getting a day off from school and meeting Carrie in the morning about the journal satisfied Christopher. He marched off down the hall with Uncle Charles's arm around his shoulders.

29

ate the next morning, Carrie was sitting at the desk in her room. She was looking over the journal while she waited for Christopher to arrive. She decided she would use her day to go through the journal slowly, page by page, with Christopher. She knew Christopher would join her as soon as he was awake, but the events of the night before obviously took their toll, and he was still sleeping.

She flipped to the back section of the journal. Jamie's notes consisted of a list of short phrases and single words:

> *Exporting and importing*
> *Location and storage*
> *Sailors/friends make the trip*
> *Payments arranged*
> *Other end—friend or foe*
> *Pub drop*
> *Storage area separate*

Location near Tri-City docks or harbor?
Codes
Cold storage and spoilage?
Labels—more than one thousand per envelope
Caviar—real product or fake
Why?

Carrie read the list several times. She even said the items out loud, but couldn't apply any meaning to Jamie's series of thoughts. While looking at this page, Carrie realized there was another entry on the back side. It was a short poem.

Sail, sail my beautiful ship
With hulls of gold and treasure
And hidden with the cargo
a package of a different measure.

Who knows, who knows
of this tale of the taking,
for the person least expected
at the heart of the making.

Discovery is easy to find,
with suspect's photo of smiles
five steps from the left with old friends
but loyalty is many more miles.

Carrie knew that Jamie wrote poetry for himself. He was criticized early in his college days by the literary magazine staff, who thought his poetry didn't follow the accepted format. It was probably why he joined the newspaper staff. As a result, Jamie never took his poetry seriously, but continued to write poems for his own amusement.

When Carrie reread the poem, she immediately spotted the photo reference. If Jamie was referring to a particular photo, it was probably part of the ashes of the studio. She was admonishing herself for not having logged more of Jamie's work, when there was a light tapping at the door. She closed the book and slid it in the top desk drawer.

As she opened the door, she lightheartedly said, "It's about time you got up!"

Charles was initially stunned and then said with a grin, "If you remember, I was out late last night. You obviously were expecting someone else."

"Sorry, I thought it was Christopher. I promised to spend time with him today. How about you? Did you get any sleep last night?"

"After I saw Christopher to his room, I went to bed, but it took awhile to fall asleep. I kept seeing the flames and thinking about the loss of Jaime's work."

"I know what you mean. I experienced the same feelings."

For someone who was up late the previous night, Charles looked great. He was dressed in a beautiful dark-blue suit, crisp white shirt, and a blue and red patterned tie. It caused Carrie to comment, "You look very dashing this morning. Are you off to meet the insurance people?"

"No, they will be here later this afternoon for a preliminary look. I'm on my way to the office for a meeting. I stopped by to ask you to go with me. After the meeting, I could show you around Faraday Press, and then we could have lunch."

"I'd love to have lunch with you and of course I'd very much like to see where magazines like *News World* are published. How about if I meet you for lunch? That way I can get a couple of things done around here and meet Christopher as promised."

Charles, just like Christopher the night before, looked over his shoulder to see if anyone was around. "May I come in?"

"Of course." Carrie stood back, and Charles entered the room. Charles sat on the very edge of the desk chair and waited for her. She closed the door and moved over to the reading chair by the window.

"I'm sure by now you've figured out that last night's fire was no accident. It was deliberately set. We are dealing with people who have murdered Jamie, mugged Simpson, chased you, and started a fire. These are very dangerous people. Instead of just waiting to see what they are going to do next, I want to try to force the issue. I've invited Simpson, Stone, Joel, a couple of Jamie's fellow workers, and even Captain Becker to my meeting this morning in the hopes of sharing information. I'd like for you to join us. Can you postpone your meeting with Christopher until later in the afternoon? I have to be home early to meet with the insurance people."

Carrie thought for a moment. "You realize there's a possibility that one of the people you've invited may be involved? You might be sharing information with the enemy." Carrie was thinking of Joel.

"I thought of that, but with Jamie's studio gone, I'm not sure where to find the next clue. I'm still completely in the dark as to why Jamie was murdered. Until we know this, we are all still in danger. We need to flush our prey from the bushes before something else happens."

"This meeting sounds like Nick Charles in a *Thin Man* movie. Get all the suspects in a room and hope someone makes a slip."

"In this situation, I wish I had Nick Charles's talent. I'm hoping just to get enough light to see where this tunnel leads." He reached out and took her hand in his. "Will you join me?"

"You know I will." Before Carrie could add anything additional, Charles stood.

"Can you be ready in fifteen minutes?"

"Sure, meet you in the kitchen."

"Hey, that reminds me. What sort of mischief were you and Christopher cooking up last night? I took your hint and didn't ask any more questions, but it looked like a serious conversation."

Carrie thought for a moment and then said, "We were discussing some of his adventures in Europe. I'll fill you in on the details in the car."

"All right. I'll get a couple of cups of coffee ready."

❧

Carrie changed her clothes into something more suitable for a business meeting. Then she sat down at the desk to write

Christopher a note. She wrote about Uncle Charles's meeting and told him she would give him all the details when she got back. She would rely on his objective viewpoint to evaluate what happened at the meeting. She was hoping this would soothe his feelings about not working on the journal. She also indicated that she sufficiently hid their "find" and to please forgive her for not revealing the location in the note. She knew he would appreciate the fact that notes can be intercepted. She folded the note and placed it in an envelope.

She went down the hallway to Christopher's room. She was stooping down to slide the note under his door when Suzanne opened her bedroom door. She stared down at Carrie, who was on bent knees.

"Good morning." Carrie tried to sound cheerful. "I'm just leaving Christopher a note. We were supposed to meet this morning, but now I need to leave before I can speak with him."

"That's very nice. I think he appreciates it when we treat him like an adult, even though he's just a child. I'm in desperate need of a cup of coffee, how about you?" Suzanne asked.

"I always need coffee in the morning," answered Carrie.

The two women walked together down the hallway. When they reached the steps, Suzanne stopped.

"You know, I just realized I'm going to need a coat or a sweater. It's chilly this morning. Tell Charles I'll be right there and if you could fix me a cup of coffee, cream, no sugar."

With those words, Suzanne turned and scooted back down the hallway. That's when Carrie realized Suzanne was also invited to Charles's meeting. She wondered when Suzanne's invitation was extended, before or after hers. *Stop that!* She thought. *It doesn't matter when she was invited. Charles is right to have her attend. She was with Jamie in Europe and may be able to add valuable information.*

❦

Charles and Carrie waited for Suzanne in the kitchen. Mrs. Cavanaugh provided Carrie with commuter coffee mugs with the Faraday Press logo, and Carrie prepared coffee for herself and Suzanne.

"It's getting late. Maybe Suzanne is waiting for us outside," suggested Charles.

Sure enough, when Carrie and Charles arrived at the car, Suzanne was seated comfortably in the front seat.

"Suzanne, I think you should drive Jamie's car to the meeting," said Charles. "I can't guarantee after the meeting I'll be able to leave to drive you home again."

"I appreciate the thought, but it's silly for us to take three different cars to the same place. Don't worry about Carrie and me. Maybe after the meeting, we girls will spend time together shopping or having lunch. We can always meet you back at the office at the end of the day or take a cab home, right, Carrie?"

Carrie and Charles exchanged glances, but there was nothing they could do. They didn't want to reveal to Suzanne they intended to have lunch and spend the afternoon with each other.

Carrie handed Suzanne her coffee and climbed into the back seat of the car. Charles shrugged his shoulders and climbed into the front seat with Suzanne. With Suzanne riding in the car, Carrie wouldn't have a chance to discuss anything with Charles. Hopefully there would be some moment during the day when they were alone, and Carrie could discuss the case with Charles.

30

araday Publishing was located right in the heart of downtown Tri-City. It was midway between the harbor area, where the Admiral Saloon was located, and Joel's office, which was in the financial district.

Charles drove past the front of the brick building, identified by the Faraday Press sign, around to the loading docks. He took a remote control from his sun visor and, with the press of a button a large metal door slowly rose. Charles pulled his car into the bay and then opened the car doors for Carrie and Suzanne. They followed him into the building.

The minute Charles opened the pressroom door Carrie's nostrils were overwhelmed by the strong smell of ink. Charles led the visitors down an aisle between two large presses that were running at full speed. Due to the tremendous thunder of the machinery, nothing was said, but Charles did wave to several employees manning the press controls above them on a metal gangway. The party of three took the elevator directly to the eighth floor. Faraday Press occupied the basement and first floor because of the size and weight of the presses and then skipped to the top four floors, which housed the editorial and administrative staff. The other floors in between were leased.

When the elevator doors opened on the eighth floor, the three passengers faced a large, modern waiting area. In the center was a horseshoe-shaped greeter station with the Faraday Press logo etched in the blond wood and outlined in black. Surrounding the desk was a series of chairs and tables in the same blond wood. On the tables were Faraday publications for the visitor to enjoy.

A young lady sitting behind the desk looked up and then smiled brightly as she recognized Charles. "Good morning, Mr. Faraday, your other guests are waiting in Conference Room A."

"Thank you, Jeanette, any messages?"

"I've already given your morning messages to Sandy." She smiled again at Charles.

"Ladies, if you will follow me."

Carrie and Suzanne followed Charles through an unmarked door behind Jeanette and found themselves in a long hallway. As they walked along, Carrie noticed that instead of artwork on the walls, covers and stories from various Faraday magazines were framed and hanging. At the end of this hallway was a smaller waiting area. Sitting behind a large mahogany L-shaped desk was a woman in her late forties with a pair of brightly colored half-frame glasses on the end of her nose. Her light hair had a stylish cut, and her dark navy dress was right out of "what a proper executive assistant should wear."

"Good morning, Sandy. May I introduce Carrie Kingsford, and of course you have already met Suzanne. Carrie, this is my executive assistant, Sandy Waxtrum. I may have the title of president, but Sandy really runs the place."

Sandy smiled at both women, but her eyes seemed to linger on Carrie. Carrie couldn't help but wonder what Charles confided to his executive assistant about her.

"Do I need to deal with any of the morning messages?"

"Nothing urgent. Everything can wait until after your meeting."

The group was once again on the move as they made a left turn into another short hallway. Midway down the corridor, Charles held the glass door of a conference room open for Carrie and Suzanne. The minute the door was open, Carrie could smell fresh coffee, and she desperately wanted another cup. The other participants were seated around the table, with their coffee and pastries. Several discussions were already in progress about the latest news and sport results from the previous day. Carrie looked at each of their faces, wondering if one of them could be a murderer. On the far side of the table, in the first seat, was Hugh Simpson. Next to him was, Jonathan Stone, and then Captain Becker. Becker was wearing his funeral suit and was engaged in conversation with a young woman whom Carrie didn't know. Perhaps she was a member of the police force since Carrie heard her mention the word "precinct." On the other side of the table were also two men Carrie didn't know, although she thought she had seen them at the Faraday wake. Suzanne sat in an empty chair next to these two men. Carrie went directly to the credenza to pour herself another cup of coffee. Charles followed her, and Carrie poured him a cup.

"I'll do introductions in a moment," Charles said, accepting the coffee from her.

"I see there's one introduction you won't have to do because he isn't here," Carrie whispered.

"Yes, I noticed our friend Joel doesn't seem to have made the meeting."

Charles no sooner spoke the words when Sandy appeared and slipped him a note. Charles looked at the note and turned it toward Carrie. It said, "Joel is unavoidably detained on a court matter and won't make the meeting." Charles placed the note in his pocket, and then he and Carrie took seats next to one another at the table.

Charles tapped on the table for order. "Shall we get started? Captain Becker has a limited amount of time, and I want him to hear as many of the comments as possible. I've called this meeting because I believe each of you may have some piece of information that could help us understand what my brother was doing at the time of his death. But before we do that, let's make sure everyone knows everyone. In order to save time, I'll just go around the table and introduce everyone."

Charles started the introductions with Simpson, Stone, and Becker. The young lady next to Becker wasn't a fellow police officer, but Linda Morton, a research associate from the magazine. Suzanne was sitting with Bill Owens, Jamie's foreign assignment editor from *News World*, and Joseph Swatski, a photographer who often went out on assignment with Jamie. With the introductions complete, Charles wasted no time in getting to the heart of the matter.

"I believe without any doubt that my brother was murdered. Secondly, I do not believe it was a random murder or the results of a bad robbery. I believe my brother was murdered because he was researching a story that uncovered a criminal act."

Captain Becker broke in. "Mr. Faraday, do you have any proof for these beliefs?"

"That's exactly why I've called this meeting, Captain Becker. I want to see if any of you has information that will support my theory. Each of you had contact with Jamie since his return from Europe." Charles paused as he looked directly at each person sitting at the table and then continued, "You may even have a piece of information you're not aware you're holding.

"Hugh, let me start with a couple of questions for you. First, did Jamie make any comments regarding the letter he left with you for Carrie, and, second, what can you tell us about your mugging?"

Hugh Simpson paused, as if he was thinking through the legal ramifications of anything he said. He placed the tips of his fingers together before responding. "Jamie asked me draw up a new will when he returned to Tri-City. Then, about thirty days ago, he returned to my office and added the section in his will about Ms. Kingsford receiving his papers. At that time he gave me an envelope to hold and said it should only be opened in the event of his death. As we now know, it contained the letter for Ms. Kingsford." Simpson paused and then added, "I should mention one other point. I asked your brother if I should keep the envelope for an indefinite period of time. He told me he hoped everything would work out within a few weeks and he would retrieve the envelope."

"No hints as to what he thought would change within a few weeks?" prodded Charles.

"No hints. Concerning your second question about the mugging, a gun was placed in my back. I was asked to hand over my briefcase. Then I was slugged."

"The man didn't ask for money or your wallet?" asked Charles.

"He only asked for my briefcase. However, as I started to regain consciousness, I heard him ask the other man if he found the letter."

"Is it true only you and Ms. Kingsford knew she took back Jamie's letter at the wake? Everyone else at the luncheon assumed you still had the letter in your possession when you left the house?" asked Becker.

"That's correct, Captain, unless Ms. Kingsford told someone."

Simpson looked across the table to Carrie.

"I told no one," Carrie verified. "Only Mr. Simpson and I knew the letter was with me. And before anyone asks, Jamie's letter left no clues. He asked me to look into his death, but said nothing about any specific threats."

"Carrie, why don't you continue and tell us about your recent encounters?" suggested Charles.

"Two men have been following me since I arrived in town. My first encounter with the men was in a downtown garage, after a lunch meeting." She caught a raised eyebrow from Charles but she wasn't sure if it was because she deliberately left out Joel's name or because she hadn't shared the incident.

The second time I was chased from Pier Eight by, I believe, the same two men. Both times, through sheer luck, I was able to escape." Carrie suddenly remembered the two men that ran her car off the road on the expressway. Since she never saw the men in the car, she decided not to mention it there, but would tell Charles later. She continued by providing the participants at the table with her limited description of the two men.

"Does the description of either of these men ring a bell with anyone?" asked Becker.

Simpson spoke. "As I mentioned, two muggers accosted me. I had the vague sense that one man was very broad, and the other man was much smaller, although I didn't actually see them. It's possible it was the same men."

Then Captain Becker cleared his throat. "It's also possible these two men were seen the night of your brother's death. One of the officers on duty now remembers seeing three men helping each other walk along the dock. Two of the three men match this description."

"And the third man?" prodded Charles.

"I'm afraid we don't have much of a description: just medium height, medium build, and gray hair."

"That sounds like most of the guys in this room, including myself," piped in Bill Owens. Everyone laughed, and the building tension in the room was broken.

Carrie was pleased that Officer Reynolds reported the additional information. She liked him, and now she knew he had integrity, too. Carrie next told the group Stephen Beeker's theory that an expert swimmer wouldn't dive in the water where Jamie's shoes were found. She produced her photographs to support the theory.

"You can see in these shots what Stephen meant." Carrie spread the pictures out on the table for everyone to see. "The yellow tape between the two pilings marks the spot where Jamie went into the water. Here's the issue. If Jamie decided to go for a swim, he would dive in from the end of the pier, not between two pilings, where the chances of hitting his head were greater."

"Ms. Kingsford, someone with alcohol in his system doesn't always follow the rules," said Becker.

"These aren't rules, Captain Becker. They are the instincts of a good swimmer. Jamie would have done this without any thought. Plus, Stephen doesn't think the alcohol in his system was sufficient to impair Jamie's judgment." Carrie was annoyed and lashed out at the good captain. "Captain Becker, why won't you admit that murder is a distinct possibility?"

"Contrary to what you may think, Ms. Kingsford, I believe murder is a real possibility. However, I'm a cop. I need proof. There's insufficient evidence to prove murder and many more facts to support accidental death. Give me something that says murder, and I'll be all over this case." Becker looked at each person sitting around the table.

Becker had effectively stopped the process. No one spoke.

Finally, Charles broke the silence. "Why don't we take a quick break? But let's come right back to the table. Since I believe Jamie was working on a story, I'd like each of you to remember the last conversation you had with Jamie that might tell us what he was investigating."

As the participants stood and headed for the restrooms or the refreshment table, Captain Becker approached Charles. "I was serious about what I just said. I need evidence, and so far all I've gotten from this meeting is more anecdotal information."

"I understand, but perhaps we'll learn more from the last conversation each person had with my brother," Charles said.

"All right, I'll stay a little bit longer, but then I need to get back on duty." Becker turned away and joined the group refilling their coffee cups.

Within a few minutes, the group reassembled at the conference table, and Charles asked for a volunteer to start.

Joseph Swatski cleared his throat. "Seeing your photos, Carrie, reminded me of the last conversation I had with Jamie. He told me he was thinking about doing a feature on the docks. Asked me if I could spare some time to take pictures. I asked what he wanted. He said nothing special just shots of the activities at the docks."

"Did you take those pictures?" asked Charles.

"No, I didn't, but there was a reason. Jamie gave me the name of a particular ship he wanted included in the pictures.

I didn't want to make two trips, especially since this wasn't an official assignment." He looked over at Bill Owens and then said, "I was going to do all the photographs the day the ship docked."

"What was the name of the ship?" asked Becker.

"It's a ship registered in Poland. I can't pronounce the name, but I have it written down at my desk."

"I'd appreciate it if you could give me the name before I leave," Becker requested.

Charles also made a note in his journal to get the name of the ship from Joseph, and then addressed Bill and Jonathan. "Did Jamie mention this story idea to either of you?"

"Jamie wouldn't come to me," said Stone. "He would go to Bill for story approval. I only get involved after stories are assigned or if there is some issue concerning the content."

"He never mentioned it to me," defended Bill, "but then Jamie wasn't officially working. Maybe he was going to flush out the idea and present it when he started back to work."

"He kind of mentioned it to me, but in a different way," said Linda quietly, as she brushed her bangs away from her glasses. "The last time I saw Jamie, he told me he was using his time off to start work on a spy thriller. He said the book was about the smuggling of military secrets, and he was going to have the thriller center around the shipping industry. He said it probably wouldn't take place in Tri-City, but he would use our docks as a reference. He asked me if I could gather information about local shipping companies, types of shipments coming into Tri-City, people he could contact and any other general reference material."

"Did you gather the material?" Becker jumped in.

"Yes, I gave him several folders about two weeks before his death. They were all labeled as to type of information"

Becker turned to Carrie. "When you were sorting Faraday's papers, did you find these folders?"

"No, I didn't. There was nothing on the docks."

"Carrie dear, you probably didn't have time to find it before the fire destroyed everything," suggested Suzanne.

"I just learned of the fire this morning," offered Becker as he looked at Charles. "I'm sorry, that there was another loss for your family."

Charles thanked him and made a brief comment about the fire to others who hadn't heard about it.

Captain Becker continued, "Do you know anything about this story, Ms. Redmond? I understand you helped Mr. Faraday with research."

"Jamie told me he might write a mystery centered in London, but that book had nothing to do with docks," Suzanne said. "I know he was considering different ideas and hadn't decided which story to write." Suzanne looked around the room for agreement on her comment.

Becker stared at Suzanne for a moment and then turned back to Linda. "Ms. Morton, can you tell us more about what was in the folders?"

Linda reviewed the type of materials she sent Jamie, including types of ships, countries of origin, types of goods imported and the inspection process. When she finished, Linda added, "It's not my job to ask the writer about the focus of his story. I simply provide research information, so

I really don't know what Jamie was going to do with the materials."

Carrie barely heard Linda's list of folders. She was thinking about the note card she found during her first trip to the studio. Did that card represent some of Jamie's notes from Linda's information on importing? More importantly, what happened to the files? She was sure Linda's files were not in the studio prior to the fire. Between the card and Jamie's journal, Carrie now believed he was writing a story and not simply gathering ideas, as Suzanne suggested.

31

The meeting ended shortly after Linda presented her information. Carrie followed Suzanne and Charles down the hallway to his office. It was obvious they weren't going to get rid of Suzanne and have time alone.

"I'm hungry. How about we have some lunch?" suggested Charles.

"Oh, yes, that sounds great," Suzanne answered and then added, "There's a lovely new French café just two blocks away. We could all go there for lunch."

"That sounds very nice, Suzanne, for some other day. Today I don't have the time. I need to catch up on a couple of items here, and then I need to get home to meet with the insurance guy. How about we order something and eat here?"

"I guess, if that's our only choice," answered a disappointed Suzanne.

Charles buzzed Sandy on the intercom and asked her to bring a menu from a local eatery.

After everyone made their selections, Sandy said, "You know there's going to be a long wait for delivery at this time of day. How about if Suzanne and I run over and pick up the food?"

"Good idea. Suzanne, would you help Sandy with the order?" asked Charles.

"I think Carrie should help us, too," Suzanne answered quickly.

"I think you two can manage the lunch," Charles said. "Besides, I can show Carrie our photographic studio, and you've already been on tour and seen our entire operation."

A disgruntled Suzanne followed Sandy out to get the lunch.

"Did you and Sandy plan to get Suzanne out of here, or was this spur of the moment?" asked a smiling Carrie.

"It wasn't planned. It's just that Sandy knows how Suzanne is always hanging around me, and Sandy does her best to run interference. Did you want to see the photo studio?"

"Yes, but not at this moment. I'd rather spend our Suzanne-free moments with you."

"Let's sit down." Charles guided her to the far side of his office, where three small sofas of a light beige color were placed around a large, low, circular table. Charles and Carrie sat on the same sofa facing one another.

"First I want to ask about that incident in the parking garage. Why didn't you mention it? Was it because you were concerned Joel had something to do with it?

"That thought initially crossed my mind, but then I realized anyone in Simpson's office knew where I would be. Then after being chased and the fire I had temporarily put that incident from my mind until today."

"Hmmm," Charles said out loud.

"What are you thinking?"

"If you were being tracked from that first day it makes me wonder…"

"You're thinking there must be a leak from someone close to the family," Carrie finished his thought." There was a moment of quiet between them and then Carrie asked, "What did you think of the meeting?"

"I was pleasantly surprised by Captain Becker," Charles said. "He seemed more receptive and cooperative, like when he provided the new information from Officer Reynolds. Maybe I've misjudged the good captain. What do you think?"

"I thought it was nice of him to even show up. It proves Becker is still interested in the case. However, we are still facing the same problem."

"What's that?" asked Charles.

"I don't mean to dampen the success of the meeting, but Becker wants hard evidence. While we did get two important pieces of information, we still don't have hard evidence. That reminds me, I didn't say anything about this in the meeting, but I did find one of Jamie's note cards in the studio with a short list of questions on importing and exporting. I think it's now clear Jamie was researching a story about the docks, even if we don't know who or what he was investigating. And a story about the docks also explains why Jamie was down at the harbor."

"There's still a problem with that theory," Charles said. "The dock that ships use for loading and unloading goods is on the opposite side of the harbor from where Jamie was found."

"Maybe Jamie's meeting was on the harbor side so as not to be seen by someone from one of the ships. We don't know who this person is or how that meeting resulted in Jamie's death, but for the first time, I feel like we're closer."

Charles still looked dejected. He thought for a moment and then asked, "You said we learned two important pieces of information. What else?"

"We've zeroed in on two of the men involved. Our description fits two of the three men spotted by Officer Reynolds. It describes one of the two men I saw in the garage. It clearly fits the two men who chased me from the Admiral's Saloon, and..." Carrie stopped herself, remembering her promise to Christopher to allow him to tell his uncle about what he saw last night. She needed to find time for Christopher to talk with Charles away from Suzanne.

"And..." prompted Charles.

"And I don't want you to be dejected." Carrie took Charles hand. "The meeting was a great success. I think it's a real possibility Jamie was murdered by one of those men. We know Jamie was working on a story about importing, which probably means he discovered a smuggling operation. The good news is we're continuing to gather puzzle pieces, and soon they will form a complete picture."

Charles nodded his head in agreement. They sat for a moment, and then Charles asked, "What about our friend

Joel. He's doing something so important he can't make the meeting?"

Carrie didn't get a chance to express her thoughts about Joel because Suzanne entered the room carrying a bag of sodas.

"You two look cozy," Suzanne said sarcastically, as she plunked her bag on the low table between the sofas.

Suzanne looked for a moment at the sofa Carrie and Charles were sharing to see if she could squeeze between them. Before Suzanne could make her decision, Sandy entered with a cardboard box containing salads and sandwiches.

"Suzanne, I think lunch would be better served at the conference table. Could you bring over the sodas?" suggested Sandy.

"That's a good suggestion, Sandy." Charles jumped up to help Sandy sort the food order. Suzanne took Charles's position on the sofa next to Carrie.

"That didn't take long," Charles whispered to Sandy.

"At the speed Suzanne was running through the carry-out line in the restaurant, I'm surprised it took this long. Sorry, I was trying to go as slowly as I could. By the way, Jeanette took a call from your mother a few minutes ago. She thought you were still in your meeting, so she took a message instead of putting the call through."

"No problem. I'll call Mother right after lunch. Sandy, won't you have your lunch with us?"

"No, thanks. I promised Jeanette I'd have lunch with her. Besides, I think two women are enough to handle at one lunch." Sandy smiled at Charles and left the room.

Suzanne monopolized the conversation during lunch, talking about restaurants and sights in Tri-City and suggesting that the three of them go sightseeing. Carrie and Charles listened politely to her chatter.

After lunch, Charles called his mother. When he returned to the table, he turned to Carrie. "Mother would like you to join her for tea this afternoon."

"Oh, that's lovely, tea with the girls," Suzanne responded.

"Oh, I'm sorry, Suzanne. Mother wants to meet with Carrie alone. After all, you've enjoyed tea with Mother several times." Charles had a way of making the rebuke quite gentle.

Charles took care of his messages while Sandy gave Carrie and Suzanne a brief tour of the building. Then the trio needed to leave so Carrie could meet with Mrs. Faraday. Suzanne once again grabbed the front seat, which left Carrie with her own thoughts in the back seat. Tea with Mrs. Faraday was one occasion when Carrie would have liked Suzanne's company. The thought of having tea alone with Mrs. Faraday wasn't something Carrie relished.

32

arrie arrived at Mrs. Faraday's room just as Mary arrived with the tea tray. Upon entering, Carrie was immediately charmed by Mrs. Faraday's rooms. The front room was soft and soothing, with a gentle feminine touch that Carrie didn't associate with the woman.

Mrs. Faraday was seated at a library desk in the corner of the room angled between the window and the opening to the bedroom. The top portion of the antique desk held a glass-enclosed bookcase, and the lower portion had four wide drawers. When the lid of the desk was lowered, it provided a writing surface and revealed several small drawers and pigeonholes for storage. The women stood for a moment until Mrs. Faraday spoke.

"Mary, don't stand there holding the tray. Please put it down on the coffee table. Carrie, please take a seat, make yourself comfortable. I'll be right with you."

Mary lowered the tray onto the coffee table that was centered between the sofa and two occasional chairs. Carrie chose one of the two mauve chairs and tried to relax as she gazed around the room. She could see the wallpaper in the bedroom was highlighted by a small rose pattern, which formed a narrow stripe against a white silk background. The solid wood furniture in the sitting room was a deep cherry color and covered with a fabric of a muted flower pattern in rose, mauve, and gray that enhanced the deep burgundy plush carpet.

"Would you like me to pour the tea, Mrs. Faraday?" asked Mary.

"No, not today, Mary. I'll take care of it. Thank you very much."

"You're welcome, ma'am," she responded, winked at Carrie, and left the room.

Carrie watched as Mrs. Faraday folded a sheet of paper, placed it in an addressed envelope, and sealed it. She rose, crossed over to the sitting area, and sat on the sofa across from Carrie. She wore a two-piece nub gray suit with a mauve-colored bow blouse. Her outfit blended perfectly with the room. She sat on the edge of the sofa as she placed a cup on a saucer and poured two cups of tea.

"Carrie, how do you take your tea: sugar, lemon, milk?"

"Just a spoonful of sugar," Carrie answered, and suddenly the lyrics from the *Mary Poppins* song played in her head. She turned her head away and looked around the room to avoid breaking into laughter.

Mrs. Faraday handed Carrie her cup of tea and offered a plate of cookies.

Carrie accepted her teacup carefully, holding the saucer with one hand and the cup with the other. She refused the cookies in order to give her full concentration to balancing her china teacup.

Mrs. Faraday fixed her own cup of tea. She took several sips that she savored before placing her cup back on the table. Carrie also took a sip from her cup and then successfully placed it on a small table next to her.

"This is a very comfortable room, Mrs. Faraday."

"Thank you. I like it. It gives me a place to get away and find a little peace of mind."

"I can understand. The colors are very calming," Carrie added.

"The room may be calming, but I'll tell you that I'm not calm. In fact, this is why I asked you to join me for tea, to discuss how I'm feeling. I have this great overwhelming feeling of dread within me. I'm worried sick about what is going on, and I'm concerned for the basic safety of my family and my home. Can you understand that?"

"I can because I'm also frightened for the people involved with this case, especially you, Charles and Christopher. And what's worse, I know I'm responsible for some of the recent activity, but I don't know why these things are happening."

"Those responsible for my son Jamie's murder must think you know something or have discovered something."

Carrie stared at Mrs. Faraday for a moment.

"You're surprised I used the word 'murder'? I never had any doubt in my mind my son was murdered. An expert swimmer doesn't drown. That is why I wanted you to come and stay with us. I hoped you would discover some evidence that would convince the police it was murder. Have you any evidence?"

"Mrs. Faraday, I don't know whether I've any more evidence now than when I first arrived. All I know is from the first night someone has been trying to stop my progress. I now believe Jamie was murdered because of a story he was investigating on smuggling. I also believe the studio was deliberately set on fire to destroy any evidence about this story."

Mrs. Faraday sat quietly as Carrie spoke and then said, "I knew it. I suspected all along Jamie was working on a story. Any ideas on what we should do next?"

"Charles had an excellent idea today, getting all the various players together to discuss what they knew. It turned out each person had a little piece of information that provided clues to the smuggling connection."

"You mean you discovered a real clue to Jamie's death?" Mrs. Faraday leaned forward as she asked the question. "What happened?"

"As we went around the room, we discovered that Jamie asked a couple of people to help him with some research about the docks. He even asked Swatski, the magazine's photographer, to take some pictures of a certain boat that was arriving. Plus, Joel told me when Jamie first came back he quizzed him about his export business. Then Christopher said his father spent time at the docks in Poland before they came home. Jamie's conversations were so casual that no one person realized he might be writing a story that put him in danger."

"A story about the docks would certainly explain why he was at the harbor the night of his death."

Mrs. Faraday made the same assumption Carrie made earlier, so Carrie added, "I'm afraid there's still a missing link. We don't know the relationship between the harbor where Jamie was murdered and the docks where ships arrive. But I feel we've made progress because everyone knew something. Even Christopher has more information to share with his uncle."

"You mean his father's journal?"

Carrie couldn't hide the surprise on her face.

"I can tell you're surprised he told me. As much as he likes secrets, the excitement of his youth often requires he share his secrets. He was bursting at the seams to tell someone he found it, and we have a good relationship. I must say he was somewhat disappointed that you didn't leave the journal for him so he could show me."

Carrie started to answer, but Mrs. Faraday raised her hand. "No need to explain to me. I know there was no way to leave something that important lying around, but you might want to remind Christopher of this."

"I'll definitely talk with him. I briefly looked at the journal this morning. It also makes references to importing or, to be more accurate, smuggling. However, there was nothing specific about what is being smuggled or who is involved. The good news is we keep gathering puzzle pieces."

"Then that's the answer of what to do next. We'll do the same thing as a family that Charles did today with Jamie's associates."

Mrs. Faraday picked up her phone. "Hello, Mrs. Cavanaugh, what are we having for dinner? Good, slice the chicken down and serve it cold, with salads and the baked rolls. Hold the hot vegetables for tomorrow night. Yes, the regular time, but we are going to eat in the study tonight." She turned back to Carrie. "Tell Charles and Christopher what we are planning, but not Suzanne."

Carrie found the comment a little unusual. She phrased her answer carefully. "Are you saying you don't want Suzanne to join us? Because I happen to think Suzanne knows more than what she's revealed."

"Oh, no, I want her there! I just don't want her to know in advance that we are going to discuss the case. I've felt for a long time that Suzanne is leaking information to someone outside this house. This someone is closely watching what we are doing."

"I'll share with Charles and Christopher our concerns about Suzanne. I especially want Christopher to hold back the information about the journal. Instead, let's use dinner to confront Suzanne and find out what she knows." After a pause, Carrie said, "I better go tell the others what we have planned." Mrs. Faraday nodded in agreement.

Carrie rose to leave when Mrs. Faraday added, "You know, Carrie, I can see now why both my sons have found you so attractive. James found you a challenge to his intellect, and Charles...well, you have touched him deeply. James made a good choice when he asked you to help solve his death. I hope Charles will make a good decision, too."

33

arrie left Mrs. Faraday's room feeling elated. She couldn't deny the positive feelings she had from the meeting.

However, Carrie couldn't dwell on the meeting with Mrs. Faraday any longer. She needed to concentrate on the upcoming dinner with Suzanne. She was deep in her own thoughts as she turned the corner in the hallway and bumped smack into Charles. He caught her before she fell to the floor.

"Well, hello! How did it go with Mother?" Charles asked.

"To be honest, it was an unexpected pleasure. We got along just fine. I was just coming to tell you what your mother and I decided. We want to share information with the family, just like you did in your meeting this morning. Where's Suzanne?"

"She's downstairs in the study," Charles said. "She's still pouting about not having tea with Mother. Why?"

Carrie spent a few seconds filling Charles in on the plan for the dinner and the approach with Suzanne. He said he would let her know that dinner was in the study and then stay downstairs to help Mrs. Cavanaugh get the study ready for the meal. Charles was about to head down the steps, but instead he turned around and gave Carrie a hug. "I knew it would go well with Mother. You two are more alike than either of you were ever willing to admit."

Carrie stood and watched him for a moment. She still wasn't sure about her personal feelings for Charles, but she was sure glad they were working together on the case.

She pulled herself back to reality and headed to Christopher's room. She barely finished knocking on the door when it was flung open.

"I was hoping it was you. It's about time you showed up." He took her by the arm and guided her to the chair. "I understand you hid the journal for security reasons, but I wish you had left me a clue. I could have been working on it during the day."

"I know you're upset with me, but when I left you the note, I thought Suzanne was going to be here with you. I didn't like writing down anything about the journal with her around. As it turned out, she went with us to your uncle's office. Anyway, I figured you would go to my room and look for the journal."

"Actually, I did sort of toss your room while you were out," he answered softly.

"Ah, I see," Carrie responded sternly. Then she broke into a grin. "You did a good job. I was in my room before having tea with your grandmother, and never knew you were there."

"Good, I was careful to put everything back where it was. I finally decided you must have taken the journal with you. I guess you shared it with the people at Uncle Charles's meeting."

"You know about the meeting?"

"Grandmother told me you all went to a meeting about my dad. I'd have liked to have gone, too, but I guess it was just for adults." He sounded down. "While you were gone, I did tell Grandmother about the journal. I felt I needed to tell someone since I didn't know where the book was."

"First of all, partner, I didn't have the book with me. It was in my room the entire time. Second, no one at the meeting was told about the journal. You found it, so you should be the one to tell your Uncle Charles about it before anyone else is told of its existence. Third, don't forget you also need to tell him about the two men and what you saw the night of the fire."

Christopher seemed relieved about the status of the journal. Then he thought about what Carrie just said. "Wait a minute! You're saying the book was in your room? I couldn't find it, and I looked everywhere."

"Obviously, you didn't look in the right place. I thought you would have found it, based on finding your father's journal."

"You hid it under the floorboards?" he asked in disbelief.

"Not exactly, since the room has wall-to-wall carpet." She took him by the hand and led him over to the fireplace in his room. She moved the fireplace set and then lifted the hearth rug.

"That's where it was? Gee, I even lifted the fireplace set. I should have looked under the rug. Can we go and get the book and go over it now before dinner?"

"I'm afraid looking at the journal will be delayed a little longer. Look, your grandmother sent me over to talk with you. At dinner, we're going to continue the meeting about your father's death."

"Oh, I see," he said dejectedly. "So you've been sent to tell me that my dinner will be sent up to my room."

"No, silly, I'm here to tell you dinner is being served in the study and don't be late."

"Really?" Christopher could barely hide his excitement.

"Really, but there's a restriction," answered Carrie.

"I knew it. I have to keep my mouth shut and listen to the adults."

"Hey, what's wrong with you? You're my partner and a full participant. The restriction has to do with Suzanne. We don't feel we can trust her. We want to be careful what we say in front of her. That's why any discussion about the journal needs to wait until we are alone with your uncle."

"Haven't I been telling you guys she couldn't be trusted? I never understood what Dad saw in her. If nobody trusts her, why are we inviting her to our meeting?"

"For the same reason your father kept her near. To find out what she knows!"

34

arrie left Christopher's room and returned to her own. She had time before the dinner with Suzanne and needed to relax. She would forget Suzanne for the moment and do some writing.

She liked the atmosphere of her room at the Faraday's. It was quiet and comfortable and the desk was a perfect size to hold her laptop and still have room for papers. It was a great place to spend some time with her character Ascot.

Carrie had used her ATM escape from her two assailants to also save Ascot from the agents who had him trapped in the alley. Now she was working on a scene where Ascot was going to meet the man who had been providing him with information. She decided this meeting would take place in a bar. She wanted the inside of the bar to be old and dark, which seemed appropriate for Ascot's secret meeting. The bar at the Admiral's Saloon gave the impression of being old.

Carrie would combine some of its characteristics with some of the features of pubs she had visited in Europe.

Ascot entered the bar. It was so dark that he was forced to stop in his tracks while his eyes adjusted to the light. Once his eyes adjusted, the room came into focus but light was still limited. The walls were covered in a dark wood paneling that no doubt had deepened in color after many years of inhaling smoke and liquor from the patrons.

Ascot spotted two men drinking beer at the bar. It was early afternoon but they were very comfortable in their seats as if they had been there for many hours. Ascot looked down the length of the long bar; there were no other customers. He looked to his right and saw an alcove that was set up for dart tournaments, but there was no one playing darts. Ascot looked at the booths that lined the right-hand wall of the bar. Although the booths had high backs, he could see no activity or hear any voices. Where was the guy he was supposed to be meeting?

He was just debating whether to leave when he saw an arm extend out from a booth at the back of the bar. Then the hand made a waving motion, inviting him to approach. Ascot started the long walk to the back of the bar. As he passed the bartender, he nodded. Finally, he reached the booth and he turned to see who was seated there. He couldn't hide his surprise when he recognized——

Carrie knew this piece of writing would need editing, but she was pleased with what she had written so far. She was sitting back relaxing when she noticed the calendar on the desk.

Good grief, I'm about to miss a deadline, she thought, realizing she needed to call her editor and ask for an extension on a photo shoot she did.

Carrie lifted the receiver on the phone near her bed and heard a conversation that was already in progress. *That's unusual*, she thought, having been under the impression that this was Jamie's private line. *I wonder where the extension is.* She was about to put the receiver down when she recognized Suzanne's voice. However, this voice was not the little girl voice she associated with Suzanne. This voice was all business.

"Did you hear something?" a soft male voice asked.

"No, but I'm using one of the cordless phones from the studio, so the base station may have been damaged in the fire. I didn't want to use one of the house lines in case someone picked up the receiver," answered Suzanne. "Anyway, as I was telling you, I don't know what that kid found. All I know is that he went to her car last night and got something out from under the seat."

"I thought your room was right over the driveway. Couldn't you see what the kid got?" asked the man on the other end of the phone line.

"It was dark. That part of the driveway isn't lit. In fact, if it weren't for the lights from the fire department equipment, I probably wouldn't have seen him at all. I could tell it was something small and easy to carry. It might have been a book, or it might have been his father's journal. The note that Carrie left for him this morning referred to whatever they found as 'it.' She seems to be encouraging Christopher's fantasies by playing detective with him."

Now Carrie knew the reason why Suzanne returned to her room that morning for a sweater. While Carrie was politely fixing Suzanne a cup of coffee in the kitchen, she was reading Christopher's note.

"Playing detective or not, she must think whatever the kid found is important. Otherwise, she would have told Christopher where she hid it," he suggested.

"But even if he found the journal, we don't know if it contains anything important," Suzanne suggested.

"I hope you're right. Except for that journal there's nothing to worry about. All the remaining papers and photos went up in smoke last night. We saw to that. We broke open every file and desk drawer before dousing them in flammable liquid. Why don't you talk to the boy? Tell him you saw him and ask him what he found. Tell him that the two of you must form an alliance to help solve his father's murder," Then he added with a snicker. "Becomes the little brat's friend."

Carrie listened carefully, hoping to identify the voice as one of the two men who chased her. Unfortunately, the second man hadn't said enough that night for Carrie to be sure it was him.

"I've tried to get along with him, but he doesn't like me. Look, I'm not sure there is anything else I can do here. Carrie has managed to gain everyone's confidence. Christopher likes her, and if I'm not mistaken, Charles is infatuated with her. I'm not sure how much longer they will let me stay."

"Then use the time you have left wisely. Find out what the kid found and keep a close eye on Carrie She's a problem we didn't plan on."

"She's not my problem! You guys were supposed to convince her to leave town before something happened to her. If you had you done your job at the harbor, she wouldn't be a problem."

Carrie gulped, now she knew Suzanne was definitely talking with one of the men who chased her. She wondered if Suzanne was naïve enough to think those men were only going to talk with her at the harbor. What on earth could Jamie have discovered that would have these people willing to kill others? Carrie forced her brain back to the phone conversation.

"I want to meet with the boss. You tell him that I want out and I want my money. I'll simply disappear, no strings attached. In fact, I'm calling the travel agency tomorrow. I want to go back to Europe," demanded Suzanne.

"I'll talk to him. I'm sure he will decide to get you out of there. But in the meantime, keep doing your job!" He paused and then added, be at the public phone booth tonight at ten, and I'll call you there with further instructions."

"All right, I'll be there. Bill, that phone better ring; no more excuses. I want to leave this house, and tomorrow won't be soon enough."

With those last words, Suzanne hung up the phone. When Carrie was sure the other party had hung up, she replaced her receiver. At least now Carrie had the proof Mrs. Faraday and Captain Becker both wanted. Suzanne was definitely connected to Jamie's murder.

Carrie went to the fireplace and removed the journal from its hiding place. She slipped the book into the band at the back of her slacks. She threw on a sweater to cover the journal's hiding place. She looked in the mirror and turned to the side to make sure the outline of the journal didn't bulge out from the fabric of the sweater. As she was fixing her makeup, she saw the determined look on her face. She would confront Suzanne Redmond with the phone conversation she just overheard. She would ask Suzanne why Jamie Faraday was murdered.

The study set-up was similar to the day of the funeral. A large folding table was added to hold the food. The jigsaw puzzle was gone and the round game table was covered with a cloth and was serving as the dining table. Mrs. Cavanaugh clearly added to the request from Mrs. Faraday for sliced chicken sandwiches. The table displayed the chicken, nicely sliced, with an assortment of cheeses along with hot rolls, a green and a pasta salad, plus chips and a relish tray. To round out the meal, there was a plate stacked with brownies, along with individual fresh fruit bowls.

When Christopher and Carrie arrived, Mrs. Faraday and Suzanne were already seated at the table, and Charles was in the process of opening a bottle of wine. Carrie helped Charles place the wine glasses on the table for each of the adults and poured a soda for Christopher.

Carrie and Charles were deciding where to sit when Suzanne spoke. "Charles, come and sit next to me."

Before Charles had a chance to respond, Christopher practically jumped from where he was standing and slid in next to Suzanne.

"Christopher, I just asked Charles to sit there."

"I know, but it's been such a long time since I had the chance to sit with you. This will be like old times. You know, when we were overseas, and I'd sit next to you at dinner." Christopher smiled innocently.

Carrie was sure Mrs. Faraday took a quick sip of wine to hide a grin from showing on her face. Christopher's quick action allowed Charles and Carrie to sit next to each other. Under other circumstances, this would have been a cozy setting for a meal. Only one lamp in the room was on low. The meal was lit by candles on the table and the light from the wood burning in the fireplace. Once the members of the group finished dinner and were eating dessert, Charles changed the direction of the dinner conversation.

"I'd like to review one more time what we know about Jamie's death. I feel we are still missing some key information."

"Oh, Charles, we spent this morning doing the same thing at your office. Can't we just have a quiet meal together without discussing Jamie's death?" Suzanne poured herself a cup of coffee.

As if his response was rehearsed, Christopher said, "I disagree. I think this is the perfect time, Uncle Charles. After all, Grandmother and I were not at your meeting. We may know something that wasn't mentioned there. Our information combined with what you learned today might be the perfect clue."

"Clues," snapped Suzanne. "This isn't a mystery book for little boys. This is real life."

"I know it's real! Even if I'm a kid, I'd like to know why my dad was murdered!" Christopher put extra emphasis on the word "murdered."

"I'll be glad to tell you what we learned today: nothing! Absolutely nothing that would change the ruling from accidental death to murder," Suzanne sneered.

They all stared as Suzanne lost her cool. Then she stopped abruptly and sweetly added, "Well we didn't."

"Suzanne, I disagree," Charles said. "I think we learned some important things today, but you were rather quiet at that meeting. I thought perhaps here, with just the family, you might have something to add."

Before Suzanne could respond, Mrs. Faraday interrupted the exchange. "I'll start." Everyone turned to face her. "My son was an expert swimmer. He wouldn't have drowned unless some other factor kept him from using his swimming skills."

"That's an interesting place to start, Mother, because Carrie took some photos of the pier area that support that conclusion." Charles summarized the information Carrie presented at the meeting. Christopher and Mrs. Faraday asked several questions, and then Suzanne inserted herself back into the conversation.

"You're right, I can share something," Suzanne said abruptly. "I'd like to know what Christopher removed from Carrie's car last night. I think it was something he took from his father's studio just before the fire started. Which reminds me, Christopher what do you know about the fire. You were wandering around just when it started."

"I didn't start that fire!" Christopher started to jump up but Carrie touched his arm and he quickly resumed his seat.

All right I won't go down that road for the moment, but you two won't deny I saw Christopher at Carrie's car?" She looked from Carrie to Christopher.

Carrie was surprised by Suzanne's forthright approach, and Charles was caught off guard by the revelation. Christopher didn't know what to do and looked to Carrie. Carrie really didn't want to talk about the journal, but decided to follow Suzanne's direct approach.

"Suzanne, that's a fair question. And, yes, we did find something, or rather Christopher did. It was Christopher's find, and he wanted to be the one to tell everyone about it. Charles, Christopher planned on telling you tonight." Christopher nodded his head in agreement. "You see, Christopher found his father's journal in the studio."

Charles raised an eyebrow and looked at the others sitting around the table. He noticed that only Suzanne shared his surprise at this announcement. "Mother, you don't seem surprised. Did you know about the journal?"

"Yes, Christopher told me this afternoon. But as Carrie mentioned, he wanted to be the one to tell you." Mrs. Faraday calmly took a sip of her coffee.

Christopher jumped to his own defense. "Uncle Charles, I didn't have time to tell you. I was asleep when you left. This was the first opportunity…"

"It's all right, Christopher, I understand," Charles interrupted.

Suzanne looked unnerved. "Christopher, I can't believe you just found Jamie's journal! You've probably had it squirreled away the whole time while playing detective." Then Suzanne thought for a moment. "Besides, I bet there isn't anything of importance in the journal. Jamie rarely used it and he wasn't writing a story," she added with emphasis.

"Suzanne, you're lying," Charles pushed back. "You and I saw Jamie use his journal right in this room, and you were there today when we learned that Jamie was starting a story about smuggling."

"Listen to your own words, Charles. He was 'starting' work on a story. That means he was just beginning. I bet there's nothing in that journal about smuggling, is there?" She looked at each of them and added, "See, I'm right, aren't I?"

Carrie didn't want anything more revealed about the journal. Instead, she wanted to confront Suzanne about the phone call. Carrie cleared her throat and said, "Suzanne, you're right, but let's not talk about the journal. Let's talk about the phone call you made just before dinner to Bill. Bill was one of the two men chasing me the other night, one of the two men who set the studio on fire, and one of the two men who killed Jamie." It was Carrie's turn to be direct.

"What phone call? I didn't make any phone call." She was clearly nervous.

"The phone call you made on Jamie's cordless phone. Apparently you weren't aware that the cordless phone line from the studio is the same line in Jamie's bedroom. When

I picked up the receiver to call my editor this afternoon, you were on the line. I heard your entire conversation." Carrie looked at Mrs. Faraday. "I think this is the proof we discussed this afternoon."

"What proof? There's no proof, because you're mistaken," she stammered. "You're just trying to put me in a bad light with the family." She looked to Charles and Mrs. Faraday for sympathy, but none was forthcoming.

Carrie continued, "Suzanne, who were you talking with on the phone? Who is the man you told about Christopher taking something from my car? Who is the man that is going to give you money and a ticket to Europe? Suzanne, it's time for the truth. Who paid you to be part of Jamie Faraday's murder?"

Suzanne jumped up from the table and moved away from the group toward the fireplace. "No, you're wrong. They didn't kill Jamie. They just wanted him to stop poking around in their business. He had no story, but he kept digging. His death wasn't murder. It was accidental. I had nothing to do with it. Charles, you know that! I was here in this study with you the night your brother was killed." She was speaking rapidly.

"That's true, Suzanne, but I think it must be obvious even to you that Jamie's death wasn't accidental. If you're working with these people, then you're an accessory. You can be charged with murder. You could go to jail," Charles said, deliberately trying to frighten her.

"I swear I had nothing to do with Jamie's death." Suzanne removed a small vase from the fireplace mantle and was turning it in her hand. "Look, I'm not saying another word until I have an understanding."

"Suzanne, come and sit down with us. Let us help you. If you cooperate and give us the names of these men, I'm sure we can limit the consequences for you," offered Mrs. Faraday as she patted Suzanne's chair.

"There will be no consequences! I want the same things from you Mrs. Faraday that Carrie overheard on the phone call. I want a ticket to Europe and some money." Suzanne looked at Mrs. Faraday, but her face showed no emotion, so she added, "I just want the money Jamie promised me in his will. Is it a deal?" Suzanne replaced the vase back on the mantle and turned to face the group.

"It's a deal," Charles said with no hesitation. "Now, what do you know?"

Suzanne headed back toward the table. But before she could reach her seat, there was the sound of glass shattering, and a gunshot stopped her progress. She briefly put her hand to her head then Suzanne Redmond slumped to the floor in a pool of red liquid.

36

Charles grabbed his mother and pulled her to the floor. Carrie, in turn, pulled Christopher from his chair on top of her.

"Everyone, stay down!" shouted Charles.

He crawled across the floor and turned off the lamp. Carrie reached up and pulled the table candles to her and extinguished them. At that moment, Mary came to the door. "What's happening? I heard glass breaking."

"Mary, don't come in! Suzanne's been shot. Get to the phone in the hall and call the police and get an ambulance." In the remaining light from the fireplace, they could all see Suzanne lying on the floor in a pool of blood. She wasn't moving.

Charles crawled over to Suzanne and hunched over her. Carrie saw her hand move slightly. Then Charles leaned close to her face, and Carrie could see Suzanne's lips moving.

Charles took her hand and held it as she struggled to whisper something to him.

"Suzanne, save your strength. Don't try to talk. We have help coming," Charles responded.

It seemed that Charles had barely finished speaking when they heard the sounds of sirens coming up the street. The first police car arrived, and when the officers realized it was a shooting, they immediately called for backup and the crime team. The ambulance arrived, and the medics worked quickly, attaching medical devices to Suzanne and getting her bundled onto a stretcher. Everyone knew Suzanne's only chance of survival was getting her to the hospital as quickly as possible.

Captain Becker arrived as Suzanne's stretcher was passing through the front door. He watched as the medics maneuvered the stretcher down the walk toward the waiting ambulance. As the ambulance departed with sirens blaring, he entered the house and took charge of the investigation by immediately snapping out orders. One of his first orders was to send officers outside the home to search the area for any evidence left by the shooter.

Before the officers left the house, Christopher piped in, "Be sure to search on the other side of the hedges at the back of the garage. You can enter the property that way and not be seen." Christopher knew from the night of the fire this was the preferred entry for the bad guys.

After Christopher's suggestion, Becker ushered or more accurately pushed the family and staff into the living room, away from the police investigation. They could see flashes of light from the study as a police photographer took camera shots of the scene. Carrie wished she had the opportunity to photograph the room before the police came. Instead they had to rely on their memories for the details of what just happened.

As they sat quietly together, Carrie looked across at Mrs. Faraday and realized she was very pale. She gave Charles a gentle nudge and nodded toward his mother. He immediately saw the ashen color of her face.

"Mother, I think you need to go up to your room and rest. If the police need a statement, they can talk to you in the morning. Christopher, would you call Dr. Nilson? Since he lives on the next block, maybe he would be willing to come over to the house and check your grandmother. Mrs. Cavanaugh, can you help me?"

"Yes, yes, of course, Mr. Charles."

Charles and Mrs. Cavanaugh guided Mrs. Faraday from her seat and toward the hallway. The policeman at the door asked them to wait while he got permission from Captain Becker for them to leave. Carrie saw that once the officer left his post, Charles didn't wait. Instead, the trio proceeded from the room and directly to the elevator.

The policeman returned and directed his question to Carrie. "Where did they go?"

"They took Mrs. Faraday upstairs to her room," answered Carrie.

"They should have waited for the official okay, even though the captain said it was fine." He looked around the room. "Where's the kid? Did he go upstairs, too?"

"No, he's over there in the corner." Carrie pointed to Christopher, who was just hanging up the phone. "He's calling the doctor for Mrs. Faraday. Officer, could you do us one more favor and let the officer at the front door know to allow Mrs. Faraday's doctor access when he arrives?"

The officer nodded and left the room again. This time he closed the living room door tightly, eliminating the opportunity for them to watch the police activities.

"I hate just sitting here. Do you think the police would mind if I went to the kitchen and finished my work?" Mary asked.

"You'll need to ask the officer on duty, Mary. However, if I were you, I'd ask the officer if it was all right if you went to the kitchen to make coffee for everyone."

Mary nodded her head, smiling. She left the room and didn't return, so Carrie assumed her approach worked.

Christopher was now sitting next to Carrie. He took a deep breath and asked, "Do you think Grandmother is all right? You know I've only one grandmother. I don't want to lose her now that I have time to spend with her."

"I'm sure she'll be fine," Carrie said trying to sound positive. "We have to remember that your grandmother is older, and all these events have been very stressful for her. We have to protect her from any more shocks and make sure she gets plenty of rest."

Christopher nodded in agreement, but seemed lost in his own thoughts.

"You know what we should do while we are sitting here?" Christopher didn't respond, but Carrie continued. "Let's review what happened. One way to help your grandmother is to solve this crime. So, tell me, what did you see? Any impressions of Suzanne or what she said?"

Christopher looked up and then said seriously, "I thought witnesses to a crime weren't supposed to talk to each other."

"You do know your crime scene procedures. On the other hand, when have you and I done anything we are supposed to do?"

It was the right thing to say because Christopher giggled. "Yeah, that's how we keep coming up with clues. We don't pay attention to the rules."

"You go first. What did you see?"

"Well, Suzanne was very sure of herself until you brought up the phone call. Then she started to fall apart. Hey, that reminds me. You never mentioned that phone call to me. Did you make that stuff up?"

"No, it was a real call. I picked it up by accident in those few minutes before I came down to dinner. That's why I didn't get a chance to tell you about it."

"That was neat the way you kept pushing her. If she hadn't been shot, I think she would have spilled her guts."

"I think she got scared when your Uncle Charles told her she could be charged as an accessory. I think, until tonight, she really believed your father's death was accidental. When it appeared it might not be…well, she wanted out. Did you notice anything else?"

"I think that's all." Christopher closed his eyes, as if he was trying to remember. "Wait a minute… I did notice something else. When she was standing by the fireplace, she kept playing with a tissue, and then I saw her stuff it in that little flower vase on the mantel."

"I noticed that, too. Maybe she was just nervous."

"From where I was sitting, it looked like Suzanne was stuffing the tissue in the vase on purpose," added Christopher.

"I was concentrating on pushing her verbally, but now that I think about it, you're right. Do you think she was hiding something in the vase?"

"It would have to be something very small. I mean, that vase is tiny," Christopher reflected.

"What was hidden?" Charles asked as he returned to the room.

Both Carrie and Christopher asked simultaneously about Mrs. Faraday's condition.

"She's a little weak. The doctor is here now and is giving her something to help her relax and sleep. He seems to think it was the shock of the shooting that affected her and nothing more serious. Dr. Nilson assures me that, with some rest, she'll be fine. Mrs. Cavanaugh is going to stay with her."

Carrie could see Christopher's shoulders relax as he heard the positive news about his grandmother.

"You two were talking about Suzanne's fascination with that small vase on the mantle?"

"You saw it, too?" Carrie asked.

"Something else I noticed was the timing of the gunshot," Charles added. "Suzanne could have been shot at any time. However, the moment she agrees to tell us what she knows, she's struck down. It's like the shooter knew what she was saying."

"Of course…that's it!" Carrie said excitedly. "I bet if the police check that vase, they are going to discover some sort of a listening device. That would explain how the shooter knew the exact moment when Suzanne was about to betray him."

"I think you're right, but a listening device would have to have a home base," Charles said. "Somewhere nearby, maybe a vehicle."

"I bet it was parked on the street behind us on the other side of the hedges. Remember, I told the police to check there," Christopher reminded them.

"That you did. Look, I'm going to see if I can talk to Becker. I'll tell him about the vase, and I'll also see if I can get an update." Charles opened the door of the room, said something to the officer in the hall, and then closed the door behind him.

37

Christopher and Carrie had little opportunity to discuss more details about the shooting before Charles was back.

"How did it go?" asked Christopher.

"Becker really is a pompous…" Charles looked at Christopher and changed his answer to, "Let's just say he has a big ego. When I told him about the possibility of a 'bug' in the vase, he acted like he already knew. However, when he went to the fireplace, he picked up the wrong vase, and I had to redirect him to the right one."

"Was there a listening device in it?" asked Carrie.

"Sure was. It was really tucked in there. Becker had to borrow tweezers from one of the lab boys to get it out. And get this: pushed down on top of the bug was a crumpled tissue. I think Suzanne stuffed the tissue on top, thinking it would cut off the transmission."

Carrie looked at Christopher and smiled. "Christopher saw Suzanne stuff that tissue in the vase."

"That was very observant of you," said Charles as he patted him on the shoulder. "Becker wants us to sit tight until he can interview us. And he doesn't want us discussing the shooting until he questions us. I think I'm going to call Simpson and ask him to come over."

When Charles went to the phone to call Simpson, Carrie looked over at Christopher. He had a big smile on his face.

"See, I knew we shouldn't talk about the shooting," he said.

"But, Christopher, there's a positive side to our rule-breaking," Carrie defended. "Because of our discussion, we gave the police a valuable piece of evidence about the bug. And they got this information sooner rather than later."

Charles returned and took the chair opposite Christopher and Carrie.

"Simpson is on his way."

"Did the Captain tell you anything else?" asked Christopher.

"I was able to pry a couple of morsels out of the good captain. He did tell me the doctors didn't waste any time getting Suzanne into surgery. They are operating now to remove the bullet in order to relieve pressure on her brain. Becker also placed a twenty-four-hour guard on Suzanne, just in case there's another attempt on her life."

Neither Carrie nor Christopher responded to the news. There was nothing they could say. Just like waiting for

Becker, they would have to wait for news about Suzanne's condition.

Charles continued, "Christopher, you'll be pleased with this information. While I was in the room, the officer who was checking the neighborhood reported back. He interviewed a man who was walking his dog on the next street. The neighbor said he saw a strange van parked for a long time. Then around the time of the shooting, it left in a hurry."

"I knew it," said Christopher confidently. "I bet they talked to old Mr. Hughes. He and his dog, Jiggles, are always out taking a walk."

"One more item: the police also found a walkie-talkie outside the study, over by the oak tree. Becker asked if it was yours, Christopher, but I was pretty sure it wasn't. I think that's how the van was communicating with the shooter."

"It's not mine, although it sounds like a neat gift idea. What else did Captain Becker say?" asked Christopher, energized by the conversation.

"I'm afraid that's it. Becker is remaining tight-lipped. I only learned about the van and the walkie-talkie because I was in the room when the officer came back."

"He just wants us to sit here and wait? I'm bored stiff," exaggerated Christopher.

"I may have something that will keep our interest until we get sprung from this room by the coppers." Carrie directed her comment to Christopher. Then she reached under the back of her sweater and pulled out Jamie's journal. She saw Charles and Christopher watching her with curiosity. "I learned this from the waiters at the Admiral's

Saloon. They keep their ticket books tucked in the back of their slacks, so their hands are free for serving. I figured this same technique would provide a perfect hiding place for the journal."

"You continue to surprise me with the things you learn while wandering around our little town." Charles moved over to sit next to her and Christopher on the sofa.

Carrie placed the journal on the coffee table. Then she carefully opened the journal, as if she were handling a rare book. She turned the pages to the final entries.

"Christopher and I discovered this page, which lists a series of words and thoughts about smuggling."

Charles picked the journal up and read the list several times before placing the journal back on the table. "This doesn't add anything more to what we learned at our meeting today, except maybe this reference to caviar," he said, pointing his finger at the entry. "It still doesn't provide us with any names."

"I found another item this morning. It's a poem Jamie wrote, and I believe it might contain a clue."

Carrie turned to the poem and handed the journal back to Charles. Charles held the book between himself and Christopher as they read the poem silently. Then Charles read the poem out loud.

"Sounds like one of my dad's photographs is a clue. But they were all burned in the fire." Christopher sounded dejected.

"Not necessarily. Copies of many of your father's photographs are also archived at Faraday Press. Based on the poem, we can start a search for group photos with at least five people," suggested Charles.

"Your father was also very clever with words, so we should also think about the meaning of the poem. In the meantime, what do you think we should do with the journal?" Carrie asked, looking at Charles.

"Let's not share the journal with Becker for now. I want more time to review the poem, and any other entries, before we turn it over to him. Put it back in the hiding place you and Christopher used today. I don't believe there's any danger tonight with all the police on site. Plus, you told Suzanne there was nothing incriminating in the journal, for anyone listening," said Charles.

"As soon as I get upstairs, I'll hide it." Carrie placed the journal back in the waistband of her slacks.

Then Christopher said, "Hey, Uncle Charles, I want to ask you something else. When you crawled over to Suzanne did she say something?"

"She was only able to get a few words out, but I heard her clearly. She said, 'He's closer than you think.' However, before she gave me a name, she fell unconscious."

Carrie said nothing as she stared in disbelief at Charles. Suzanne said the exact same words Ascot said in her dream. Another strange coincidence?

Christopher repeated the words out loud and then added, "It sure sounds like it's someone we know."

Before they could create a list of possible suspects Captain Becker entered the room to take their statements. Simpson was right behind him.

38

It was a late night by the time Christopher, Carrie, and Charles finished giving their statements to Becker and the police finished their work in the study. Carrie was exhausted and slept late.

When she went down for breakfast, she learned from Mrs. Cavanaugh that Charles went to the office. She was sure he was starting the search of archived photographs.

Sleeping late had its advantages because while she was resting, she had an idea. She decided to call Charles at the office and share her plan. After she dialed the number, she wondered if Sandy Waxtrum would put through her call. Carrie was sure Charles received many unwanted calls and solicitations, which Sandy no doubt screened out. When she reached Sandy, she identified herself and asked to speak with Charles. She was prepared to go into further detail about the purpose of her call, but it wasn't necessary.

"Oh, yes, how are you, Ms. Kingsford? Please hold I'll ring Mr. Faraday." Carrie was sure her heart skipped a beat when she realized Charles must have instructed Sandy that she was a priority call. She decided she liked the idea of being a priority in Charles Faraday's life.

"Good morning. What a pleasant surprise!"

"Speaking of surprises, I can't believe, after last night, you were up early and off to the office."

"I wanted to get started looking for photos. Thousands of them are boxed and stored, not to mention the newer shots housed on digital files. What are you up to this morning?"

"I was wondering if you've heard from Joel."

"Not a word, but we're definitely on the same wavelength. I left another message for him this morning. The person answering the phone initially indicated he was available. Once I identified who I was, suddenly she remembered Joel was in a meeting and not taking calls. It's pretty clear he's trying to avoid me."

"Today's airwaves carried a brief story about the shooting," Carrie said. "You would have thought that news would have generated a phone call from Joel."

"Do you think Joel was involved last night?" Charles asked, as if he was struggling with his own answer.

"No, I don't, and I also don't believe Joel was involved with Jamie's death, but I think he knows something he's not telling us. Why would he break into the studio unless there was something he wanted? What do you think?"

"I know for someone who was interested in all the details of this case a few weeks ago, he's quickly lost interest. Of course, it's going to be tough to confront him if we can't talk with him."

"That's why I'm calling. I've an idea. If he won't come to us, how about we go to him?"

"What makes you think if he won't take my calls, he'll talk to us in person?"

"We aren't going to his office. When Joel and I ate lunch, we ate at the Harbor Net Restaurant. You said he eats at that restaurant almost every day around one o'clock and the restaurant reserves the same table for him. How about if we get there early? We tell the manager we're Joel's guests, they seat us at his table, and when he comes in…well, I don't think he'll want to make a scene at his favorite restaurant."

"And if for some reason he doesn't show?"

"Then you and I have lunch together."

"Sounds like a win-win situation to me," said Charles.

At twelve-thirty, Carrie and Charles were seated at Joel's favorite table enjoying a bottle of his favorite white zinfandel wine. On cue at one o'clock, Joel Wheeler was escorted to his table. Apparently the maître d' never mentioned he had guests waiting because there was no disguising the surprised look on his face when Joel saw Charles and Carrie at the table. His natural inclination was to back away from the table, but the maître d' blocked his path.

"Hello, Joel. We got here a little early, so we went ahead and ordered the wine. Hope you don't mind?"

Sensing Joel's panic, Charles stood and shook his hand, keeping a tight grip on his arm. The maître d' never sensed anything was wrong as he pulled a chair out for Joel. Charles released his grip as Joel took the seat. Assuming a friendly lunch among associates was underway, the maître d' returned to his position at the front door.

"You know, Charles, I don't remember inviting you and Carrie for lunch. I use my lunch time to refresh both my body and my mind, and I would prefer to eat alone," He emphasized the word alone.

"Joel, we would have respected your privacy if you had returned any of my phone calls. Since you didn't call me, we thought this would be a pleasant way to return an item you lost," Charles said, still smiling.

Carrie reached into her handbag and placed the pocket-knife on the table. Joel reached for it, but Carrie quickly covered it with the palm of her hand. Joel recovered and said, "I only wanted to see if it was mine. That's a very popular knife. Many people own them."

"It's yours, Joel. Popular or not, most people don't have their knives engraved with the initials J.W. Secondly, most people wouldn't have lost their knife while breaking into Jamie's studio."

The same waiter who took their order when Carrie lunched with Joel appeared. "The usual, Mr. Wheeler?" he asked politely.

"What?" he snapped. "No, I don't think I want anything today."

"Now, Joel, you need to refresh your body and mind. Besides, you'll just get hungry watching us eat." Carrie turned to the waiter and said, "I think we'll have three cups of the New England clam chowder and three crab cake sandwiches on rolls, with sides of slaw."

When the waiter received no additional instructions from Joel, he left with the order.

"Excellent choice, Carrie," Charles said, taking another sip of wine.

"You two think you're cute. Well, I don't have time for this."

"Then let's cut the nonsense. Joel, in the scuffle with me the other night, your knife dropped out of your pocket." Charles said. "But if you don't want to talk with us, perhaps you would prefer telling the police why you broke into Jamie's studio? I'm sure the police will also ask you about the recent fire at the studio and Suzanne's shooting last night."

Joel had been avoiding eye contact, but now he looked directly at Charles. "What are you talking about? Are you saying Suzanne's been shot?" Joel was genuinely surprised.

"It was in the morning papers and on the air this morning about the shooting at our home last night," confirmed Charles.

"Honest, I didn't hear anything about it. I listen to CDs on my ride in and then read the newspaper at the office. But this morning I was working on a brief and didn't have time to read the paper."

"Suzanne was shot just as she was about to reveal the name of my brother's murderer."

"That means that Suzanne was working with…" Joel didn't finish his sentence, but took the extra wine glass on the table and grabbed the bottle of zinfandel. He filled his glass to the brim and took a large gulp of the wine. "It's not what you think. I'm not tied in any way to your brother's murder, and I didn't know anything about Suzanne being shot."

"I noticed you are now saying 'murder,'" Carrie said. "Before when we met, you tried hard to convince me Jamie's death was an accident."

"That's because I was worried about you. I didn't want you poking around the way Jamie was poking around. He hadn't changed over the years. He would dig and dig until he found something, even if what he discovered had nothing to do with his original story idea."

"So, what did my brother find out about you?"

Joel looked around to make sure no one was listening and then lowered his voice. "All right, but I need your assurance that everything I say stays between us. No cops!"

Charles and Carrie exchanged a glance.

"You've got my guarantee, providing what you tell us isn't directly linked to my brother's death."

"It isn't. What about you, Carrie? Will you agree to keep what I say between us?"

"Of course, I agree," she confirmed.

Joel looked from Charles to Carrie, satisfying himself he had their promises, and then continued. "Jamie was researching a story on the importing and exporting of goods. He contacted me when he returned to the States because he came across my name."

"What do you mean he came across your name?" asked Charles.

"I don't know the details. Jamie never told me. He simply said he heard my name mentioned in certain circles in relation to exporting items out of Europe."

"Joel, I'm going to be brutally honest with you. We know Jamie was working on a story not about the business of importing and exporting, but about smuggling. I think Jamie probably was on the trail of stolen goods and how they arrive in Tri-City. I think he heard your name mentioned in relation to stolen goods. What type of importing business are you running?" demanded Carrie?

"Absolutely not! I don't smuggle!" Joel started playing with the stem of his wine glass.

"Joel, we said we would protect you, but only if you're honest with us," said Charles sternly.

"Alright, there have been times when people want to get an item out of a country and they contact a legitimate import/export dealer like me to help them."

"Joel, let me see if I understand. These items you help people get in and out of the country aren't stolen?" asked Carrie in disbelief.

"Shh, not so loud." Joel checked again to see if anyone was listening to the conversation. The nearest table was a group of tourists who were thoroughly engrossed in their experience of opening and eating hard-shell crabs. Satisfied no one was paying any attention to them, Joel continued, "Not stolen goods exactly. I'm talking about private collectors who want to get a piece they own out of a country. I helped them get their item packed with a shipment of something else. Look, the majority of my business is the normal importing of items. I've helped out with these special deliveries only a couple of times." Joel took another large gulp of wine. "We are a port city. I do a great deal of legal work for the shipping industry, and these couple of 'special deals' can't become public knowledge, do you understand?"

Charles ignored Joel's justification of his business practices and asked, "I assume you're substituting the word 'normal' for the word 'legal'? So my brother finds out about your little side business and confronts you. You're worried about the loss of your import business and the possibility of being disbarred, so you..."

The conversation ceased when the waiter brought their plates of food. Joel refilled his wine glass, and Charles ordered another bottle of zinfandel. When the waiter left, Joel continued. "No, you're wrong. That's not the way it was. Jamie also made a deal with me. You remember, Carrie, how Jamie was always making deals?"

Carrie nodded her head, remembering Jamie's methods.

Joel continued. "Jamie promised that if I helped him with some inside information about importing, he would never mention my sideline deals to anyone."

"Jamie would have required more of a deal than just some information about importing," said Carrie.

Joel briefly stared at Carrie and then smiled. "Yeah, he did. I promised I'd stop any questionable activities in the future. Since these transactions aren't the majority of my business, it was easy for me to agree."

"Now that sounds like a Jamie deal," Charles said. "He wouldn't say you were wrong, but he would figure out a way to get you back on the right path."

"Exactly. That was Jamie, and that was our deal."

For a man who originally didn't want any lunch, Joel now dug into his food with a vengeance. Carrie and Charles had barely touched their soup, and Joel was already attacking his crab cake sandwich.

"If you had a deal from Jamie, why did you break into the studio?" asked Charles.

"I had a promise from Jamie, no one else. I was afraid he might have mentioned me in his notes. All I was trying to do was make sure there was nothing around to implicate me."

"But, Joel, you knew I was going through Jamie's papers. Why didn't you say something when we ate lunch? I'd have honored Jamie's deal, and it would have saved us all this aggravation."

"To be honest, when we started reminiscing, I couldn't get past the old memories. I kept remembering your sense of right and wrong. I wasn't sure I could trust you not to turn me in to the authorities."

"You'll be glad to know I've mellowed. I've learned there are all kinds of shades of gray, but let's get back to your meeting with Jamie. What kind of questions was Jamie asking?"

"As you suspected, his questions all concerned smuggling. What was the best way to hide an item? How did the person receiving the item get it? Was there someone on board the ship or someone at customs working with the smugglers? What happens at customs? What were the penalties if you got caught? Questions like that."

"Did Jamie say what types of goods he thought were being smuggled? Drugs?" asked Charles.

"I don't think it was drugs because he never asked any question specifically related to drugs." Joel was silent, but then an idea flashed across his face. "Wait a minute. Now that you mention it, Jamie did say one thing. When we were talking about penalties, he asked if the penalty for smuggling weapons or drugs differed from smuggling consumer goods."

"Consumer goods," Carrie said. "I wonder what type of consumer goods." Then Carrie remembered Jamie's list. Her eyes meet Charles and confirmed they were both thinking of the reference to caviar on Jamie's list.

"I've no idea. Jamie never mentioned details. It may only have been a research question to give him a better understanding of the process." Joel paused and then added, "So, what happens now?"

"We finish our lunch, and Carrie and I keep looking for clues," offered Charles.

"Good! If it's all right with you two, I think I'll head back to the office. You don't mind picking up the check, do you, Charles?" Joel stood and emptied his glass of wine and left. He stopped by the maître d' stand on the way out and pointed back to the table. Joel, no doubt, was making sure he knew Charles was paying the bill.

After Joel departed, Charles asked, "What do you think?"

"I think for the first time since this whole thing started, we know the reason for Jamie's murder," said Carrie sadly.

"We do? I'm afraid you will have to enlighten me," said Charles.

"Joel reminded me of the way Jamie would make those deals. I think Jamie discovered who was behind the smuggling. I think he confronted this person, just like he confronted Joel. He offered this person the opportunity to stop the smuggling. In exchange, Jamie wouldn't write the story, and he would forget what he discovered. Just in case the person didn't follow through on the promise, Jamie kept a couple of aces up his sleeve. His aces were me and his journal."

"It also means one other thing."

"What's that, Charles?"

"If it was someone he didn't know, he would have simply written the story and exposed the person. I think this is what Suzanne meant by this person being 'closer than you think.' Jamie knew the person who murdered him."

39

The next day was Saturday and Mrs. Cavanaugh's day off. She decided to spend her afternoon playing cards with Mrs. Faraday. Mrs. Faraday was feeling much better, but remained in her room for extra rest.

Although Mrs. Cavanaugh was in the house, the one thing she didn't do on her day off was cook. It was a school day for Mary, and she wouldn't be back until the afternoon. So Christopher suggested ordering Chinese food for lunch. The ladies were sent a tray with a selection of Chinese food. Christopher, Carrie, and Charles sat at the kitchen table and shared the cartons of food.

"Uncle Charles, did you call the hospital today to check on Suzanne?"

"I did. She came through the surgery, but is still unconscious. The doctors feel the next seventy-two hours are critical to her recovery. But I have some other interesting news. I had a call from Becker today. Becker lifted Suzanne's prints from that vase she was handling and ran a check. He got a hit. Her crimes were mostly teenage pranks, but they were enough to get her fingerprints on file. Here's the interesting part: her name is Suzanne Renwick, not Redmond. Maybe that's why Jonathan's search didn't turn up much."

"I knew it!" Christopher said. "I knew she was a phony. I could tell. She was always looking over her shoulder, as if she expected to be nabbed."

Carrie looked at Christopher in amazement. She continued to be impressed with Christopher's power of observation. "Was Becker able to trace any family for her?" she asked.

"Yes, her parents live in Chicago, and Becker said they are a nice middle-class couple. They were receiving postcards from Suzanne while she was in Europe. Then she wrote to tell them she would be returning to the States and would let them know where she was. They were waiting to hear from her."

"She probably didn't tell them where she was for fear they would show up at our house and blow her cover," said Christopher.

"Now, Christopher, be nice," said Charles.

"Sorry, it's just that everything I thought about her is coming true."

Carrie turned back to Charles. "You said Becker called you. Is he now sharing information?"

"I think he wanted to see if we knew more about Suzanne than what we previously stated. However, he did offer an apology for his abrupt behavior last night. He said he appears abrupt when he's concentrating on a crime."

"Maybe Becker was just feeling guilty since he didn't spot Suzanne as a phony. In fact, I wish one of us discovered the truth sooner. Maybe we could have saved her from being shot," said Carrie.

"Don't feel guilty," said Charles. "We only had suspicions and no real evidence of her involvement until you overheard that phone call. I believe Jamie was suspicious, and that's why he brought her home. Mother and I had suspicions, which is why we allowed her to stay. But suspicions don't count."

"I know. I just wish there was a different outcome," answered Carrie.

"I think her associates knew Suzanne's usefulness was ending. That's why they were listening last night. At least, with the shooting happening here, we were able to get immediate medical help for her. That medical help is probably what saved her life," concluded Charles. "I just wish she had told us more before she was shot."

"Me, too, because other than looking for photos, we don't have any more clues," stated Christopher.

"Well, I have a next step. I've been thinking about talking to that kid at the Admiral's Saloon."

"Do you mean Ben?" supplied Carrie.

"That's the one. The more I think about him, the more I believe he may know more."

"Good idea," Carrie said. "I'll go with you."

"Yeah, me, too," piped in Christopher.

"Whoa! Both of you get to stay right here. I want to approach it from a different angle. I want to find out what

Ben knows about the docks of Tri-City. Maybe importers eat at the restaurant."

"Charles, I don't like the idea of you going there alone. You see, the more I think about my adventure at the harbor, the more I think it may have been Ben who alerted those two men. I told him I was looking into Jamie's death, I gave him my name, and I told him I was going to the pier. The timing was just right between my leaving the restaurant, visiting the pier, and those two guys showing up by my car."

"That's why I'm not going alone. I'm calling Jonathan Stone to go with me. He knows more about Tri-City than anyone I know. He can help me ask Ben the right questions about the docks." Charles went to his study to call Stone.

Carrie and Christopher sat silently as Charles made his arrangements to meet Stone at the Admiral's Saloon.

"All set." He returned to the table. "Hey, before I go, I'd like to take one more look at that poem in Jamie's journal. Could you get it for me?"

"I just happen to have it here." Carrie reached into her jacket pocket and pulled out the journal. "I thought we might want to take another look at it."

Charles took the book and flipped to the page with the poem. Carrie slid her chair next to Charles, and Christopher came and looked over their shoulders.

"Have you figured out the meaning, Uncle Charles?"

"Not really. I just wanted to memorize some of Jamie's thoughts. Its funny how certain words come up in a conversation about a particular industry." He handed the book back to Carrie. "Okay, I'm on my way."

Charles wanted to give Carrie a goodbye kiss, but he realized Christopher was in the room, so he gave her a quick kiss on the forehead.

"Good heavens, Uncle Charles, give her a proper kiss. I'll turn my back if you're embarrassed." And Christopher turned around.

"Well, you heard the man," said Carrie.

After giving Carrie a "proper kiss," Charles gave Christopher a light punch on the shoulder and went out the kitchen door. Christopher and Carrie watched his car pull away.

"You're okay that your uncle and I like each other?"

"I think it's great! I like the idea of having you around, and I can tell Uncle Charles feels the same way. How about having some ice cream?"

Carrie fixed a couple of dishes of ice cream to go with their almond cookies. When they were seated at the table, Christopher said, "I think Uncle Charles knows something he's not telling us."

"I thought the same thing. What do you think he's up to?" Carrie asked. "Maybe he saw a clue in the poem."

While they ate their cookies and ice cream, Carrie opened the journal to the poem and read it out loud. "Do you hear anything that we may have missed?"

"The lines about shipping sound okay, but that stuff about the picture hanging and five from the left doesn't fit."

"I agree. I think your father was trying to tell us there's a picture, and the person we're after is five places from the left."

"Maybe Uncle Charles found the photo," replied Christopher.

"I was just thinking. Did your father give you any pictures to hold?"

"The only pictures I have are ones from our vacations. And those photos are of Dad, me, and sometimes Suzanne. Dad's poem implies it's a group of people, like a class picture, where everyone lines up."

"That's it! A group shot where everyone lines up and smiles. Come on." Carrie jumped up from the table, ran out of the kitchen, and headed for the hallway.

"Hey, where are we going?" Christopher asked as he ran after her.

They both took the hallway steps two at a time and flew down the hallway to Carrie's room. Once inside, Carrie went right to the wall. Hanging in plain view was the picture of the launch of the *News World* magazine. She counted five from the left. Then she stood and looked in disbelief at Christopher.

"Christopher, five from the left is Jonathan Stone!"

40

"Joel?"

"Yes."

"It's Carrie."

"I know who it is, but I didn't expect to hear from you. I thought we finished our discussion at lunch yesterday." With his deep voice Carrie couldn't tell if he was annoyed or apprehensive about more questions.

"Now, Joel, don't be that way. Charles and I learned a great deal yesterday, and we can't thank you enough for your honesty and cooperation," Carrie said in a low, calming voice.

"In that case, I'm glad I helped." Joel's tone changed. "To be honest, our talk helped me, too. I feel the burden of worrying about my couple of importing indiscretions was lifted. You must believe me when I say that I've stopped those activities, and I also trust you and Charles will keep your promise."

"I assure you, Charles and I will keep our word. We have no interest in anything other than solving Jamie's murder."

After a silence, Joel said, "Carrie, I hope when all this is settled, we can still be friends."

"Joel, we'll always be friends. We go back too far and have too many wonderful memories to allow one incident to affect our friendship."

"That's good to know. I assume you're calling for a reason."

"Charles and I have one more question. We were wondering if anyone else who worked with Jamie, or knew the Faraday family, contacted you about importing."

"Is it important? I don't like revealing my client names."

"Joel, it's very important. It could literally be a life-or-death situation."

"You mean this person could be in danger, like Jamie?"

Carrie decided not to tell Joel she suspected this person could be the villain and not the victim. Instead she said, "Yes, someone could be in danger."

"There's one person, but please don't let him know I gave you his name. I've helped Jonathan Stone a couple of times."

"How did you help him?" Carrie felt a sinking feeling in her stomach as Joel verified what Carrie already suspected.

"Jonathan contacted me to help him bring in some items from Europe. But, Carrie, I wasn't doing anything unusual with Jonathan, if you know what I mean. He had purchased some items in Europe, and I was just facilitating some straight importing for him. Do you think he's in danger?"

"I don't know, Joel, but I better check this out right away. I'll talk to you soon, and thanks."

"Carrie, wait, be careful! I don't know what's happening, but I don't want to pick up the paper and read about any more murders."

"Thanks, Joel, I have to go. I'll take care, and I'll be in touch."

When Carrie hung up, her heart was racing. She needed to get to Charles.

41

Carrie tried Charles's cell phone. There was no answer, and she wasn't comfortable leaving a message. She decided to drive to the Admiral's Saloon. Christopher wanted to go, but Carrie convinced him he needed to be in charge at the house and to warn Uncle Charles in case he called.

As Carrie was driving to the saloon, she hoped her conclusions about Stone were incorrect. Carrie pushed her speed, but once she entered the city limits, she was slowed by the traffic lights on every corner. When she reached the harbor area, she drove past the parking lot on Pier Eight. She didn't want to take a chance that her two friends were still hanging around. Instead, she drove to High Seas Street and parked in the residential section.

Carrie locked her car and started her walk to the restaurant, keeping an alert eye. Pedestrian traffic was light until she reached Harbor Avenue, and then she encountered crowds of tourists enjoying the harbor. She blended in with the walkers until she reached the Admiral's Saloon. Once inside, she slipped onto a stool at the far end of the bar. Her seat was hidden by a large group standing around drinking beer. From her perch, Carrie could see virtually everyone entering or leaving the bar.

"What can I get you? We have some great beers on tap," stated the bartender, who was decked out in a clean, crisp white shirt and black bow tie. He wiped the space in front of her and placed a square cardboard coaster advertising a light beer down on the bar.

Carrie looked at a table tent on the bar that advertised a frozen drink of the month. "I'm not much of a beer drinker, but I'll have one of those strawberry daiquiris you're featuring."

"Coming right up." After a quick whir on the blender, the bartender returned with Carrie's drink and a mixed bowl of nuts and pretzels.

"Is Ben working tonight? He waited on me the last time, and I liked his service."

"Yup, he's working, but you may have to wait for one of his tables."

"Why do you say that? It doesn't look that busy in the dining room," observed Carrie.

"You're the third person within the last thirty minutes asking for one of Ben's tables. Two gentlemen said they were also pleased with Ben's previous service."

"Two guys at one table? Ben can certainly handle two tables at a time."

"No, the gentlemen weren't together, and each server has a limited number of tables for single seating. Unfortunately for you, both men were seated within the last fifteen minutes. You should sip your drink slowly."

Carrie wondered who these guys could be. Charles and Jonathan wouldn't ask for separate tables Maybe they were just two businessmen who wanted Ben to wait on them. Of course, that seemed like an odd coincidence.

"You know, maybe when Ben comes down to pick up drinks for his tables, I'll just say hi. That way I can have my dinner at the bar and another one of your delicious daiquiris," Carrie suggested. She was thinking she was in a better position to watch the traffic from her bar stool.

The bartender nodded his head in agreement with her suggestion. "Sounds like a plan to me. When Ben comes by, I'll send him your way. Let me know when you're ready to order another drink or dinner." The bartender left to serve several couples who sat at the bar a few seats away from Carrie.

Carrie moved two stools away from the new arrivals, closer to the dining area. She continued to sip her drink while she angled her position to better see the people in the dining room. She saw no signs of Charles or Jonathan Stone. Did they change their plans? Was Jonathan Stone aware he was a suspect? More importantly, did Charles know Jonathan was a suspect? She didn't like waiting and was debating what to do next when she saw Ben enter the waiting area from a door marked "Management Offices." He wasn't dressed in the usual Admiral's Saloon garb, but in street clothes. Carrie jumped up and quickly threw a ten-dollar bill on the bar as she realized Ben was leaving the restaurant.

"Ben, wait a minute!" Carrie called after him.

He looked over his shoulder and said, "Sorry, got to run."

Carrie could see panic on his face, but it was also obvious he didn't recognize her. "Ben, it's me, Carrie Kingsford. We spoke the other night. Where are you going?"

"Me? I'm, uh, I...I don't feel well," he stammered. "I'm going home."

Just as Ben was about to escape through the front door, a large group of people entered and blocked his way. While Ben waited to get past, Carrie grabbed his arm.

"Hey, let me go. Who are you, anyway?"

"I told you. I'm Carrie Kingsford. Remember, we talked about Jamie Faraday's death the other night." Panic returned to his eyes. "Ben, if you're in danger, you shouldn't just walk out of here without protection."

He pulled her over to the side, away from the incoming patrons. "I know I'm in danger. That's why I'm getting the hell out of here."

"Has Charles Faraday been here to talk with you?" Carrie asked.

"No. Who's he?"

"He's Jamie Faraday's brother. He was coming to talk with you. He would have been here with another man or maybe even the police," she stated.

"The police! Why would the police want me?"

"Blackmail is usually considered police business."

"Blackmail? I don't know what you're talking about!" Ben shot back.

"Cut the crap, Ben," Carrie said. "This murder case is in its final act. We are about to nail the murderer of Jamie Faraday. So far, all you're in trouble for is a couple of blackmail payments. The police won't care about these payments if you help nail a murderer."

"Look, you're wrong. I'm not a blackmailer. I may have gotten paid for providing some information, but I certainly have nothing to do with any murder."

"Then why don't you tell me the whole story?"

"All right, I'll talk, but not here." He looked around again at the faces of the incoming patrons. "We need to leave here."

They went out of the restaurant, and Ben turned left toward the main downtown area.

"My car is the other way," Carrie offered. "We could talk in the car, and then I'll drive you somewhere safe."

"No, there's a small pub nearby. They don't do dinners or happy hour, so they won't be busy at this time. We can talk there."

The little voice in Carrie's head kept asking, *Where is everyone?* She saw no signs of Charles and Jonathan. Why was Ben in such a hurry to get away from the restaurant? Ben walked quickly along the boardwalk, dodging in and out between people as he walked against the flow of traffic. Carrie found it difficult to keep up with him and was just about to tell Ben to slow down when she recognized Officer Reynolds coming their way. She felt relief at seeing his friendly face. Carrie raised her hand and waved, just as

Ben made a quick right turn down a side street and headed back toward Harbor Avenue. Officer Reynolds waved back, but Carrie didn't know if his wave was a friendly gesture or if he recognized her.

Midway down the block was a refurbished row house with a single wooden door. Over the top of the door was a swinging pub sign advertising the Dancing Sailor. The sign portrayed a sailor with his leg raised, as if he was doing a jig. Ben entered the pub, and Carrie followed.

The low lighting and the deep-brown wood walls and furniture made the place so dark that Carrie was momentarily blinded. As Carrie's eyes began to adjust to the lack of light, she saw an open area to her left with a series of dartboards on the wall. Around the three adjoining walls was a ledge to hold drinks and snacks for the players. The brightly lettered sign near the dartboards indicated tournaments were held Monday through Friday nights, starting at eight. This was Saturday, so no dart games tonight.

Since the pub was located in an old row house, the building was longer than wide. Next to the dart area was a bar that took up half the length of the remaining floor space. At the end of the bar, the room opened up again. On the right side of the room across from the bar were a series of high-back booths and several small tables. Ben was right about the place providing privacy at that hour of the day. Only one couple was seated at the end of the bar nearest the door.

Ben's eyes must have adjusted to the light quicker, or maybe he was more familiar with the layout. Carrie saw him standing at a booth almost at the back of the pub. She nodded to the bartender as she passed him on her way to join Ben. And then she stopped in her tracks. She was inside a bar that was almost exactly like the one she created for Ascot in her book. Was it possible that her mind had some vision into the future? She walked more slowly toward the back, where Ben stood. In her book, Ascot was surprised by whom he saw sitting in the booth.

Carrie had reached Ben and she turned to look at the person sitting in the booth. She couldn't hide her shock. She quickly spun around in an attempt to escape, but her path was blocked by two men who came up behind her. One was tall and heavy, like a football player. The other man was short and very thin.

42

"Thanks for the warning, Mr. Stone. I think I got away from the restaurant just in time. Two men arrived and requested my tables, and then this lady asked for me, but no one else," said Ben.

"Ah, Ms. Kingsford, I was hoping to catch up with you! I'm always glad to have additional guests when I throw a party. Please, join Charles," offered Jonathan Stone as he pointed to the other side of the booth.

Carrie slid in next to Charles. When she looked at him, she saw his cheek was bruised.

"Charles, you're hurt!"

"It's nothing, just a bump." Charles was clearly surprised by Carrie's arrival. "Carrie, what are you doing here?"

"I came to warn you, but it looks like I didn't do a very good job."

"That's all right. I didn't do a very good job, either." Charles looked away from Carrie at the young man standing next to Jonathan. "I assume this is Ben from the Admiral's Saloon."

"Hey, who is this guy?" demanded Ben.

Jonathan Stone decided to play the perfect host by providing introductions.

"Ben, I'd like you to meet Charles Faraday, Jamie Faraday's brother. Obviously, you've already met Carrie Kingsford, and you know me. Ben, come, sit down here." Stone patted the wooden seat next to him.

Ben wasn't sure about Stone's offer to sit next to him, but Stone's two associates helped him decide. They stood beside Ben, and the bigger man placed a hand on his shoulder. Ben slid in next to Stone.

"Shall we get started?" offered Jonathan.

"Wait a minute!" Charles interrupted. "You haven't finished your introductions. We don't know the names of these gentlemen."

Carrie wasn't sure their names were important, considering the circumstances, but decided to play along with Charles's request. "Yes, I'd also like to meet these gentlemen. Although I feel I already know them, having experienced so many close encounters."

"Of course, my dear," Jonathan said, addressing Carrie. "This is Mr. Tomas Petrovich. I met him on a trip to Eastern Europe." Petrovich, the bigger man, stood to attention, clicked his heels, and bowed slightly to the group. "And this is Mr. Bill Genello, whom I've known for many years from my early days in New York." Mr. Genello looked at his fingernails and grinned. It was a nasty grin. "Now, everyone knows everyone, and it does make it more pleasant," said Jonathan.

Carrie heard a noise and looked back over her shoulder. The couple sitting at the bar was leaving. The bartender followed them to the door, flipped the "Open" sign to "Closed," and locked the door.

"All set, Mr. Stone. The place is all yours," the bartender said as he passed the booth and took the stairs at the back of the pub, leaving Stone and his group alone on the first floor.

"Now, folks, it is important for me to understand how much you two know and what evidence led you to me."

"Look, Mr. Stone, if I could just get my money, I'll be out of here," Ben said.

"You're right, Ben, it's time for your payoff." Stone nodded to Petrovich, who in one quick motion snapped his hand against the back of Ben's neck. Petrovich and Genello pulled Ben from his seat and dragged him to the back room.

"Jonathan, there's no need to hurt the boy," Carrie said. "He really doesn't know anything about the murder."

"He knows we were together, and I can't have him tell the police even the little bit he knows," answered Stone. "Oh, my dear, I'm so sorry. I'm afraid I'm not only going to have to deal with Ben, but both of you as well."

43

"Before you 'deal with us,' as you put it, I have one question for you," Charles said. "Does Ben know you murdered my brother?"

"No, as a matter of fact, he doesn't. What he saw was a brief meeting between me and Jamie at the Admiral's Saloon bar the night of the murder. Unfortunately, he heard Jamie call me by name. Fortunately for me, the police didn't question him about that night. I went back the next night and talked with Ben. I was able to convince him that Jamie and I were working on a story together. After all, would I come back to talk with him if I had anything to do with the death? I told him there was a possibility the death wasn't an accident, and I was investigating what happened. I gave him a nice tip and promised him more money if he would let me know if anyone started nosing around. You see, Ben was convinced I was one of the good guys in this whole affair."

"Ah, so it was Ben who alerted you I was at the Admiral's Saloon? That's how Petrovich and Genello were waiting for me at my car," confirmed Carrie.

"Yes, the boys were having a terrible time trying to catch you. They missed you on the highway."

Stone just verified the nagging feeling Carrie always had that her incident on the highway was not a coincidence. "I wondered about that encounter," said Carrie.

"Then they missed you in the garage the day you lunched with Joel and again the night you met Ben." Genello reached over and lightly tapped Stone on the shoulder. "Yes, yes I remember. The boys would like me to ask where you hid the night they chased you." Stone's tone remained light and friendly.

Carrie looked at Charles. "I guess it doesn't matter if I tell. I hid in a bank's ATM lobby and used the customer service phone to call the police."

"My, my, you are a clever girl. Boys, you will have to add ATMs to the list of places to check when you are chasing someone." Stone returned his attention to the couple. "Now back to my original question. How much do you two know about what Jamie was doing?" His tone changed.

"Not enough to understand why you murdered my brother. Of course, I know you didn't do it. Which of these two goons did your dirty work?"

Petrovich stepped forward and nodded to the group.

Charles continued, "I assume you were the one that decided to try to make it look like an accident. Jonathan, come clean and tell us what happened that night."

"Unfortunately, I was responsible for your brother's death. Your brother just wouldn't stop digging into smuggling at the harbor. His research coupled with his idealized sense of right and wrong made him a big problem for my business."

"What kind of a business are you running that you have to hire thugs to murder people?" Charles demanded.

Stone looked from Carrie to Charles. "I guess it won't hurt at this time to tell you about my caviar business. I really haven't had the opportunity to share my success story with anyone."

Stone was obviously pleased that Charles had asked the question. However, Carrie wondered why Charles seemed so determined to keep Stone talking. It was clear now what happened to Jamie would happen to them. Perhaps Charles was trying to delay their ultimate fate.

"While your brother was in Poland, he notified Bill Owens he had a tip about smuggling and thought it would make a great story. Owens asked me, and I approved the idea."

"Good grief, Jonathan, if Jamie asked about working on a story that would affect your business, why didn't you stop him?" Carrie asked.

"There were several reasons, my dear. First, Jamie's original story was not specific to the caviar business. It had more to do with political corruption. Second, I thought with Jamie's research expertise, I could learn more about law enforcement techniques for spotting illegal imports. Third, if Jamie's investigation led to my business, it meant I had a weak link that needed to be fixed."

"Jonathan, who are you working for?" Charles asked. "Who is supporting this little sideline of yours?"

"Who's supporting me? Don't be ridiculous!" Stone huffed. "No one is supporting me. I'm in charge. People work for me!"

Carrie remembered Jamie's wake and her first impressions of Stone as he munched on a toast point with caviar. She couldn't help but wonder if the caviar was provided by Stone.

"Did serving as general manager for the magazine help you find contacts to run your business? How many Faraday employees are helping you in this sideline?" Charles was lightly tapping his fingers on the tabletop.

"You'll be glad to know, Charles, that no members of your staff met my standards for employment. Although, I admit, I occasionally used the overseas staff to take small packages back and forth for me. Of course, they thought these packages were just personal gifts between friends."

Charles asked point blank, "What else are you importing besides caviar—military documents, art, or drugs?"

"Good heavens, no. I'm not a criminal! I'm a businessman. You may not believe this, but caviar has become quite a tasty little business for me." Stone laughed heartily at his little joke. He quickly regained his composure and added, "Since the fall of the Communist-controlled governments, the strict regulations regarding caviar exports have become lax. As a result, more people around the world, including Tri-City residents, want caviar. The profits are huge, but, alas, there is a limited supply."

"Jonathan, what are you saying?" asked Charles. "Are you smuggling real caviar, or are you producing fake caviar to sell?"

"Both," Jonathan replied. "Most consumers are fascinated by the aura surrounding Russian caviar. However, except for the most experienced connoisseur, the average person can't tell one fish egg from another. This leaves the market wide open for some blending of less expensive eggs. I have sources that provide me with authentic Russian labels, so no one is the wiser. Of course, I also import black market Russian caviar for those special affairs where someone might know the difference."

"Did Jamie discover a shipment of your caviar on a dock in Europe?" asked Carrie. "Is that what led him to your smuggling activities?"

"Actually, if he had discovered a caviar shipment for me, I doubt if anything would have happened. He would have teased me about my expensive tastes. No, what he discovered was a shipment of the fake Russian labels. One of our reporters was dropping off some material for Jamie and picking up a package of labels for me. The idiot got the packages mixed. With a little backtracking, Jamie found one of my caviar sources in Poland. It didn't take him long to put together what I was doing when he found Polish caviar in a tin with one of my fake Russian labels."

"You're saying this…this, as you call it, 'little caviar business' cost my brother his life!"

Carrie sensed the emotion rising within Charles. She was afraid he might do something foolish. She reached over and gently touched his arm. She felt him relax.

"You two still don't understand that my 'little business' is worth millions. However, I'll tell you that no one was ever supposed to be hurt," he added softly.

Stone looked down at his suit jacket and carefully picked off a speck of lint. Then he turned his eyes to Carrie. "Carrie, don't you have any questions about my business?"

"I was wondering if Joel works with you since he also does importing." The minute Carrie asked the question, she regretted it, realizing she may have just placed Joel in danger.

"I've used Joel as a backup. If I couldn't get a shipment out of a particular location, I'd check with Joel to see if he had a contact. But Joel assumed my shipments were legitimate."

Charles and Carrie exchanged a quick glance. Wouldn't Stone be surprised to learn that Joel had a little secret, too?

Carrie was about to ask another question when she felt Charles take her hand underneath the table and squeeze it gently. Suddenly everything seemed fine. If it was time for her to die, she was glad she was with Charles.

Stone, seeing there were no more questions, said, "Since I have been open about my business, I hope you will be equally open in telling me how you learned I was involved. Should we continue our civilized approach and have Carrie go first?"

Carrie's mind raced quickly to create a plausible response of how she discovered Stone. She didn't want to involve anyone else or reveal any evidence. She carefully selected her words. "I think you're going to be terribly disappointed. I'm afraid I didn't know you were involved." She decided to play to his ego. "You see, I was thinking about the night Mr. Petrovich and Mr. Genello chased me. I was positive I wasn't followed from the house, which meant someone alerted them to my presence at the harbor. The logical person was Ben, and I came here tonight to confront him. He said he would talk with me but not at the restaurant, and I foolishly followed him here to the pub."

"You're telling me that you weren't looking for me, but just tagging along with Ben?" he asked with genuine surprise.

"I warned you my explanation wasn't anything spectacular. Only now do I realize how stupid my actions were."

Carrie couldn't get a reading on whether Jonathan accepted her explanation, but he turned away from her and asked Charles, "What about you?"

Charles looked at Carrie. "It's all right, I feel equally shortsighted." Charles then turned to Stone. "Is it correct for me to assume Suzanne was working for you and the listening device was yours?"

Jonathan nodded his head in agreement to Charles' question and then added, "I met Suzanne through Bill Genello. They were friends when Suzanne worked in New York. She wanted to travel in Europe and I wanted someone to keep an eye on Jamie while he researched his smuggling story. So I hired her. I told Suzanne that I needed someone to keep Jamie on track with his deadlines, but she was never to let Jamie know she worked for the magazine."

"She never realized she worked for you and not the company?" asked Charles.

"I think she suspected when I had her hide the listening device in the study. She didn't like spying on you. But I told her with Carrie in town, I needed her help to know the progress you were making with the murder investigation. In her little girl way she thought she was helping to solve the murder. Of course, it was this same device that helped us realize Suzanne was about to tell all. Unfortunately, this revelation caused Mr. Petrovich to shoot her. But let's not linger on the unpleasant. Charles, I want to hear about the journal."

"The journal? You heard through the listening device that the journal is of no value to you, Jonathan. The journal contains no names or clues about what was being smuggled. I wanted you to meet me at the Admiral's Saloon to help me question this kid, Ben. Unfortunately, you jumped to the conclusion that we were closing in on you."

"Perhaps." Jonathan's answer was pensive.

Carrie could tell he wasn't pleased with the implication he had jumped to a wrong conclusion.

Jonathan continued. "Jamie went to Simpson for his will and the letter for Carrie. Do you think Jamie confided in Simpson?"

"I'm telling you Jamie didn't tell anyone anything! You know how he worked. He kept his cards close until he sat down to write the final story. In fact, I bet Jamie wasn't planning on writing a story." Charles said this and then carefully waited for Jonathan's reaction. "Didn't he tell you he wouldn't write the story?

"Your brother did make an offer that if I stopped smuggling the caviar, he wouldn't write the story. Jamie also jumped to a wrong conclusion. He thought I'd agree to his offer out of fear of losing my job and my income. He had no way of knowing I was making more from smuggling than from my editor's job." Jonathan paused and then added, "Although I still find it difficult to believe I was wrong in assuming you both knew I was involved."

"I wouldn't have asked you to investigate Suzanne's background or asked for your help tonight if I thought you were the murderer? I figured Ben had more information, and hoped he would lead us to the murderer." Charles looked directly at Jonathan. "Now that you understand how we came to be sitting across the table from you, what are you going to do with us?"

"That's a problem. I do hate to be the bearer of bad news, but I don't see any way I can leave you two around to tell your story." Jonathan made a clicking sound with his tongue, indicating his regret.

After Jonathan's comment, Carrie could feel the tears welling up in her eyes. Charles must have sensed her feelings because he reached over and gave her a kiss. Then he nuzzled her neck and whispered softly in her ear, "Where are we?"

His question wasn't what Carrie expected, and she pulled back and looked at his face. Charles gave her another quick kiss.

"That was lovely, but I'm afraid it's time to go," said Jonathan. Petrovich and Genello, who were sitting quietly at a nearby table, now jumped to their feet.

"Where are we going?" asked Charles, with desperation sounding in his voice for the first time.

"I have a place where you won't be found for quite a while," Jonathan answered. "Perhaps people will think the two of you ran off together."

"Why not here?" retorted Charles.

"Customers will be arriving shortly, and murder is not on the menu. This place also provides another little side income for me. I don't want it shut down during a subsequent police investigation into your disappearance."

"Carrie, did you drive here?" Charles asked.

"What? Oh, no. Ben and I walked the couple of blocks from the Admiral's Saloon." Then it dawned on Carrie why Charles whispered the question. He really didn't know where they were. "How did you get here?" she asked in return.

"Jonathan met me at the office, and the guys were waiting in the parking lot with the van. Petrovich and I sat in the back, where there wasn't much of a view."

"Oh Charles, that means you missed the sign out front. It reminds me of the pubs in London, where the pictures on the sign have such cute names. This sign has a British sailor doing a jig. Which makes sense, since the name of the pub is the Dancing Sailor." Upon saying the name, Carrie could see Charles relax.

Then Jonathan chimed in. "The picture really does help identify the place. Many times I've had deliveries brought by foreign sailors who don't speak much English, and the sign makes it easy for them to find the pub. But enough of this chatter, we really must go."

Petrovich helped Carrie out of the booth. Then Charles slid across the seat. As he went to stand, he slipped toward the floor. "Sorry, my leg seems to have gone asleep."

"Really, Charles, this is no time for you to try to delay." Jonathan no sooner finished the words than they heard pounding on the front door. Jonathan nodded for Petrovich and Genello to check out the sound.

44

efore Petrovich and Genello reached the front of the pub, there was a cracking sound and the front door burst open. As the police entered the front, there was pounding on the back door.

Petrovich and Genello took cover behind the bar and exchanged gunfire with the police. Charles knocked over a table and pulled Carrie behind it for cover. Out of the corner of his eye, Charles saw Jonathan run to the flight of stairs the bartender used earlier. The battle seemed endless to the couple crouched behind the wooden table. Then they heard a loud pop and saw a cloud of smoke rising. This was followed by the sounds of coughing and choking, as Petrovich and Genello emerged from their hiding place behind the bar with their hands raised.

"Tear gas," said Charles. "Try to avoid breathing deeply."

"Did you know the police were coming?" asked Carrie. "Is that why you wanted me to say the name of the pub?"

"Jonathan wasn't the only one with a listening device. I'm wearing a police wire," Charles responded. "The only problem was I didn't know where we were since Stone brought me in through the back door." Carrie started to ask more questions, but Charles said, "I'll tell you more about it later. Right now I'm going after Jonathan."

"Charles, be careful. You can't be sure Jonathan doesn't have a gun or isn't going to get one."

"My foremost thought is to return to you. As soon as the police get back here, send them after me." With those words, Charles left Carrie and went after Stone.

Carrie decided not to wait for the police to reach her. The gas was beginning to drift toward the back of the room. She got up from her position behind the table and went to the back door to let the rest of the police enter. When she arrived in the back room, she saw Ben bound and gagged, lying in a heap in a corner. She didn't stop to help him since the pounding on the door continued.

"Wait a minute. It's Carrie Kingsford. I'm trying to get the door unlocked."

Carrie struggled with several bolts and locks before she was finally able to free the door. The police rushed in, led by Captain Becker.

"Are you all right, Ms. Kingsford?"

"Yes, I'm fine, but this young man will need some medical attention," she said, pointing to Ben.

"Call the paramedics," Becker ordered the officer behind him. "What's the situation out front?"

"When the tear gas exploded, Jonathan's two men surrendered. However, as you broke through the front door, Jonathan headed for the upstairs. And a bartender went upstairs about twenty minutes ago."

"Where is Mr. Faraday?"

"He went after Jonathan," responded Carrie. "He wants you to follow."

"He shouldn't have done that!" Becker was clearly annoyed with this news.

"This way," Carrie said. She led Becker and two officers into the main pub.

Becker yelled to an officer approaching from the front, "Everything under control up there?"

"All set, Captain. Bad guys in custody," the officer answered as she lifted her gas mask.

Becker motioned for Carrie to lead on. She quickly took Becker and his officers to the bottom of the steps leading to the second floor. Carrie started to follow Becker up the steps, but he turned and stopped her. "No, you wait here! Officer Reynolds, please make sure Ms. Kingsford stays put."

Carrie had no chance to protest. Becker and the officer went up the steps as Officer Reynolds took hold of Carrie's arm.

"Ah, Ms. Kingsford, we meet again," said Officer Reynolds with a broad grin. "In case the tear gas drifts back, perhaps it would be better if we sit at a table closer to the back door so we get some fresh air." Officer Reynolds led her to a table closest to the back room and pulled out a chair for her.

Carrie sat, as directed. She was helpless and frustrated, not knowing what was happening to Charles. She said a silent prayer asking that Charles be kept safe.

45

harles followed Stone up the back steps of the pub. He approached the second floor slowly, hugging the railing of the steps. Charles reminded himself not to be a hero. He only wanted to follow Stone so he could tell the police where he went.

As he neared the top of the steps and his head became visible through the spokes of the banister, he watched for any signs of Stone or the bartender. There was no movement. Instead, he discovered four closed doors along a hallway that ran the length of the building.

He approached the first room. He stood to the side of the door, using the wall as protection. He turned the knob and flung the door inward. It hit the back wall and snapped back toward him. He looked in and saw a storage room. Lining the walls of the room were gray shelving units holding various supplies for the pub. He saw no place for anyone to hide. He left the door open to this room and slid along the hallway to the next one.

He listened. All he heard was the continuing commotion from downstairs. He repeated his method for opening the door and this time gazed into a lavish office. There was no sign of Stone, but Charles knew he had been there. The wall safe was open, a desk drawer had been dumped, and several file drawers were ajar. A fire in the fireplace was still burning the remains of several folders. Charles dropped to the floor and scanned the area to see if Stone might be hiding under the desk or behind the sofa. Once Charles was convinced Stone was gone, he went directly to the fireplace. He took the poker, moved the burning files onto the slate grate, and stomped on them to extinguish the fire. Hopefully, some of the information could be saved. He then moved to the desk and looked at the remaining contents in the drawer. There was only one item of interest: an empty cartridge box. Charles knew that Stone was now armed.

Charles reentered the hallway. He could no longer hear gunfire, but he continued to hear banging. The police must be at the back door. *Carrie will tell the police I'm upstairs and help will follow*, he assured himself. *Two more doors to go*, he thought as he listened at the third door. He thought he heard a sound. Charles repeated the process of throwing the door open, only this time it didn't hit the wall. Someone was behind the door. Charles quickly pushed against the door with his full weight. He heard the sound of a groan. At the same time, a bullet skimmed across the wood of a banquet table located in the center of the room. From behind the door, a hand holding a gun appeared. Charles kept pressure on the door as he wrestled the gun away. Once Charles had control of the gun, he pulled the person from behind the door. It was the bartender, and although his nose was bleeding, he came out swinging. Charles ducked, then hit him with all his might and was surprised when he knocked him out. He didn't have time to tie him up. He hoped his punch would keep him out of the way until the police got there. Charles took the bartender's gun and went back into the hallway.

The last door was straight ahead. Charles could feel an adrenaline rush. This was the only place Stone could be. He approached the door cautiously. He listened. He heard only silence. However, unlike the other doors on the floor, this one opened out into the hallway. Charles steadied his gun and then swung the door out toward him. As he glanced into the blackness, he saw a set of steps going up to the roof. At the top was another closed door. Charles quickly took the steps and found the door at the top locked. He looked at the gun in his hand. *They do this in the movies. Let's see if it works in real life.*

He retreated back a couple of steps to avoid a ricochet and fired directly at the lock. The door swung open to reveal the roof of the building.

Charles flattened himself against the top step for cover. He was blinded as to what was to the left, right, and behind the door of the roof. He could only see a small section of open space in front of him. Charles decided there was only one way to find out where Stone was hiding and that was to go out on the roof. He exited the door and leaned his back against the wall of the roof entrance. No signs of Stone. He slowly moved to the edge of his cover and cast his eyes to the left. There was a large ventilation unit, which would be a perfect hiding place. Charles was debating what to do next when he felt something poke him in the side.

"Bad mistake, Charles. You should have stayed downstairs." Jonathan Stone leveled a gun at Charles. "Raise your hands, please." Charles complied and Stone took his gun. "Charles, having a gun is so out of character for you. Where did you get it?"

"I took it from the bartender you left downstairs. It's over, Jonathan. The police are right behind me."

"I think Petrovich and Genello will keep the police busy long enough for me to escape."

"You're wrong, Jonathan. The gunfire has stopped. That means Petrovich and Genello are in custody. You're a smart businessman. It's time to cut your losses."

Jonathan cocked his head and listened. "Cut my losses and do what? Go to jail for the rest of my life? Even though Petrovich was responsible for Jamie's murder and shooting Suzanne, I'm still an accessory. There is also the matter of the illegal caviar."

"What's the alternative?" Charles asked.

"For right now, we are going to move to the other side of the roof." Stone gave Charles a couple of pokes in the back.

Charles moved as slowly as he dared to the other side. Stone walked to the edge of the roof and looked over. He seemed pleased. He then directed Charles to move backward.

"Jonathan, what are you planning?"

"Did I ever tell you I was quite an athlete in my younger days? In college I was on the track-and-field team and quite good at the long jump."

"College was a long time ago," Charles responded.

"True, but I've always kept in good shape. Keeping in shape is something you should consider, Charles. I never see you doing any exercise."

Charles ignored his comment and said, "Jonathan, this is crazy. Suppose you make it to the other roof. Then what? You think the police aren't surrounding the entire area? You're just prolonging the inevitable, and you may get hurt. Get a good lawyer instead."

"I have a good lawyer. He helped me buy the building next door. That's my escape route. Since the police are here, they obviously know more than what you admitted. But that's okay, regardless of what I said downstairs, I wasn't going to kill you and Carrie. I was going to detain you while I finished my arrangements to leave Tri-City. And Charles, I never meant to hurt Jamie. Please believe me."

With these words, Stone started to run across the roof. Charles was amazed at the speed Stone generated in such a short distance. There was a gap in the roof edging, which allowed him a straight shot. He went through the gap effortlessly.

Charles was so focused on Stone he never heard the noises behind him. Stone was airborne when the first police shot was fired.

Charles yelled, "No, don't shoot him. Quickly! Send someone to the house next door!"

Stone was hit by that first bullet. He grabbed his upper arm. Charles was close enough to see the blood seeping through Stone's fingers. As the next police shot was fired, Stone hit the roof of the building next door and rolled several times.

Charles ran to the edge of the roof. He could no longer see Stone. He must have made it to the staircase leading down into the building. It was the last time Charles would see Jonathan Stone.

46

A week had passed since the events at the Dancing Sailor pub. Genello and Petrovich were behind bars, without bail. Suzanne's parents arrived and were making arrangements to take her home for a long convalescence. Jonathan Stone was still at large and it was believed he was no longer in Tri-City.

On Saturday night, Captain Becker joined the Faradays and Carrie for dinner. After a quiet meal, they were sitting in the study having coffee and Becker was finally sharing information with the family about the case. Christopher would normally avoid coffee in the study, but that night he wanted to hear all the details from Becker.

Mrs. Faraday, who was looking and feeling much better, took a sip from her mint aperitif and let out a small sigh. "I know we have all the answers to this horrible nightmare, but I still can't believe that Jonathan Stone was the person responsible for all of this mayhem. Do you think he will ever be captured?"

"I personally think we'll never hear from Jonathan again," Charles answered. "With his connections from his importing business, he could be hiding in any number of places."

"Maybe he went back to Poland" suggested Christopher.

"Perhaps, but I'd bet on a Latin American country," answered Becker.

"Really!" responded Mrs. Faraday. "Somehow, I can't see Jonathan Stone with his sophisticated sense of style in some Latin American country."

"Ah, but there are several Latin American countries—Uruguay, Argentina, and Paraguay for example—with communities very much like Europe," offered Carrie.

"Captain Becker, do you have a way of searching these countries for Mr. Stone?" Christopher asked. "Can you bring him back for trial?"

Christopher finished his soda and was concentrating his energies on cracking pieces of ice in his mouth.

"We really can't do anything until we have a lead as to where he's hiding. Then we can request the help of the local police and start a long process to bring him back. But, Christopher, I wouldn't hold out much hope of ever finding Stone, unless he makes another mistake."

"Surely the local police would know if a wealthy American suddenly appears in their community?" asked Mrs. Faraday. Then she turned to Christopher. "Please, either put the glass down or pour yourself more soda, but stop cracking that ice."

Christopher looked embarrassed, but jumped up and poured himself another glass of soda.

"Here's what I think," Becker said. "First, I don't think Stone is in a small town. I'll bet he's living in one of the larger cities in South America so his arrival wouldn't alert the police. Second, Stone was a man of great intelligence who planned everything down to the smallest detail. He's probably been to this city before and established another identity for himself." Becker drank his coffee and continued. "He has a place to live, financial relationships, and friends. He simply tells his friends he's retired from business in the United States. And, finally, he has probably altered his appearance, perhaps a mustache or beard, dyed hair, or even shaved his head, different glasses, casual clothing, et cetera. These changes are all designed to make him different from any police photo we might send."

"So Mr. Stone is gone forever," said a dejected Christopher.

"I believe so. If it's any help to you, Christopher, it doesn't appear that Stone was actually responsible for your father's death."

"Can we be sure of that?" asked Charles.

Becker leaned forward. "Once Genello found out that Stone wasn't around to help him, he started spilling his guts. He turned state's evidence against Petrovich in exchange for a lesser charge. Genello claims Stone scheduled a meeting to cut a deal with Jamie not to write the story. I think Stone wanted the deal with your brother to buy some time until he could he could finalize everything and clear out of

Tri-City. Anyway, according to Genello, Petrovich didn't like Jamie's deal and pushed him. Jamie fell backward, hit his head on the piling and went into the water. Genello had already knocked the light out on the pier, so in the dark and with the fog, they couldn't find Jamie. When they finally spotted him and pulled him out of the water, it was too late. They left the area by faking that drunken routine that Officer Reynolds saw."

"What about Suzanne?" asked Mrs. Faraday. "Did this Petrovich also shoot her?"

"According to Genello, he and Stone were listening in the van and Petrovich was outside the window. When Stone heard Suzanne start to crack he asked Petrovich to provide a diversion so they could get Suzanne out of the house. However, Petrovich decided on a different outcome for Suzanne."

Mrs. Faraday shook her head as she heard the details. "So this one man with no regard for human life is responsible for all this tragedy."

Becker nodded in agreement. "Mr. Faraday, we went along with your plan to catch Stone, but I'm not sure I understand all the clues that led you to him."

Christopher jumped in. "My dad left clues in his journal. I mean, he wrote clues in a poem. I kept searching for it. He hid the journal in the floor of the studio, and I found it the night of the fire!"

Becker looked astonished as the information rolled out of Christopher. "There was a journal? Why wasn't I shown this journal?" demanded Becker.

"It was just a book my dad kept notes in." Christopher was trying to provide an explanation to please Becker.

"Christopher, perhaps you should let your uncle explain to Captain Becker," offered Mrs. Faraday.

Christopher looked dejected, but Charles came to his rescue. "I think Christopher can handle this, Mother. After all, it was his relentless search for the journal that gave us the final clue. Go ahead, Christopher, but talk slowly, using complete sentences."

Christopher placed his soda glass on the coaster, sat up straight, and folded his hands. "You see, my dad used a small notebook for jotting down story ideas. I knew if there was any place we would find a clue, it would be in his notebook." Christopher then explained how he kept searching for the journal and finally discovered it under the studio floorboards. "We didn't give you the book because it didn't seem to have any real clues in it. But there was this poem, and we finally figured out the line about the photo in the poem pointed to Mr. Stone. That's when Uncle Charles contacted you, and Carrie followed Uncle Charles."

Becker looked at Christopher and then turned to Charles with a raised eyebrow. "Christopher is right," Charles validated. "I was searching for a group picture in the Faraday photo archives that matched the one described in the poem. I discovered the same photo that Carrie and Christopher found hanging in Jamie's bedroom. We all came to the same conclusion at pretty much the same moment. The poem referenced the fifth person, and that was Stone. That's when I contacted you, and, well…you all know the rest."

Becker smiled at the group and finished the last of his coffee. "Well, I guess that's all. Anything else I can answer for you?" offered Becker.

"I'm still a little vague about what happened between Charles leaving here and everyone ending up in the pub," Mrs. Faraday said.

"When Charles left here, he was going to meet Jonathan at the Admiral's Saloon. When I got to the saloon, no one was around, except for two men who requested Ben's tables. Did those men work for you?" asked Carrie.

"Yes, they're detectives in my unit. Our original plan called for Charles and Stone to go to the Admiral's Saloon and get seated in Ben's area. We knew if Stone was meeting with Mr. Faraday in the saloon, he would leave Petrovich and Genello behind. The hope was Ben would reveal something that would allow Charles to confront Stone with Jamie's murder. We wired Charles in order to capture Stone's confession."

"What went wrong?"

"We assumed Stone would go with Charles because he would think he was helping to solve the case," said Becker. "Instead, Stone either smelled the trap or realized he couldn't walk into the Admiral's Saloon since Ben knew him."

"My mistake was allowing Jonathan to talk me into picking him up at the office," Charles reflected. "Petrovich and Genello overpowered me and threw me in the back of the van, where there was virtually no conversation and no windows.

Becker knew I was with Jonathan, but had no idea where we were going."

"You can imagine how I felt," Becker said. "I involved a civilian in a dangerous situation and had no way to find him. We took a chance that Stone had a location near the Admiral's Saloon. So we drove to the harbor and waited. Then Officer Reynolds told us he saw you, and we moved our surveillance to that spot, but there are lots of bars and businesses on that street. That's how once you said the name of the pub, Ms. Kingsford, we arrived so quickly."

"Speaking of the Dancing Sailor, what's the status of Jonathan's holdings?" asked Mrs. Faraday.

"As I mentioned, even before Jamie was killed, Stone was in the process of liquidating everything he owned. Ownership of the pub and the building next door was already transferred to his sister, who lives in New York. Of course, we are trying to trace his other holdings and businesses, but it's very hard. We've asked your friend Mr. Wheeler for assistance. He's been a great help since he knows about importing."

Charles and Carrie exchanged a brief glance, but said nothing.

Becker continued. "As you know he does legal work for several importing businesses in Tri-City and provided us with valuable information about how he thinks Stone's import business worked. With the exception of those couple of folders you saved from the fireplace at the pub, we retrieved nothing of value from the office."

"Did those folders provide any leads?" asked Charles.

"The folders contained a list of arrival dates for his caviar shipments, along with some limited information about the ships and the producers of the caviar. It may provide the international authorities with some leads about the smuggling operation, but nothing to help us track Stone."

Becker waited, but there were no additional questions.

"Well, folks, I guess that's about it." Becker stood to leave.

Mrs. Faraday stood and shook Becker's hand. "Thank you, Captain Becker, for keeping the case open and pursuing it to the end."

"You're welcome, ma'am. I don't like unsolved cases. Of course, I prefer not to have cases to solve in the first place." Becker then turned to Christopher. "Goodnight, Christopher. Your father would be proud of the way you solved this case."

Christopher beamed with the compliment and shook his hand. "Thank you, Captain Becker."

Carrie and Charles walked Captain Becker out to his car. They held hands as they watched Becker slowly navigate the driveway to the street.

"What do you think about Joel being such a good little helper to the police?" Carrie asked.

"I'm glad he's helping," Charles replied. "It's good for cleansing his guilt, and maybe he also realizes how close he came to being on the wrong side of the law."

"You know what's really interesting? I don't think Jamie knew anything about Joel's side business. I really think Jamie contacted Joel looking for some help, but Joel had a guilty conscience. Jamie was a good reporter and probably sensed Joel was into something. Jamie pushed and Joel spilled his guts. Of course, Jamie took the opportunity to make a deal with Joel to get him to stop his illegal activities. Because of his success with Joel, Jamie probably thought a similar offer to Jonathan would work, too."

"Well, if Genello's confession to Becker is correct, it sounds like Jamie's negotiations with Stone would have been equally successful. It's a shame Petrovich has such a quick temper," Charles added.

"It makes you wonder why things turn out the way they do. If it weren't for Petrovich, Jamie would be here. Suzanne wouldn't be facing months of recovery. Jonathan would have quietly started a new life with no one the wiser. And then there's Joel. The last thing he said to me was that he hoped when all this was over, we could all still be friends."

"There's another good thing that happened in all this turmoil. It brought Carrie Kingsford back to Tri-City and back to the Faradays." Charles squeezed her hand.

"What a sweet compliment. But with everything all wrapped up on the case, I need to get back to my life." Carrie turned back toward the house.

"I don't think things are wrapped up," said Charles, as he placed his arm around her shoulders.

"What do you mean?" Carrie asked. "We have answers to all our questions."

"No, I think one question still needs an answer. I would like to know if you would be willing to stay here with me." Charles bent down and kissed her.

Carrie rested her head on his shoulder. "Perhaps I could stay a little longer."

Made in the USA
Middletown, DE
15 March 2025

72725098R00184